For Howard —
Good friend with
thanks for your input
on this book. Enjoy
the read! All the
best all the time.
Clive
Rosengren
11/15/18

MARTINI SHOT

AN EDDIE COLLINS MYSTERY

CLIVE ROSENGREN

coffeetownpress

Kenmore, WA

coffeetownpress

For more information go to: www.coffeetownpress.com
www.cliverosengren.com

Cover design by Aubrey Anderson

Martini Shot
Copyright © 2018 by Clive Rosengren

ISBN: 978-1-60381-760-8 (Trade Paper)
ISBN: 978-1-60381-755-4 (eBook)

Library of Congress Control Number: 2018950035

Printed in the United States of America

ACKNOWLEDGMENTS

------- ◆ -------

SINCE THE AUTHOR HAS HAD NO experience whatsoever raising a twelve-year old girl, my thanks to two people who have: Howard Dallin and his daughter, Maggy Perry. Howard has raised two, as has Maggy. Thanks to both of them for their input in my attempts to find the voice for Kelly Robinson.

Once again thanks to my friend Brad Whitmore for his thoughts and suggestions on this manuscript. You continue to provide invaluable insight on Eddie Collins and the people around him.

The author would be remiss without again thanking the members of Monday Mayhem, my writing group, and first firewall in fleshing out this story. Thanks to Jenn Ashton, Carole Beers, Sharon Dean, Michael Niemann, and Tim Wohlforth.

CHAPTER ONE

———◆———

T. S. ELIOT GOT IT WRONG when he called April the cruelest month. He'd obviously never been in the San Fernando Valley in mid-July. It was late Monday morning and the mercury hovered around a hundred and one as my car crept along Ventura Boulevard in search of a parking space. I could swear my teeth were sweating. My shirt had wet half moons at the armpits, testing the strength of my Old Spice. Beads of perspiration trickled down my neck, in defiance of the air conditioner that groaned like a heifer in labor.

I turned onto a side street, squeezed into a gap dangerously close to a fire hydrant, then cracked the windows, picked up my photo and resume and slid into the inferno. I donned my summer porkpie. The small brim provided no help from the midday glare. Sunglasses would have helped, but while getting into my car I'd dropped my keys, bent over to retrieve them and promptly stepped on the glasses that had slid from my shirt pocket. All in all, it was starting to be one of those days where one shouldn't even bother to take the plow out of the shed.

And then I rounded a corner and bumped into Santa Claus.

We mumbled apologies and continued on. I turned to see the sidewalk ahead of me filled with the jolly old St. Nicks, some in complete regalia, some not. One fellow wore Birkenstocks and plaid Bermuda shorts, but passed muster by covering his potbelly with a flaming red tee shirt. A full white beard and a red hat provided the finishing touches.

I was on my way to an audition for a television bank commercial. I was to be a security guard. Obviously the Santas were there for something else. There must have been twenty of them in the waiting room, sitting in theater seats against the walls. The rest of the space was filled with carpeted benches.

Interspersed with the Santas were fifteen would-be security guards, all my type. Par for the course at these cattle calls.

And par for the course with respect to my pursuit of the Hollywood gold ring. I was used to it. I'm in my early forties, with a full head of hair and reasonably good looks. Yeah, perhaps a little too much paunch and traces of wrinkles around the eyes, but that's to be expected in a character actor, one who is right for all sorts of roles, from security guard to bartender to business executive. I've learned to accept the fact that at many of these auditions I'm just another face in the crowd. Today wasn't any different. In fact, only fifteen competitors were pretty good odds at landing the job.

The casting office had four audition rooms, numbered appropriately. Several of my rivals wore uniform caps and shirts, making me feel under-dressed. I signed in, found a seat between two of the jolly Kris Kringles and listened to them compare notes on their agents. One of my competitors, with whom I'd done a job a few years back, caught my eye from across the room. I gave him a nod and looked over the commercial's storyboard. The gist of the ad had the guard doing a double take after seeing an old woman brandishing a pistol. Double takes I can do. Even with sweaty armpits.

A reedy young woman opened door number three and called out, "Eddie Collins." As I doffed my porkpie she ushered me into the room and I stood in front of a bored director and two somnambulating clients. I double taked my heart out, but I must have been under-whelming. They gave me the impression I had interrupted their day. I signed out, wished one of the Santas good luck and headed for the front door.

From behind me I heard, "Hey, Eddie."

I turned as Roy Dickerson walked up. He stood about my height, but had me by more than a few pounds. He wasn't in full Santa uniform, but did have a false beard and a red hat.

"Hey, Roy, what's going on? How long did it take you to grow the beard?"

He pulled it down over his mouth. "As long as it takes to shell out fifteen ninety-five. Why aren't you here for Santa?"

"I don't believe in him."

"Except when the residuals start coming in."

"True that."

"Hey, you still hanging out your private eye shingle?"

"Yeah, why?"

"I maybe got a job for you." He turned when he heard his name called by a young man wearing an elf's hat who was sticking his head out of door number one. "Ah, crap. Can you wait up for me?"

"You got it."

He clapped me on the shoulder and walked toward the elf. I found a corner of the room and listened to more conversation from the Santas. They all seemed to know each other from print advertising gigs and department store bookings. But from the gist of what they were saying, I didn't think they were bona-fide actors. With all those genuine white beards, it seemed to me that their opportunities would be limited.

My cellphone rang and the display indicated it was Mavis Werner, my secretary. "Hey, Kiddo, what's up?" I said, and started for the front door, ceding defeat from the Santa serenade.

"Are you through with your audition?"

"Yeah. They weren't impressed." The building next door had an awning and a little patch of shade, which I promptly claimed. "What's up?"

"You're not going to believe this."

"Steven Spielberg wants to hire me."

"Uh, not today."

"Then what?"

"They're laying new carpet in the hallway."

"You're kidding."

"Believe it."

I and my fellow tenants of the building that housed my office on Hollywood Boulevard had been begging the owner for years to get rid of what he has always referred to as carpet.

"Great news."

"The color's kind of crappy, though."

"Anything's an improvement."

"Well, maybe." I watched a Santa emerge from the casting office and pull off the top part of his costume like a snake shedding his skin. "But hey, listen," Mavis continued. "The reason I called is the mail came. I thought you'd want to know there's a letter here from a James Robinson in Cincinnati."

Her mention of the city brought me up short. Events from several years back bubbled up in my memory and made me recall a name I hadn't thought of in a while.

After a moment of dead air Mavis said, "Eddie, you there?"

"Yeah. I heard you."

"Isn't Cincinnati where that daughter of yours is? The one that was adopted? Kelly Robinson, right?"

"Correct on all three counts."

"So who do you suppose this James Robinson is?"

"My guess would be the father."

"Do you want me to open it?"

"Nah, I'll look at it when I get back."

"Okay."

She hung up and I put the cellphone back in my pocket. I pulled out a handkerchief and swabbed the lining of my hat. Across the street two young guys started arguing over a parking space. Given the temperature, the scene had all the ingredients for escalation.

Kelly Robinson. Some years ago, after my ex wife, Elaine Weddington, had been murdered by a couple of jealous actresses, a scumbag of a producer had informed me of the existence of a daughter. She had been given up for adoption without my knowledge or consent. In fact, I wasn't even aware of Elaine's pregnancy before we split up. I was told the child's adoptive father was a teacher and the mother a realtor. I've never seen the girl, save for a picture given to me by my ex's boyfriend. Over the years I've wrestled with my feelings regarding the girl. From time to time I'd entertained thoughts of making contact with her, but had never followed through. I'd always thought it wasn't my place to insinuate myself into her life. So now I couldn't help but wonder why I'd gotten a letter from someone bearing the girl's name. True, James Robinson could be someone entirely different, but the coincidence was too obvious.

Roy Dickerson came out of the casting office and stuck his red hat into a pocket of his cargo shorts. He pulled out a pack of some kind of black foreign cigarettes and a lighter and walked up to me.

"You ace it, Roy?"

"Doubt it. Can't compete with all those guys in full uniform. I swear to God one of these times someone is going to show up with Rudolph and a midget."

I had to chuckle at the image. "That's why I told my agent not to send me out on those things."

"Good idea," he said. He stuck a cigarette in his mouth and flicked his Zippo. A bit of a breeze caught a spark from the cancer stick and blew it into his fake beard. It started to smolder. He looked down, saw the wisps of smoke and yanked the beard from his face, stomped on it and threw the thing in a nearby trash bin. "Goddammit, there's money down the toilet."

"You better grow your own, Roy."

"You kiddin' me? I tried once. My wife told me it gave her hives."

I laughed as he shook his head and grinned. "So what's this about a job?" I said.

"Can we get out of this heat?"

"Absolutely." I pointed across the street. "There's a Mickey D's. Something cold would be good."

"Let's do it."

We stepped off the curb and waited for traffic, then hustled across Ventura Boulevard. The two combatants for the parking space had apparently settled their differences. They were taking selfies of the two of them.

I pulled the door open and was met with a welcome blast of cold air. We ordered large sodas. Roy grabbed a handful of napkins and we squeezed ourselves onto two immovable chairs. Roy wiped his face. "Dammit, but I hate hot weather."

"I hear you," I said. I sucked down some soda and waited while he checked his cellphone. "So, who needs a PI, Roy?"

"I've got an uncle who lives out at the Motion Picture Country Home in Woodland Hills. You been there?"

"Visited once."

"His name is Benjamin Roth. Ever hear of him?"

I sipped my drink and thought for a moment. "Might have. An actor, right?"

"Yeah, he goes back a long time. Used to be a contract player at Universal. He worked all the time."

"Okay, I think I remember him. Little guy, right?"

Roy nodded and slurped up some soda. "And feisty. At least he used to be."

"And he wants a PI?"

"Maybe."

"Why?"

"He's got a son, Jack. My cousin. Ben disowned him years ago."

"What for?"

"I don't know for sure. He's never wanted to talk about it. But I'm out there the other day looking in on him and he starts asking me if I've seen Jack. I tell him I haven't. Then he begins wondering what happened to him. Long story short, Ben tells me he wants to see his son again."

I pulled a notebook from my pocket and jotted down the name. "This Jack. Same last name? Roth?"

"No, he changed it to Callahan. His mother's maiden name."

"Why?"

"Jack never said for sure. For a while he flirted with the idea of going into the business. Maybe he figured he wanted to make it on his own name."

"You suppose that ticked off the old man?"

"Possibly. Ben's always kind of danced around the reason. My uncle's in his early nineties. He's going downhill and I think he maybe wants to make amends. Hell, I don't know, could be he's got some money to leave him or something."

"How long ago did your uncle disown him?"

"Eight years."

"So the guy could be dead."

"Yeah, who knows?"

"How old is he?"

"Thirty-six, I think. Ben had sort of a May-December thing with Jack's mother. I think she'd barely turned twenty-one when she had him."

"And Jack hasn't been heard from since?"

"Not a peep."

I made some notes and took a pull on the straw. Outside on Ventura Boulevard, an ambulance screamed by. "So, what do you want to do, Roy?"

"Why don't we drive out there tomorrow and you can talk to him."

"Okay." I slid my notebook and pen across the table. "Write down the address and I'll meet you there."

Roy scribbled it on a page and slid the notebook back. "How about ten-thirty or so?"

"Sounds good," I said. We finished our drinks and squeezed out from behind the table. A blast furnace greeted us when we opened the door.

"I bet you could fry a goddamn egg on the sidewalk," Roy said, as he fished out another cigarette and fired it up. "In fact, didn't they do that in a movie once?"

"Yup. ... *tick... tick ... tick ...* with Jim Brown and George Kennedy."

"Christ, Collins, you're a walking encyclopedia."

"Nah, just a movie junkie." We scoped out the traffic and lumbered across Ventura. "Good luck with the Santa spot, Roy. Hope you land it."

"Thanks. If I get the callback I'll have to buy another beard."

We shook hands, and I walked back to my car. The possibility of getting another client pleased me. Now the question remained whether or not a letter from one James Robinson would do the same.

CHAPTER TWO

---◆---

AFTER I LEFT ROY DICKERSON I popped into a Rite Aid and replaced my sunglasses. Nearby a roach coach was parked, so I grabbed a burrito for lunch. My mistake was taking it with me on the ride back into Hollywood. The aroma drove me nuts as I made my way down Cahuenga Boulevard, windows up and air conditioning whining.

One of the other tenants on my floor of the building is the Elite Talent Agency, whose clientele are models. A particularly attractive member of that group waited by the elevator. I'd seen her before. She was tall, California blonde, wore high heels and a skirt whose length demanded I behave myself.

"Hello, Mr. Collins," she purred.

"Hi there. Miriam, isn't it?"

"That's right."

"Hot enough for you?"

"Disgusting. I'm wearing too many clothes." She glanced at me with a twinkle in her eye and a small smile made for mischief.

"Not going there," I said.

She laughed and tossed her golden curls. I followed her inside the elevator and we started the rumbling ascent. We traded small talk as the car grunted its way upward and finally stopped on our floor. The door creaked open and we stepped out onto a psychedelic surface that cried out for a strong dose of Dramamine. There were yellow and green swirls and splotches that would make Jackson Pollock burn his brushes.

Lenny Daye, another one of my neighbors, the major-domo behind *Pecs 'n Abs* magazine, stood outside his office door, hands on hips, glaring at the new carpet.

"Eddie, look at this!"

"Well, at least it's new, Lenny."

"I guess. Stay indoors if you're hung over, honey." He turned to Miriam as she walked past him on her way to the talent agency. "Hi, sweetheart. With those heels of yours, I wouldn't look down."

I opened my office door and saw Mavis behind her computer. She looked up and said, "Well, what do you think?"

I shook my head. "Lenny's ready to have a fit."

She handed me a letter and I walked into my office and put it and the burrito on my desk. I hung my hat on a peg and pawed through a beaded curtain into my living quarters, a studio apartment overlooking Hollywood Boulevard. I popped open a can of beer, filled a glass and went back to my desk. Mavis sat in a chair in front of it, a piece of paper in her hand and a look of anticipation on her face.

I pointed to what she was holding and said, "What's that?"

"After I talked to you on the phone, I did some noodling online." She slid the sheet across the desk. It was a sample copy of a California Certificate of Live Birth. Several boxes were highlighted in yellow. "Elaine never told you she put the girl up for adoption, did she?"

"I had no idea she was even pregnant," I said, as I unwrapped the burrito and took a bite.

"So you don't know if your name is on the birth certificate?"

"That's right. What are you getting at?"

"If your name isn't on it, then how do you suppose this James Robinson found you? And how does he know you're the birth father?"

I looked at her as I swallowed and took a sip of beer. "Maybe Goldberg told him." Goldberg was Sam Goldberg, a sleaze-ball producer I'd gotten tangled up with when my ex and I were calling it quits. "He knew about the baby. I was told he set up a trust fund for the girl, so who the hell knows what he might have told Robinson."

"Why would he set up a trust fund? From what you've told me, Sam Goldberg didn't strike me as being that generous."

"Yeah, I know," I said. I took another bite of the burrito. "Elaine was his bread and butter there for a few years. Her pictures made him money. Maybe he figured he owed her."

"Yeah, maybe," she said. "And maybe he didn't talk to Robinson." She pointed to the letter. "That still doesn't explain how this guy in Cincinnati knows you're the birth father."

"Hey, look, we're putting the cart before the horse here, aren't we? We may be looking at a coincidence with a capital C. This guy may not even be Kelly's adoptive father."

"Well, there's only one way to find out," she said.

I bit off another small chunk of the burrito. "I assume you want to hear what he says?"

"If that's okay."

"Fine by me."

"But you better not drool burrito all over the letter."

"Roger that." I took a swallow of beer and very deliberately slid the glass and the food over to one side of the desk. "Your wish is my command." I slit open the top of the envelope, pulled out a single sheet of personalized stationery and began to read.

Dear Mr. Collins: Please accept my apologies for this letter coming to you from out of the blue, as it were. Twelve years ago in Los Angeles my wife Betty and I adopted our daughter Kelly. Her birth certificate listed Elaine Weddington as the birth mother, and Eddie Collins as the father. I therefore hope I do indeed have the right Eddie Collins.

"Well, that wipes out the coincidence with a capital C," I said.

"And that means Elaine put your name on the birth certificate," Mavis added. She pointed to one of the highlighted boxes. "Only one parent had to sign it."

"I'm surprised she even bothered to list me," I said, as I sipped from my beer glass and tried not to dredge up old resentments. I continued reading.

I did some online research and was able to learn the circumstances surrounding Ms. Weddington's death. If the two of you were still married at the time, my condolences on your loss. We recently told our daughter that she was adopted, and while we didn't provide her with all the details of Ms. Weddington's death, Kelly was nevertheless a bit upset to learn that she was murdered. Those feelings have persisted, so much so that she has now expressed a desire to learn more about her birth parents.

My wife is a real estate agent and will ironically be attending her high school class reunion in Los Angeles this coming weekend. Since I teach high school English, I, along with Kelly, am able to accompany her. If, in fact, you are Kelly's birth father, would you consent to meeting us and our daughter? Perhaps you could provide Kelly with more complete information about her birth mother?

I again apologize for the suddenness of this letter. If you're the right person, could you please give me a call? If not, please pardon the intrusion.

Sincerely, James Robinson.

His phone numbers were at the top of the page. I folded the letter and replaced it in the envelope, then took a bite from my burrito and looked at Mavis.

"Wow," she said. "That is out of the blue, isn't it?"

"To say the least. This weekend? That's cutting it pretty close. And why didn't he just call?"

"I don't know, Eddie. Maybe he figured a letter would be more formal or something. Are you going to phone him back?"

"I don't know. Think I should?"

"You've told me you've thought about the girl in the past. Now's your chance to find out who she is."

"I've just landed a missing persons case. It's going to tie me up for a few days."

"Good grief, there's such a thing as multi-tasking, you know."

"Yeah, yeah," I said, and took a sip of beer. "But she's twelve. I don't have the first clue about how to relate to someone that young."

"Oh, for Pete's sake, she's not going to move in with you. And besides, her parents are going to be with her."

Mavis was right. I'd often thought of this daughter, who up until now existed only as a name and a snapshot. Faced with the reality of seeing her in person, I didn't know if I had the nerve to carry through with it.

"What if the kid's resentful?" I said. "I mean, finding out your birth parents didn't want you can't be the most gratifying fact for a twelve-year old to deal with."

Mavis reached for the sample certificate and looked at it for a long moment. "No, I don't suppose it is. But for twelve years, she's probably been in a very nurturing environment. It seems to me any resentments would have been smoothed over by this James and Betty Robinson."

I took another bite of the burrito and chewed. "What did you have for breakfast, kiddo? You're making a hell of a lot of sense here all of a sudden."

"No, you're just listening for a change. Look at it this way, Eddie. You're the only person who can tell her who her mother was and how she died. Elaine still lives on film. You can show the girl one of her movies."

"That's true. If I can stand to watch it."

"Oh, phooey. Bad vibes, boss man. Kelly isn't going to appreciate that. And furthermore, I don't think you really mean it." She stood up and started back to her office. "Give the man a call already."

She was right again. Despite the acrimony surrounding the breakup with my ex, I had come to realize that my behavior back then was a contributing factor. Elaine's murder had saddened me deeply and any lingering anger I had needed to be squelched.

I finished off the burrito and the beer and took the glass back into my apartment. Mavis was on her computer as I handed her the sample birth certificate and looked at the clock on her desk. "One-thirty here. That means, what, four-thirty in Cincinnati?"

"That's right."

"July, so he's probably not in school."

"Did he provide a cell number?"

"Yeah."

"You're more likely to get him that way."

"Right," I said, and went back into my office. I pulled out the letter and saw the cell number at the top of the page. Mavis stood in the doorway as I pushed the speakerphone button and dialed. It rang two times and then was picked up.

"Hello," a deep voice said.

"James Robinson?"

"Speaking."

"Mr. Robinson, this is Eddie Collins calling. I just got your letter. You've reached the right person."

"Oh, thank goodness. And thank you for responding. I would have phoned, but with all the telemarketers and robo calls these days, I thought I might not be able to reach you. I hope you didn't mind the letter."

"Not at all. I read it just a few minutes ago."

Are you agreeable to meeting our daughter?"

"I must admit a little hesitation, but yes, I'd like that." Mavis flashed me a thumbs-up from the doorway. "When do you plan to be in town?"

"We're flying in on Friday. We'll be staying at the Sportsman's Lodge in the Valley. Do you know it?"

"Very well."

"Betty graduated from Van Nuys high, so Sportsman's seemed to be the most convenient place."

"Good choice," I said, and gave him both my office and cellphone numbers.

"As I mentioned, we were able to learn of Miss Weddington's passing," he said. "Were the two of you still together?"

"No, in fact we had split up by the time Kelly was born. I should tell you that I didn't know of her birth until just a few years ago."

There was silence on the other end of the line. "I see," Robinson finally said. "So this is really coming as a surprise to you, isn't it?"

"It certainly is. Let me ask you this. What does Kelly know about Elaine?"

"That she was an actress. In fact, we've watched one of her movies. So she knows what she looked like. She had quite a career."

"She did," I said.

"My Internet search revealed that you also are an actor. Still in the business?"

"Sometimes I wonder, but my agent reminds me from time to time." I heard a chuckle on the other end of the line. "I also operate my own private investigation office."

"Really?" he said. "Interesting. I hope we're not interrupting a case."

"Well, matter of fact, I just took on a client, but it's not something that I can't work around." I glanced over at Mavis and saw her give me a smile.

"That's very intriguing, Mr. Collins. Kelly should get a kick out of your dual careers."

"Well, I'll look forward to meeting her, along with you and your wife. Give me a call when you get here."

"I certainly will, Mr. Collins," Robinson said, then broke the connection.

I folded the letter and replaced it in the envelope.

"Well, that wasn't so bad, was it?" Mavis said.

"Better than an hour in a dentist's chair. She's seen one of Elaine's movies, so it's not like I'll have to introduce her to a complete stranger."

"But she's still going to want to know what her mother was like, Eddie. You haven't forgotten that, have you?"

"No," I said, as I leaned back in my chair. "There were some good times." And there had been. It wasn't going to kill me to share those memories. Despite my trepidations, I figured I owed it to Kelly Robinson for her to learn more about the woman who had brought her into this world.

Chapter Three

———◆———

THE OFFICIAL NAME IS THE MOTION Picture & Television Country House and Hospital. In 1940 the actor Jean Hersholt bought forty acres of land out in Woodland Hills from Bob's Good Earth Real Estate. The following year little Mary Pickford was one of the ground-breakers for the first buildings. Mr. Hersholt now has an honorary Oscar periodically bestowed in his name.

The list of residents over the years is mind-boggling. Larry Fine, one of the Three Stooges, lived there. So did Norma Shearer, once the reigning queen of Hollywood and wife of MGM boy wonder Irving G. Thalberg. Johnny Weismuller, Tarzan number six resided there for a while, but had to be transferred because of his tendency to roam the halls at night letting loose with the ape-man's famous yell. Living out his last years was also Dick Wilson, otherwise known as Mr. Whipple, who, in 504 television commercials, kept imploring us to "Don't Squeeze the Charmin."

As I left the Ventura Freeway at Mulholland I couldn't help but picture the surreal scenario of Tarzan and Mr. Whipple sitting down together over morning oatmeal. I hung a right on Spielberg Drive and found the parking lot. Roy Dickerson leaned against his car, cigarette smoke swirling around his straw hat.

"Morning," he said.

"Why are you standing out in this heat?"

He held up one of his black cigarettes. "I can't smoke these closer than fifty feet. Surprised they didn't make me go to Encino."

"Well, they look pretty potent. What the hell are they?"

"Sobranie Black Russians," he replied. "Cost me an arm and a leg."

"So you need that Santa spot. Did you get the callback?"

"My phone damn sure didn't ring."

"Maybe it will today." I clapped him on the shoulder. "You talk to your uncle?"

"I called him last night. He said he'd be here. As if he's got anyplace else to go." He stepped on his cigarette butt and gestured for me to follow him. "He's in the Katzenberg Pavilions," he said, dropping the name of one of the major supporters of the facility. We walked past the Wasserman Koi Pond, named after Lew Wasserman, former head of Universal and once one of the major power brokers in Hollywood.

"You ever get the feeling you're walking among ghosts?" I said.

"Christ, yes. I mean, the Roddy McDowell Rose Garden? Not to mention the John Ford Chapel, the Edith Head Plaza. Then don't forget the Louis B. Mayer Theater and the Douglas Fairbanks Lounge. It goes on and on. Creepy, man."

"So, I suppose you've already made your reservation, right?"

He chuckled. "Oh, hell yeah. With that waiting list, I'm gonna get right on it."

We entered the Katzenberg Pavilions and encountered two elderly ladies in wheelchairs. They interrupted their conversation and smiled as we approached and then said good morning. The air in the building was cool and I could detect the faint trace of air freshener. Framed portraits hung on the walls of the hallway. I glanced at a couple of them and recognized faces from a bygone era. No doubt former residents.

We came to Ben Roth's room and Roy tapped on the door and pushed it open. The unit was small, but comfortable. Characteristic of most retirement homes, the furniture looked like it was furnished by the facility, not the resident. A bathroom was off to the left and a bed around a corner to the right. A writing desk sat against one wall and a sofa with a coffee table occupied the opposite side of the room. Ben had a brown leather recliner that faced a television in one corner that was tuned in to a baseball game. The sound was muted. Outside a sliding glass door was a small round table and ice cream chairs on a concrete slab. Several pictures hung on the walls, the only visible trace of a life before retirement.

Ben Roth sat in a chair in front of the desk. He wore a loud Hawaiian shirt with palm trees and flamingos and parrots fighting for turf. His trousers were wrinkled and he had slippers on his feet. He was a small man, curly gray hair cut short with little of it left on the top of his head. He was bent over, fiddling with the hem of his shirt.

"Hey, Ben, what are you doing?" Roy said.

"Trying to get rid of this goddamn thread," he replied. "That's what I get for buying something made in Bangladesh, for crissakes."

Roy squatted down in front of him. "Don't pull on it. Haven't you got a scissors?"

"Nah. They probably think I'm on some sort of suicide watch or something."

Roy grinned at me and reached into his pants pocket. He pulled out a small penknife and opened a tiny pair of scissors. "Here, let me get it." He snipped off the stray thread and dropped it in a wastebasket next to the desk.

"That's a nifty little unit," Ben said. "Where'd you get it?"

"REI."

"Hah! Made in America!" He chuckled and reached out and playfully slapped Roy on one cheek. "What brings you to the land of the almost dead?"

"Bubbling over with optimism today, are we?" Roy said.

"I've been to the crapper twice already. I'm all bubbled out."

Roy stood and gestured to me. "This is Eddie Collins. He's a private investigator."

Ben looked at me over his shoulder. "A gumshoe, huh?" He stuck out a bony hand as he looked me over. "Glad to meet you, Eddie Collins." We shook hands. His grip was surprisingly firm. "You're better looking than Bogie."

"Thank you, sir."

"Probably can't drink like him, though."

"You got me there."

He laughed and pushed himself out of his chair. Roy grabbed his elbow and helped him over to his recliner. "You here looking for work?"

"Roy told me you might want some help locating your son," I said.

He sank down in the chair and let out a huge sigh. "Against my better judgment, but yeah, I think it's time to mend some fences. You gonna bankrupt me, Gumshoe?"

"I doubt it," I said.

"Well, here's the poop. The kid pissed me off a while back and I kicked his ass out."

"What did he do?" I said.

"Why you asking?" he replied.

Roy sat down on the sofa. "It'll probably help Eddie to know that. Don't you think?"

The old man eyed me as I sat down next to Roy. "Maybe so. You're not going to go blabbing all over town, are you?"

"Client confidentiality, Ben," I said.

"Yeah, I heard that before." He continued to eye me and I started to feel like I was in a line-up. "All right, Shamus. Here's more poop. I gave him some money to invest in a movie he said he was going to produce. The damn thing went belly up and he took me to the cleaners."

"How much did you give him?" Roy said.

"None of your damn business. But it was plenty. Jack may think so, but I ain't made of money." Ben picked up the remote and turned off the ballgame. "He did something else, too, but..." He left the sentence dangling and looked out the glass door.

"But what?" Roy said.

"Aw, nothin'. Forget it."

"Come on, Ben," Roy said. "You gonna hire a private eye, the guy's gotta have all the pertinent information about the person he's looking for."

"Bullshit! I want to see the kid, that's all. You got his name, what more do you need?"

Roy and I looked at each other as Ben pulled out a handkerchief and wiped his nose. I shrugged my shoulders and Roy gave me a nod.

"Any idea at all where he may be?" I said.

"If I did, I wouldn't be talking to you, would I?"

I shook my head and took out my notebook. There was going to be no pussyfooting around with Ben Roth. "His name's Jack Callahan, right?" I said.

"Yeah, and that didn't exactly sit right with me either. Thought he was being so goddamn smart changing his name. Hell, it's done right by me for ninety-some years. Snot-nose kid."

"Do you know what the name of the film was or the company that was going to do it?" I said.

He pointed in the direction of his bed. "Yeah, there's an envelope in the night table over there. Pull it out, Roy."

Roy retrieved a manila envelope and handed it to Ben. He pulled out some papers and a pair of reading glasses from his shirt pocket.

"Some outfit in the valley." He handed me the piece of paper. "Copy it down."

The paper looked to be some sort of informal deal memo with a letterhead reading *Punch Productions* and an address in Van Nuys. I wrote down the information and handed the paper back to him. "What about Jack's mother, Ben? She have any idea where he could be?"

He stuffed the piece of paper in the envelope and laid it on the small table next to his recliner. "My ex and me don't exactly communicate. She lives up in Ojai. I called her and asked. She said she don't where the kid is and hung up on me. So much for that."

"What's her name?" I said.

"You don't listen so good, do you? She doesn't know a damn thing."

"Her name is Maureen Callahan," Roy said. "I'll give you her address. It's in my phone."

Ben looked at both of us and uttered a grunt. "Ganging up on me, huh? Both of you."

"We want to find Jack," Roy said. "That's all."

"Yeah, yeah, yeah," he muttered.

"Do you have a picture of him?" I said.

"On the other night table," he replied. Roy got up and brought back a four-by-six photo of a smiling young man with a round face and reddish-brown hair.

"Good looking kid," I said, as I removed the photo from its frame.

"Takes after his mother," Ben said. "I never got a second look from the ladies."

"That's not what I've heard," Roy said.

"Yeah, well, you heard wrong." Ben scooted to the edge of the recliner. "So, Gumshoe, you got a piece of paper for me to sign or something? Contract? Deed to all my property? I've already given away the fatted calf."

"I'll send you my standard contract." I handed him one of my cards. "In the meantime, here's my card. My cellphone number's on the back."

He took the card and put it in his shirt pocket and stood up. "Well, you're going to need a retainer, aren't you?" He shuffled back to his desk and sat down.

"Not really necessary," I said.

"Hogwash! Never heard of a gumshoe who didn't want a retainer. What, you got a trust fund or something?"

"Eddie's an actor, Ben," Roy said.

He turned to look at me. "An actor? Good Christ, what am I getting myself into?" He pulled open a drawer. "Well, then, you damn sure need a retainer."

I looked at Roy and he flashed me a grin and shrugged his shoulders. Ben tore off a check and handed it to me. "Here, Eddie the actor gumshoe. Don't spend it all in one place."

I looked at the check and saw that it was more than generous. "Thanks, Ben, I'll do my best to find your son."

"You damn well better. I've got your card. I'll send out a posse if you don't." He put the checkbook back in the drawer and stood up. "All right, then. Now if you'll excuse me, it's time for mystery meat. I'd invite you two to lunch, but I don't believe in inflicting punishment on innocent people."

I laid the picture frame on the coffee table and Roy and I started for the door.

"Hey, Gumshoe," Ben said.

"Yeah, Ben."

"When you find Jack tell him it's all right. I'll bury the hatchet. Won't be long before I take the big sleep. We need to be friends before I do."

"You got it," I said, and we left the room.

We got no more than fifty feet from the pavilion when the black cigarette came out of the pack and smoke started billowing.

"What do you suppose he didn't want to tell us?" I said.

"Beats the hell out of me. I wasn't around Jack all that often, but I never knew of anything he'd hide from his old man."

"Was Jack in any of the unions? SAG, directors' guild, writers'?"

"Come to think of it, at one point he might have got his SAG card. Don't know if it's still active."

"I'll check it out. You said you had his mother's phone number?"

"Oh, yeah." Roy pulled out his cell, found the number and showed it to me. I made a note of the information, got his phone number and handed him another one of my cards.

"Thanks for taking this on, Eddie. Ben can be a little rough around the edges, but his heart's in the right place."

"I'll keep you posted," I said.

He walked back to his car with tendrils of smoke whirling around his head. I waited for a light on the Mulholland on-ramp and stuck a CD in the player. Tom T. Hall joined me on the ride with "Old Dogs, Children And Watermelon Wine." I had the old dog with Ben Roth. His son Jack and Kelly Robinson were the children. I didn't know where watermelon wine fit in. In fact, I didn't even know there was such a beverage.

It had indeed been a couple of interesting days.

CHAPTER FOUR

———◆———

BEN ROTH HAD HIDDEN SOMETHING FROM us concerning his son. However, since he'd told me he wanted to mend some fences, whatever the omission was couldn't have been that important. Or could it? I mulled over the question as I headed east on the Ventura Freeway where traffic was surprisingly light. I got off at the Van Nuys exit and parked under a solitary tree in a supermarket parking lot.

"Collins Investigations," Mavis said when she picked up the phone.

"Hey, kiddo, anything going on?"

"Lenny is threatening the landlord with a petition to get the carpet changed."

"Yeah, well, good luck with that."

"You'd think with the way he usually dresses he'd like it."

"Good point," I said. "Maybe he doesn't like the competition. Hey listen, can you do a couple of computer searches for me?"

"You know, Eddie, you can do that on your cellphone."

"And go blind trying to read the screen? Besides, how else can I justify the huge salary I pay you?"

I could hear a chuckle on the other end of the line. "I'm just jerking you around, boss man. What do you need?"

"The first is for a guy by the name of Jack Callahan. He could be an actor, maybe a film director or producer. See if he turns up in any of the guild rosters."

"Spelled like it sounds?"

"Right. The second is for a company called Punch Productions. The address Roth gave me is on Moorpark in Van Nuys.

"Okay. Where are you now?"

"I found a patch of shade outside a Ralph's up in the Valley. Gonna grab a bite and see if this Punch Productions is still around."

"How was Ben Roth?"

"He's a pistol. I'll give you the whole picture when I get back." I broke the connection, cracked the windows a tad and shut the car off.

There was a little deli on the other side of the lot. Their pastrami sandwiches are legendary. The one I dug into didn't disappoint. I sat at a small table under an umbrella in front of the place. Three pigeons tussled over the last crumbs as I watched two kids skate-boarding down an alley to my right. They jostled with each other until one of them hit a pothole and took a header. He lay there for a bit, not getting any sympathy from his friend.

Just as I began to think the kid might need some help, my cell chirped, announcing the arrival of a text. The screen said it was from Carla Rizzoli, an actress I'd once dated, who, some months back, had become a client. She'd hired me to find her brother. Unfortunately, I had killed a man in self-defense. The shooting had messed with my head, but a therapist finally convinced me that I shouldn't continue to carry the guilt. The positive outcome of the whole incident was that Carla had now re-entered my life, which probably violates every rule in the PI handbook. But I lost my copy years ago, so I don't give a damn.

The text said *off @ 6. dinner?*

I tapped out sounds good. *i have news. will pick u up.*

goody. see you then, shamus, came the reply. I grinned at her insistence in calling me that. I must confess I'd gotten very used to it. I also copped to now being comfortable with texting in incomplete sentences, something which undoubtedly would cause my former English teachers to cringe in dismay.

The fallen skate-boarder finally got to his feet and I finished my cold soda and headed back to my car. The Moorpark address for Punch Productions was a nondescript red brick building sandwiched between a dry cleaners and a convenience store. A sign above the door indicated the current occupant was Big Wheel Bikes, not Punch Productions. I parked across the street and walked back. Inside there were various bicycles in racks, along with shelves of accessories. Seats, lights, helmets, reflectors, you name it.

A young man stood behind the counter dressed in a tee shirt with some reference to Lance Armstrong emblazoned across the front of it. His blond hair was tied back in a ponytail and earrings hung from both lobes. He had a thick bushy mustache and a soul patch in the middle of his face.

"Howdy," he said.

"Afternoon. How long have you guys been at this location?"

"Six years in March."

"Do you know if a company by the name of Punch Productions was here before you moved in?"

"I don't know, man. The building was empty when we got here." He leaned on the counter and fiddled with his soul patch. "You looking for somebody?"

"Yeah, as a matter of fact," I said, and handed him the picture of Jack Callahan. "This guy look at all familiar?"

"You a cop?"

"Private. You want to see my license?"

"No, man, if you say so." He held the picture in front of his face for a couple of moments and said, "Nope. Never seen the dude before."

"His name's Jack Callahan. Ring a bell?"

"Sorry."

"Thanks for your help," I said and turned to go. "How much do these bikes run?"

"Depends on what you want."

I pointed to one of the models. "How about that one?"

"That's a Niner RIP 9 RDO. On sale for twenty-one ninety-nine."

"As in twenty-one hundred dollars?"

"That's right."

"I could buy a used car for that."

"But then you'd still have a used car," the kid said, with a lopsided grin on his face. He had me, so I pushed open the door and stood on the sidewalk and glanced at my used car. I decided I preferred four wheels, not two.

The info Ben Roth had given me was out of date. Hopefully Mavis's search would provide another address for Punch Productions. To the right of Big Wheel Bikes was Century Cleaners. A swarthy, middle-aged man with dark stubble on his face had one hand pressed against a button that hung from the ceiling by a thick cord. A rack of plastic dry cleaning bags rotated in an oval arc. He had a pencil behind one ear, wore a wrinkled black shirt and khaki trousers. When he saw me he took his hand off the button and the bags stopped. He walked up to the counter.

"Yes, sir?" he said, in an accent which my ear told me he originally hailed from someplace in the Middle East. "Help you?"

"Your neighbor next door used to be Punch Productions. Have you been here long enough to remember them?"

"Fifteen years. Yes, I remember. Very bad neighbor."

"Why is that?"

"Strange people. In and out all day."

"What kind of people? How were they strange?"

"Women. Looked like hookers. Some of the men, too. You know what I mean?"

"Yeah, I think so." I held up Callahan's picture. "Does this guy look familiar?"

He nodded vigorously and handed the photo back to me. "Yes, yes, he was one of the men."

"You're sure?"

"Yes, sure. He would bring me clothes."

"To be dry cleaned?"

"Yes." He rubbed the top of his head. "Odd clothes."

"How do mean odd?"

"Bright colors. Very loud. Crazy patterns. Shouldn't be on the street with such clothes."

"This dry cleaning you did? I don't suppose you'd still have an address for him?"

"Oh, no, sir. Too long ago. Sorry."

"Thanks for your time," I said, and started for the door, but he stopped me.

"Excuse me, but one more thing."

"What's that?"

"Well, long time ago now, but I think there was some sort of killing once."

"What happened?"

"One night I'm in back doing books, and I hear sirens. All sorts of noise. I go to front door. Two, maybe three police cars. Ambulance. Cops have people in handcuffs. I remember now. This guy in picture? He's one of them."

"In handcuffs?"

"Yes."

I handed him the picture again. "This guy?"

"Yes, yes, that guy. He come in here many times. I don't forget."

"How do you know there was a killing?"

"They roll somebody out in one of those black bags. You know, zippered up?"

I fished out one of my cards and gave it to him. "Would you give me a call if you happen to remember anything else about him?"

"Yeah, sure, will do."

He slid the card into a drawer and I walked back out into the heat. I put my new sunglasses on and glanced up and down Moorpark. So Jack Callahan had been led away in handcuffs. According to Ben Roth, his son supposedly was in business with Punch Productions, where someone had apparently been killed. It begged the question what kind of business. It also made me wonder if that fact was what Roth had kept from me and Roy Dickerson. I don't imagine a father would boast about a son being arrested, even if he had disowned said son.

CHAPTER FIVE

———— ♦ ————

I PULLED INTO THE ALLEY BEHIND my building and found a truck partially blocking it. Huge rolls of carpet protruded from the rear door of the vehicle. After some jockeying I squeezed into my parking space next to Lenny Daye's Volkswagen. The door of the building was propped open with a concrete block. As I started for the entrance, two carpet layers came bursting through the opening with a roll over their shoulders.

"Whoa, sorry," the guy at the front end said.

I backed up and they came on through. "Did your boss pick out the carpet?" I said.

"No, sir. You gotta blame the owner of the building for that one."

"You get much call for this pattern?"

"Once. Some club on the Sunset Strip."

They continued through the door and started for their truck. The guy on the rear end called over his shoulder, "You'll get used to it."

"I'll take your word for it," I said, and turned the corner and punched the button for my floor. The psychedelic sight that greeted me when I stepped out of the elevator convinced me the guy was talking through his hat.

Mavis stuck her head out of her little inner sanctum when I pushed open the office door. "Hey, Eddie. Got some reading material for you."

"From both searches?"

"One of them wasn't too successful. There's a couple of folders on your desk."

I hung my porkpie on its peg and sat down. "That Moorpark address for Punch Productions turned out to be a bust."

"Well, I found a few more," she said, as she flipped open the folder and set down her cup of coffee and pulled up a chair. "Did you know that Punch Productions is the name of Dustin Hoffman's production company?"

"I did not."

"He sure as heck hasn't got anything to do with this, has he?"

"I'd bet my last dollar on it." I showed her the picture Ben Roth had given me. "This is the guy I'm looking for. I talked to the owner of a dry cleaner's next door. He told me several years ago that a Punch Productions was there. He also said the guy in the picture was hauled off in handcuffs one night."

"Does Ben Roth know that?"

"I doubt it."

I looked at the list of hits for Punch Productions. Two entries caught my eye. One was up in San Fernando and another had a Torrance address. Mavis had done a Google search for both of them, but it hadn't yielded much information on either.

She flipped open the second folder and slid it in front of me. "I got more hits on Jack Callahan. Most of them I didn't think were valid. A Chicago Blackhawks hockey player, for instance."

That left me with a list of thirteen possibilities. Some of them had phone numbers. "Did you happen to call any of these?" I said.

"No. I figured you'd want to look at them first."

"Thanks. Good work."

"The contract for Ben Roth went out with the mail. I think he was joking, but the mailman said he liked the carpet."

"He's probably been out in the heat too long."

She sipped on her cup of coffee. "So what was this Ben Roth like?"

I leaned back in my chair and gave her my impression of my newest client. She sipped and laughed at some of the comments he'd made to Roy and me.

"You think he might know about his son's arrest and didn't want to tell you?" she said.

"Could be. His kid being carted off in cuffs is something he wouldn't be proud of."

Mavis finished off her coffee and stood up. "I've got to make a run out to Venice. You need me for anything else today?"

"No, you go ahead. What's in Venice?"

"This little old grandmother by the name of Lucy Fallon has a set of glasses with the Lennon sisters on them. Remember the Lennon sisters?"

"How could I forget?"

"She wants to sell them, and I need to check 'em out."

"Big call for the Lennon sisters, is there?"

"You never know, Eddie."

And I never do. Mavis's Internet trade in antiques and collectibles constantly leaves me in awe of the tendency for some people to collect what might otherwise be called junk.

She went into her office and I pawed my way through the beaded curtain into my apartment, grabbed a bottle of water from the mini-fridge and returned to the desk. I heard the front door open and Mavis called out, "See you tomorrow, Eddie."

"Okay," I said. "Thanks again for this stuff." The door closed and I sank down in my desk chair, propped my feet up and started scanning the computer printouts. Several of the hits for Punch Productions had the variation of "Sucker Punch Productions." I called a few of them. One offered real estate management services and another one in the south bay defined themselves as a music promoter. A few more provided nothing of significance. An animation house, a video game producer.

I picked up the phone and dialed the number for Punch Productions up in San Fernando. After three rings someone picked up and a gravelly voice said, "Punch Productions."

"Yeah, hi. I'm looking for a guy by the name of Jack Callahan. I was told he might work for you?"

There was a long pause on the other end of the line. "Who the hell is this?" the voice said.

"The name's Bob Huntsman. I'm with Provident Resources. We're trying to get in touch with Mr. Callahan regarding some financial investments. Do you know where I can reach him?"

"No, I don't, and if you find him tell him to go fuck himself." The call ended abruptly.

I hung up and gazed at the poster of Bogie and Bacall hanging over my desk. So, I now had a link between one Jack Callahan and a Punch Productions. Of course, it might not be my Jack Callahan, but the coincidence of him being connected to the name of a company Ben Roth had given me was at least a starting point. I wrote the address and phone number in my notebook and shifted my attention to the file with the Jack Callahan hits.

The Jack Callahan in Pomona was a retired fire fighter. The one in Boyle Heights didn't have a clue who Ben Roth was. Three calls went to voice mail, and a fourth to a bartender in Hollywood, who sounded similar to the person with the gravel road for a voice. My eyes started to sag, and with a concession to my encroaching middle age, I pulled down Mr. Murphy's bed and sought forty winks before meeting Carla.

THAT PI HANDBOOK I'D LOST A long time ago no doubt frowned on a gumshoe taking a nap while on a case. Tough. The snooze was badly needed. That same handbook also probably didn't recommend a PI being involved with an exotic dancer by the name of Velvet La Rose. Again, tough. Besides, I don't think of Carla Rizzoli in those terms. She's an aspiring actress currently keeping the wolf away from the door at "Chez Cherie" in Glendale. That's where I was headed with some serious Eric Clapton for company.

The case involving Carla's brother Frankie some months back had resulted in her being shot in the leg. Not a good thing to happen to a dancer. Some strenuous physical therapy had restored her ability to tantalize and tease while draping herself around a pole. Her reappearance in my life had caught me by surprise, and for a time I did admit to being a little gun shy of getting involved with her again. However, the spark had reignited the feelings we had for each other, and we were getting more comfortable with each other as the months went by.

I turned into the parking lot as a commuter train came barreling past on the tracks next to the club. The bouncer was Mickey Lund, a gentle bear of a man with a blond ponytail hanging down his back. He sported a neatly-trimmed beard and his blue eyes didn't miss a trick. We'd gotten to know each other pretty well over the weeks since Carla had started at the club. His face broke into a huge grin, and he stuck out a hand whose wrist was circled with gold and silver bracelets.

"Hey, Eddie, how ya doin'?"

"Can't complain, Mickey."

"Carla's in her last set. Go on in." I started to reach into my pocket but he stopped me. "Naw, naw, your money's no good."

"Thanks," I said, and walked down a short hallway into the lounge. A sparse crowd was scattered among several tables alongside sort of a runway where Carla did her thing. Soft red light spilled over the stage and rock music with a pulsating beat poured through speakers mounted in the corners of the ceiling.

Carla saw me enter and beckoned for me to take a table next to the stage. I'd seen her dance numerous times, but had always sequestered myself in a corner of the room. I've had ample opportunity to see her with her clothes off, so I didn't feel the need to sit close and drool like everyone else.

When I indicated I'd take a seat in the corner she shook her head in time to the music and pointed to a table next to the runway. I got some catcalls for my hesitance from a couple of patrons as I shrugged my shoulders and took a seat.

She shimmied herself toward me, turned her back and pointed to her left leg, the one where she'd been shot. The bullet had resulted in a small blossom that was now covered by a tattoo of a red rose. I hadn't seen the ink before and gave her a thumbs-up, then pulled a five-spot from my pocket and stuck it under the red garter around her thigh. She bent down, took off my porkpie and planted a kiss on the top of my head. My sheepish grin provoked more catcalls.

She finished her set and pointed toward the lobby.

I was checking my cellphone and listening to Mickey carding two young guys when Carla bounced up to me. She had a tote bag slung over one shoulder and wore denim shorts and a red tank top. She looked even more alluring than she had onstage.

"Hey, you," she said and planted a kiss on me, then flashed the back of her leg. "So you like the tattoo?"

"I do. When did that happen?"

"The other day. Now we've got to get one for you."

I narrowed my eyelids and looked at her. "Would you put a bumper sticker on a Bentley?"

She doubled over and burst into laughter. When she straightened up she punched me on the shoulder. We said goodbye to Mickey and headed for the parking lot.

"What's your news?" she said.

"Food first."

"Good. I've got some too."

"News?"

"Yup."

I looked at her, expecting some elaboration, but she very coyly smiled and moved her fingers over her lips, zipping them shut, as it were.

We left her car in the parking lot and drove to a nearby Olive Garden. A perky young waitress took our order and a carafe of red wine soon arrived. We clinked glasses and Carla asked about my news. I related the contents of the letter I'd received from James Robinson and our subsequent phone call.

"Oh, Eddie, that's great." When I didn't respond immediately she continued. "Well, isn't it?"

"I guess," I said, and expressed the reservations I'd previously shared with Mavis.

She took one of my hands in hers. "You don't have to worry. The fact that she wants to meet you tells me it's going to be a treat for both of you."

"From your lips to God's ears," I said.

"When is this happening?"

"They're flying in on Friday."

"Wow. That soon. Are you going to let me meet her?"

"If you give up on the idea of putting a tattoo on me."

She stuck her tongue out at me and we leaned back as our waitress deposited a basket of crunchy bread in front of us. For several moments we dipped chunks in olive oil, both of us nodding our heads in approval.

"So what's your news?" I said. "Does it have something to do with that tattoo?"

"Yes it does. It's a present to myself."

I broke off another chunk of bread and thought for a moment. "Wait a minute. I haven't missed a birthday or something have I?"

She grabbed her wine glass. "Nope. I just thought I needed to celebrate a little."

"Celebrate what?"

"I landed a part in a pilot."

"Really?" A huge grin broke out on her face and I quickly followed suit. "Why the hell did it take you so long to tell me?"

"I didn't want to do it over the phone."

"That's terrific," I said, as we clinked our glasses. "Tell me all about it."

A pilot is one episode of a television show that is more or less an audition before the networks and the powers that be. Carla went on to tell me that hers was an hour show about a female detective agency. *Charlie's Angels* without the glitz. Carla was one of the detectives, a street-wise young woman with attitude.

"That is super news," I said. "Here's to at least thirteen episodes." She laughed and we toasted. Our waitress appeared and we ordered another carafe. "What about the club? They going to let you go?"

"They are. The manager is a sweetheart."

"When do you shoot?"

"They haven't told me yet. Should be soon, though." She sipped from her wine glass as I broke off another chunk of bread.

"I've got some more news," I said.

"What?"

"Nothing like landing a TV pilot, but I do have another case."

She leaned over the table. "Well, look at you. My private eye is alive and well." I chuckled and sopped up some olive oil. "Who and what?" she asked.

"Another missing person," I said. The waitress appeared with our food, along with more wine. As we dug into our pasta, I proceeded to tell her about meeting Roy Dickerson at the audition and Ben Roth.

"There are going to be a lot of Jack Callahans, aren't there?" Carla said.

"You're right. Most of them are dead ends. But I think I may have linked one of them to this Punch Productions. That's the name of the company Ben told me his son was hooked up with."

She put down her fork and stared at me with a puzzled look on her face. "Punch Productions?"

"Yeah, why?"

"Viv, one of the girls I worked with at the Follies did something for a

Punch Productions a while back."

The Follies she mentioned was Feline Follies, the club where Carla had danced before Chez Cherie. It had subsequently been shuttered due to the owners' involvement in drug smuggling and money laundering.

"There's more than one Punch Productions," I said. "Might not be the one I'm thinking of."

"True," she said, as she took her cellphone from her bag. "Where's it located?"

"Up in San Fernando." I pulled out my notebook and showed her the address.

She pushed some keys on the phone and put it to her ear. After a moment she said, "Viv? Hi, it's Carla." I sipped my wine and listened as the two women traded pleasantries. "Hey, listen, Viv, didn't you do something with a Punch Productions one time?" Carla listened and relayed the San Fernando address. She glanced at me and a surprised look washed over her face. "Thanks, Viv." Pause. "Yeah, let's get together soon. Bye, hon." She broke the connection and put the phone back in her tote bag.

"What'd she say?" I said.

Carla poured some wine into her glass. "Yeah, Viv got offered something from them, but she took a walk after she showed up."

"Why?"

"They didn't tell her at the audition, but the company was a porn film company."

"Really?"

"Yeah. Gay porn."

Her comment caught me with a forkful of pasta headed for my mouth. I slowly chewed and thought of another reason why Ben Roth might have clammed up about his son.

CHAPTER SIX

———— ◆ ————

CARLA PARKED IN MY ASSIGNED SPACE and waited behind the wheel while I found room on the street. I pushed the button for the elevator. She leaned into me and I put my arms around her, a gesture that was becoming more and more natural for me.

"Brace yourself when we get up there," I said.

"Why?"

"You'll see."

The door opened on my floor and she let out a gasp when she saw the carpet. "Oh, my God! You should hang a disco ball and charge admission."

"Not a bad idea," I said, as I stuck my key in the office door.

"Good thing Mavis isn't here," Carla said.

"Why do you say that?"

"Well, I just remembered the first time I stayed over. How she freaked out when she saw me in the morning?"

I laughed as I recalled the moment. Mavis had come through the front door with the usual pronouncement of her arrival. I'd been at my desk and Carla was sitting in one of the client chairs. Mavis came through the door in mid-sentence and stopped short when she saw I had a guest. The look on her face gave new definition to the word surprise. She couldn't have been caught more off guard if she'd seen a nun at a roulette wheel. I introduced them. They shook hands, Mavis somewhat reluctantly. Carla had initially felt intimidated, but in subsequent meetings she'd discovered Mavis's Internet buying and selling. Now they chatted away like magpies, making girly-girl talk as if they'd grown up together.

"The way you two carry on together, I feel like I'm wearing a blazer at a state dinner."

"Oh, you poor neglected soul," she said. She began tickling me as I pushed open the door of the office and checked the answering machine. No calls. I stopped the tickling by wrapping my arms around her and wrestling her back into my apartment. She kicked off her shoes and flopped down on Mr. Murphy's bed.

Since Carla and I had become an item, the subject of moving in together hadn't come up, but I was willing to bet it eventually would. Given the size of my digs, the odds favored me becoming the mover, but I didn't relish the idea of leaving Hollywood. Since she was also a renter, it seemed to me we could work out a compromise. She lived out by the Sony lot, and if this pilot of hers saw the light of day, being closer to the center of the action in Hollywood would be to her advantage. At least that was the potential plan of action I had formulated.

I fluffed up a pillow and laid down beside her. She had the TV remote in her hand and turned on the set.

"Movie?"

"Sure," I replied.

She propped herself up on one elbow and looked down at me. "That's not exactly a ringing endorsement."

"Sorry. I was thinking about what your friend Viv told you over the phone."

"About Punch Productions?"

"Right."

"You didn't know what kind of a film company it was?"

"Not a clue."

"This Jack Callahan's father didn't tell you?"

"I don't think he knew either. All Ben Roth told me was the name of the company and that his son had invested some of the old man's money in it. And that the money was squandered."

Carla tapped the remote on my chest. "And that's what pissed him off?"

"There was something else, but Ben wouldn't tell me what it was."

Carla sat up and crossed her legs in a lotus position. "If Punch Productions is a gay porn film company, this Jack Callahan could be gay, right?"

"I suppose."

"So that's part of why the old man was pissed off?"

"The fact that his kid's gay?"

"Yes."

"Possibly."

"Even in this day and age?"

"Roth is in his nineties, Carla. Another generation. Maybe he isn't comfortable with it."

"Time for him to get on the planet," she said. I laughed and she turned off the television set. "But that doesn't explain the handcuffs and the killing at the dry cleaners."

"You're right," I said.

"Which probably means you're going to find out why he was arrested. If he was."

She had kind of a half-grin on her face as she sat there tapping the remote on my chest.

"Why the twenty questions all of a sudden?" I said.

"On the job training, Shamus. If I'm going to play a detective on TV I've got to start acting like one."

"Oh, brother, here it comes. I charge for my services, you know."

"We can work something out."

"This mean you going to quit draping yourself around a pole?"

"Not entirely." She dropped the remote on my chest, stood up and started swaying her hips and undoing the button on the front of her shorts.

On the job training. Yeah, right.

THE ADDRESS I HAD FOR PUNCH Productions up in San Fernando was just off Maclay Street, a neighborhood populated with warehouses and commercial storefronts. I parked across the street from a concrete building with the word "Punch" embossed on a sign to the right of the front door. The building was painted white, very plain and unassuming. But then, if you're operating a porn film company, the less attraction you draw to yourself the better.

I grabbed the picture of Jack Callahan, opened the trunk and picked up a leather portfolio filled with phony legal-looking papers and slipped the photo among them. As I crossed the street, I wondered whether or not I would have to disguise my voice, in case I encountered the man who had sounded like steel wheels on a stretch of gravel.

My concern was unfounded. Behind a receptionist's desk sat a very attractive woman with a few years on her that suited her nicely. A nameplate on the lip of the desk read Doris Barnes. She had a head of blond hair styled in some semblance of a beehive. Reading glasses on a chain dangled from around her neck. Tear-drop earrings dangled almost to the collar of a pale blue blouse. Her lips were red with lipstick, and eyes with lashes like spider webs looked up at me as I pulled the door open.

Off to the left of the front door was a coffee table flanked by two threadbare sofas. Two young men sprawled over them. On one, a beefy black man with serious corn rows flipped through a magazine. He was dressed in black jeans and a black wife-beater. A gold chain hung around his neck. On the other sofa, a pale-faced kid slouched. He probably hadn't yet seen the business end of a razor. He stared off into space as if he wanted to be somewhere else. Two guys looking for work, perhaps?

The receptionist looked up as I approached and said, "May I help you, honey?" Her voice was as far away from gravel as you could get. The words oozed out, almost dripping with honeysuckle, like she'd just stepped out from Tara in *Gone With the Wind*.

"Yes, ma'am," I said. "The name's Clark Butler. I'm with Provident Resources and I'm looking for a gentleman by the name of Jack Callahan. I'm led to believe that he works for Punch Productions. I hope I've got the correct address."

"Well, sugar, unless someone messed with that little ol' sign out there, you've got the right place. I don't believe I've heard that name before, though. Mebbe you're thinking of some other Punch?" She smiled and batted those spider webs at me.

I unzipped the portfolio and looked inside. "No, don't think so. This is Punch Productions, right? A film company?"

"It certainly is, darlin'." She reached for a bottle of Diet Coke with a straw sticking out of it and slurped. "I sure don't mean to be a doubtin' Doris here, but could it be you're barking up the wrong magnolia tree?"

"For his sake, I hope not. There's some money involved. It could be his if I find him."

"Well, now, if I was to change my mind and say I know this Jack Callahan fella, could I get some kind of a finder's fee?" She laughed and batted the eyelashes again, giving me the impression she could probably be a lot of fun after she got off work.

"Well, Doris, I would dearly love to do that, but Mr. Callahan would no doubt object."

"Wouldn't he, though?" she said.

"Tell me, what kind of films do you do here at Punch?" The spider webs narrowed slightly as she looked at me.

"Don't go spreadin' this around, but we make films that are…how shall I say this? Of a somewhat 'adult' type?" She made air quotes on the word adult, and winked a spider web.

"I see," I said, and looked at the two guys on the sofa. Both of them had taken notice of my conversation with Doris. I leaned over the desk and whispered. "Are those guys actors of some type?"

"Of some type, yes," she replied. "But lookin' at you, Mr. Butler, I don't think you're that type, so you probably wouldn't be interested in the films we do here at Punch. You get my drift?" She smiled and flashed me another web wink.

"I believe I do, Doris. And I thank you for your time."

"Anytime, sugar," she said and slurped some more Diet Coke.

I tipped my hat to her and pulled the front door open. I was slipping on my sunglasses when I heard the voice behind me.

"Hey, Mister."

I turned to see the black guy with corn-rows walking toward me.

"What do you really want Jack Callahan for?" he asked.

"Just what I said. He might have some money coming to him."

"Bullshit. Clark Butler? Yeah, right. And I'm Hattie McDaniel. C'mon, man."

He'd caught me. I was obviously talking to a movie buff. "You know Jack Callahan?"

"I might. Show me some ID. Mr. Butler."

"Okay, you got me," I said, as I pulled out a business card and handed it to him.

"A private dick. I might have known."

"So tell me about Jack Callahan." I opened the portfolio and pulled out the picture. "This Jack Callahan. You know him?"

The guy looked at the photo and handed it back to me. "I've seen him around."

"Where?"

"West Hollywood."

"Where in West Hollywood?"

"Where do you think?"

"You tell me."

"The dude is gay, man. Figure it out. Why you looking for him?"

"You ever hear of client confidentiality?"

"Which means you ain't gonna tell me."

"That's about it. So where in West Hollywood does he hang out?"

"The Abbey, Fubar, Rage, you name it." He sidled up to me and ran a fingertip along the front of my shirt. "I could help you look if you'd like."

I pushed the fingertip aside and stepped back. "You figured me wrong, pal. I come down on the other side of the fence."

"Too bad," he said, with a smile on his face.

"If you happen to see Jack Callahan, give me a call, will you?"

"Yeah, I'll think about it." He turned around and started back into Punch.

"One more thing," I said. He stopped before opening the door. "You have anything to do with this place when it was on Moorpark?"

"Not much. Before my time, if you know what I mean."

"There was a police action there and this Jack Callahan was apparently arrested. If you know him, did he ever say anything about that?"

"No, man. Not to me."

"Thanks," I said, and he went back into the building. I zipped up my fake portfolio and headed for my car. West Hollywood, especially the stretch along Santa Monica Boulevard, is almost wall-to-wall gay bars and nightclubs. As I opened the trunk I wondered what would be the best way to circulate through the area without getting hit on to the point where it got uncomfortable. Then the answer jumped out at me: my neighbor Lenny Daye. The perfect tour guide. I fired up the car, hung a U-turn and drove half a block before my cellphone went off. I pulled over and fumbled it out of my pocket, but didn't recognize the number. "Hello?"

"Hey, Eddie, it's Roy Dickerson."

"How ya doin', Roy? You land that Santa spot?"

"Not yet. But I did get a callback. Against my better judgment I'm buying another fake beard and a hat."

"There ya go. Good luck."

"Thanks. Hey, listen, the reason I'm calling. You made any progress on finding Jack?"

"A little. Found a place where he used to work and maybe got a line on where he hangs out."

"Terrific."

"Let me ask you something. How close are, or were, you and Jack?"

After a moment or two of silence he said, "Aw, I don't know. Close as cousins get, I guess. Why?"

"Far as you know, Roy, is your cousin a gay man?"

"What?"

"Is he gay?"

There was a pause on the other end of the line before Roy uttered a laugh. "Christ, not that I'm aware of. If he is, he's hidden it pretty well. Not only from me, but from his old man."

"You think that might be what Roth didn't tell us?"

Silence again. "Could be. Did you ask Ben?"

"Not yet."

"Let me know what he says."

"Will do," I said. "Get that damn commercial. Let me hear a ho, ho, ho."

"Fuck you," he said, then laughed and broke the connection.

A delivery truck had boxed me in. As I waited, I thought about the fact of Jack Callahan being gay. In today's zeitgeist it wasn't as much of a social taboo as it was years ago, but to someone like Ben Roth, who grew up in a different era, having a gay son still might be something he would frown upon. Maybe he wanted to make amends, which was the real reason for wanting to reconnect with Jack. I hoped that was the case.

The truck driver was taking his own sweet time letting me get out of my parking space. I needed to talk to Lenny and see if he would help me prowl the West Hollywood gay neighborhood, but before that, the reason for Jack Callahan's arrest was still something that needed answering. There was only one person to help me with that. Charlie Rivers.

I looked at my watch and had an idea where he might be at this time of day. Charlie never missed a lunch. I picked up the phone, scrolled through my contacts and punched in a number.

Chapter Seven

———◆———

THE SIGN OUTSIDE NORM'S ON LA Cienega proclaims "Where life happens." I don't know how that relates to having a patty melt for lunch, but if you don't collapse outside the front door, I guess there's truth in advertising. Over the years I've gotten to be on a first-name basis with some of the people in the LAPD's Hollywood Station. One of them, Debbie Stander, usually knows the whereabouts of Lieutenant Charlie Rivers. That's because he tells her. And then she tells me. Today's call to her put him at this LA landmark a bit north of the Beverly Center. Fortune smiled on me as a Subaru backed out and left me a space in the crowded parking lot.

A hostess asked me how many and I pointed to a corner booth where Charlie sat. A copy of the *Los Angeles Times* was spread out next to him and he was working on a salad. He wore a short-sleeved blue shirt and a loose red tie. As I approached, he looked up and a frown broke out on his face. I folded myself into the booth opposite him.

"How's the salad?"

"Not bad. Until you got here."

"You on a diet?"

"I'm always on a diet."

A waitress walked up with a menu. She put it down and promptly picked it up again when I ordered a patty melt on sourdough, slaw, and a cup of coffee.

Charlie put down his fork and sipped from a glass of iced tea. "How'd you find me?"

"Debbie."

He shook his head. "Woman needs a transfer. Why didn't you just call?"

"I figured I'd spook you."

"You figured right." He stabbed a piece of chicken and looked at me. "What do you want?"

"Nice to see you, too, Charlie." I put a finger on his check and slid it over to my side of the table.

"Are you bribing a police officer, Mr. Collins?"

"Naw, just buying you lunch."

"I'll ask again. What do you want?"

"I need to see an arrest report."

"Send a check or money order for twenty-four bucks to LAPD with the name of the arrestee, date and type of crime. You can get the address online. Better yet, call Debbie. She's a font of information."

"Red tape, Charlie."

"Protocol, Eddie."

He filled a fork with lettuce and a chunk of tomato, then chewed and stared at me, a trace of smugness on his face. The waitress appeared with my coffee and walked off. Charlie still stared. I peeled the top off a container of cream and poured it into the cup. As I stirred, I listened to two old guys in the next booth discussing the merits of Viagra versus Cialis. I guess life does happen at Norm's.

I took a sip of the coffee, then reached in my pocket and pulled out my money clip. I separated a twenty and a five and pushed the bills across the table. He looked at them, then me, and his eyes narrowed to a squint.

"I don't know if you're aware of this, Charlie, but I'm acquainted with a guy who's acquainted with a guy who works in the front office of the Rams."

He swallowed and sipped iced tea, but couldn't hold back the grin that broke out at the corners of his mouth. "You know, Collins, people sometimes refer to me as a teddy bear. I tell them they're full of crap. Why doesn't it work with you?"

"Well, Charlie, I've been told I have the guile of Svengali. Maybe they're right."

He shook his head and pulled a notebook and a pen from his shirt pocket. "Of all the gumshoes in this town, I have to know one that uses guile and Svengali in the same sentence. Spill."

At that moment the waitress appeared with my food and I waited until she walked off. "Jack Callahan," I said. "Arrested at a company by the name of Punch Productions on Moorpark up in the Valley." Charlie jotted and I took a mouthful of the patty melt. I looked at my notebook and gave him the address, approximate date and the rest of the information the guy at the dry cleaners had given me.

"Okay, look," he said. "Since this date goes back a while, I'll cut you some slack. But if you've got an apparent murder here, Hollywood Division hasn't got a homicide desk anymore."

"Since when?"

"Since just recently. How come you don't know that, given the fact that you're such a hot-shot detective?"

"So who handles them now?"

"West, or Robbery Homicide."

"That kinda cuts into your territory, doesn't it?"

He put his fork down and sipped from his iced tea glass. "Well, in case you haven't heard, people are still beating up on people, stealing cars, and generally getting into trouble, so I don't think I'll be put out to pasture. Plus the fact, it gives me more time to fend off pests otherwise known as private detectives. You catch my drift?"

I nodded, took a bite of the sandwich and thought about what he'd just told me. The relationship I'd cultivated with Charlie over the years was invaluable. I didn't relish it being compromised in any way. "Well, look, all I need are names and addresses."

He stabbed some lettuce, chewed, and looked at his notes. "Is this Callahan doing time?"

"That I don't know. I'm inclined to say he's not."

"And why are you so inclined?"

"Someone told me they'd seen him."

"Recently?"

"That was my impression."

"Why are you looking for him?"

"His old man wants to find him."

He jotted some more in his notebook. "You got a fax in that hole in the wall you call an office?"

I gave it to him, along with my cell number. We ate for a moment or two, making small talk about this and that and the weather. The two old guys seemed to agree on Viagra and then got up from their booth and shuffled out the front door. Charlie finished his salad and his iced tea and reached in his pocket.

"I'll leave the tip. How much?"

"Keep your money, Charlie."

"You'll bill your client anyway, right? Expenses?"

"Yeah, hadn't thought of that."

He picked up the twenty and the five I'd slid across the table. "Put these back in your wallet. Bribing a police officer could put your PI ticket in jeopardy." He pushed himself to the edge of the booth and stood up. "I'll poke around and shoot you a fax."

"Appreciate it."

He took a step or two and stopped. "But speaking of bribes, the fifty-yard line would be good."

"I'll see what I can do."

LENNY DAYE'S VOLKSWAGEN WAS IN THE parking lot of my building. Unless he was out wandering the Boulevard, that meant he would be in his office. With Jack Callahan's picture clutched in one hand I stuck my head into Collins Investigations, told Mavis I was on the premises, then pushed my way into the office of *Pecs 'n Abs* magazine, Lenny's thriving little enterprise. Copies of the publication were strewn across a coffee table in front of a couple of canvas director's chairs. Generous amounts of those particular male body parts were displayed on the covers. Whether or not other parts of the male anatomy were on display between said covers, I couldn't tell you. Potted plants stood in the corners of the room and some soft rock drifted from speakers in the ceiling. Lenny's endeavor had launched a few years back. He didn't have much of a payroll, choosing to do most of the work himself, but he did employ someone to answer phones.

That someone was Billy Perkins. His sartorial flamboyance tried to emulate his employer, but fell short. Nevertheless, his hair was black and full of gelled spikes. Hardware hung from around his neck and punctured his ears. His shirt was green and yellow. Loud green and yellow. He looked up from a computer as I opened the door.

"Hi, Eddie," he said.

"You trying to compete with the carpet," I said, pointing to his shirt.

"Oh, my God, can you believe it? I've been eating Dramamine like candy."

"Your boss in?"

"Yes, he is." He picked up the phone, punched a button and said, "Your neighbor wants to see you."

Billy hung up and a few seconds later Lenny flung open the door to his office like he was Tallulah Bankhead making an entrance. Faded jeans that must have been painted on covered his legs. He wore an Hawaiian shirt with more flora and fauna on it than an Amazon rain forest.

"Eddie, darling, don't tell me! You have finally agreed to be my centerfold!"

"If you put me in your magazine, Lenny, your subscribers will storm the office with torches and pitchforks."

"Yours or mine?"

"Both."

"Oooh, I love it."

"You got a minute, Lenny?"

"For you, honey, absolutely."

With another dramatic flourish he gestured for me to enter and then shut the door behind him. Lenny's sanctuary was cluttered with headshots of hunks and assorted copies of magazines and newspapers, many of them the competition. Posters dotted the walls, shots of fashion models, both male and female. His desktop held more clutter, which he shoved to one side as he sat down and folded his hands under his chin.

"What's up?" he said.

"Do you hang around any of those clubs in West Hollywood?"

"By 'those,' do you mean gay clubs?"

"That's right. The ones along Santa Monica."

"Not as much as I used to, but I've been known to drop in from time to time. When I get the urge to roll around in the mud."

I handed him the photo of Callahan. "This guy look at all familiar?"

"No. He's kinda cute, though." He handed the photo back to me. "Who is he?"

"His name is Jack Callahan. His old man is a client of mine, and he wants me to find him."

Lenny leaned back in his chair and locked his hands behind his head. "How does that fit in with West Hollywood?"

"I have reason to believe he's gay."

"Well, why didn't you say so in the first place? Now I'm all ears. Tell, tell."

"I'll buy you dinner if you help me out."

"Restaurant of my choice?"

"You name it."

He leaned over his desk again. "What do you need?"

"I want you to take me along on a swing through some of those clubs."

"Oh, my God, Eddie, are you sure?"

"Yeah. Why?"

"I know you sometimes channel Sam Spade, but those places are pretty in-your-face. Are you sure you're up for it?" He cocked his head and grinned. "Figuratively speaking, of course."

"That's why you're going to walk point for me."

"I don't know whether to feel flattered or threatened. When do you want to do this?"

"Tonight. You have plans?"

"I was going to organize my spice rack, but that can wait. What time?"

"Whenever's good for you."

"I shall knock on your portal at eight. That all right?"

"I'll see you then," I said, and got out of my chair. "What do you think I should wear? I can't compete with your wardrobe."

"Oh, for God's sake, Eddie, don't even try. Some leather might be good. I'd leave the plaid shirt behind, though."

I said hello to one of the Elite Talent Agency's clients as I closed Lenny's office door. A redhead with legs that were meant for dancing. She smiled and pointed to the carpet.

"Does your landlord have it in for you, Mr. Collins?"

"Kinda looks like it, doesn't it?"

I pushed open my office door. Mavis was on her computer, a frown on her face.

"What's the matter?" I said.

"I'm bidding with some doofus up in Sacramento."

I assumed she was on eBay, which is where she gets most of these so-called antiques and collectibles she deals with. "Bidding on what?"

"Howdy Doody and Buffalo Bob bobble heads."

I shook my head and picked up the mail. Bills and a residual for $4.26. Terrific. I had a brief thought of signing the check over to Mavis to help pay for the bobble heads.

"There's a fax from Charlie Rivers on your desk."

"Thanks." I hung my porkpie on its peg, went into my apartment to hit the head and came back to my desk and looked at Charlie's fax. The cover sheet read, "*Here you go. Not much. Hope it helps. Thanks for lunch.*"

I propped my feet up on the desk and started to look over the sheets. Gunfire had been reported by someone walking in the alley behind Punch Productions. Police arrived to find one Jeremy Tipton dead from a GSW to upper torso. The crime scene appeared to be a bedroom scene for a movie. Lights and camera equipment were found in the room. A loaded 9mm lay nearby. Jack Callahan was found lying several feet away from the victim, dazed, suffering from lacerations on both arms. There were no other persons at the crime scene.

Mavis suddenly erupted with a "Yes!" from her office. She bounced into the doorway and said, "Howdy Doody's on his way."

"I'm very happy for you," I said, which prompted her don't-mess-with-me look. I decided to keep any further editorial comments to myself and instead told her of my intention to go prowling with Lenny that evening.

"Are you going to behave yourself?"

"Depends on how drunk I get."

"Yeah, well, that's all you need."

"I'm just going to ask questions and show a picture of the guy. Which reminds me." I handed her the photo of Jack Callahan. "Make me a copy of this, will you?"

"Can do," she said, as she grabbed it and went back to her office.

I turned my attention back to the fax. Callahan had been arrested and held over for questioning. The 9mm turned out to be registered to a Tabatha

Preston. Callahan's prints weren't on the firearm and there was no trace of gun shot residue on his hands or clothing. LAPD grilled him for as long as they could without charging him and he was eventually released due to a lack of evidence. No witnesses. He said that the lacerations on his arms were the result of a prior scuffle with Preston and a Bart Helms. Tabatha Preston had subsequently been tried, but was acquitted. I couldn't find anything as to whether or not the case was ever solved.

That was it. Nothing to point to Callahan being involved in the murder. So there had to be something else that had made Ben Roth disown his son. Based on what the guy with the corn rows had told me outside of Punch Productions, it seemed highly likely that Ben had kicked his son out because he was gay. Maybe my foray into West Hollywood would provide an answer. But would it help bridge a gap between father and son? That remained to be seen.

CHAPTER EIGHT

———◆———

THERE WAS, INDEED, SOMETHING LEATHER IN my closet. A vest I'd bought for some long-forgotten audition. It was black, and when I put it on I felt I was ready for the O.K. Corral. A simple red, striped shirt and a pair of khakis completed the outfit. Lenny, however, insisted I ditch the porkpie. Reluctantly, I agreed and tossed it on Mavis's desk as we headed for the parking lot. Lenny's Volkswagen would be easier to park, so we opted for his car. As usual, his attire didn't disappoint. A red paisley shirt was tucked into black leather trousers. He wore black, calf-high boots on his feet and jewelry hung from his neck.

"Where do you buy your clothes?" I said, as we moved into the right lane on La Brea, heading south.

"A great little boutique on Melrose. Funky, inexpensive. There's all kinds of them down there. The bling is paste, anywhere I can find it."

"Sorry, I'm short on bling." I said.

"Oh, you'll be fine, honey." We caught a red light on Sunset, waited for three cars and turned right. "Now, how are we going to proceed here, Mister Private Eye?"

I handed him the extra photo of Callahan that Mavis had made. "Without being too obvious, just casually show the picture and ask if they know him."

"Why am I looking for him?"

"A family member wants to find him. His father is sick."

"Well, is he? The father, I mean."

I'd told Lenny a little about why I was looking for Jack Callahan, but not everything. "Ben Roth is still alive. In his nineties, but still kicking."

"Sounds familiar. Kicking someone out because he's gay."

"I don't know that for sure."

"I'd bet my last dollar on it."

A red light caught us at Crescent Heights. Lenny stared straight ahead with a look on his face that I hadn't seen before.

"Is that what happened to you?" I asked, and immediately regretted saying it. "Sorry, none of my business."

"No, it's okay, Eddie. And yes, that's what happened to me."

"How old were you?"

"Eighteen. My Gawd, that's twenty years ago already."

"This was in Bakersfield, right?"

"Fresno. Same environment. Dust and rednecks." He took a deep breath and looked off to his left. "I'd known I was gay for a few years. But in a strict Catholic family with an old man who drooled over professional wrestlers, having a faggot for a son was unheard of. I mean, he thought Haystack Calhoun and Killer Kowalski were minor gods."

"How'd your mother feel?"

"She was okay with me coming out, bless her soul. Not so my dad. He basically told me to get lost and come back when I'd 'straightened myself' out, as he put it. So I did. Got lost, I mean. The other ain't gonna happen." He laughed as the light changed and we began moving toward the Sunset Strip. "My dad died three years ago, and it was a real chore for me to even go to the funeral. Good thing my boyfriend was with me."

"I didn't know you're with someone."

"I'm not now. That was then. Dear Tommy."

"What happened?"

"He moved on, to put it politely." Lenny slapped me on the shoulder. "For fuck's sake, what is this, True Confessions?"

"Aw, you're right. My nose is out of joint."

"Well, since you started it, Mavis tells me there's a girlfriend. True?"

"True. Carla Rizzoli. An actress."

"That's not all, dear, at least according to your secretary. Hmmmm?"

"Sounds like someone else's nose is out of joint. Okay. Carla also works as a dancer. But she just landed a pilot, so maybe she'll be done with wrapping herself around a pole."

"Good for her. And you," Lenny said. La Cienega appeared and we hung a left. "So we should do this separately?" he continued. "Ask our questions? Not hang together?"

"I think so. If we get too obvious, we might blow the whole thing."

"Not in public, dear." I turned to look at him and he laughed. "I'm sorry, Eddie, it's just my potty mouth. I promise I'll be good." I finally got his double entendre and shook my head as he let loose with what could best be described as a cackle. Lenny was having fun and I was glad he was in a good mood because I was admittedly heading into uncharted waters.

We turned right on Santa Monica Boulevard and started looking for a place to park. "There should be valet parking, right?" I said.

"No way, Jose. The last time I was down here I let someone park my car and he stunk it up with the smell of his cologne."

I chuckled and looked off to my right at the sidewalk full of pedestrians. I was about to gaze front again when something caught my eye. Strolling along Santa Monica Boulevard was Roy Dickerson.

"What the hell?" I said, as I turned to look over my shoulder.

"What's the matter?"

"Just saw a guy I know."

"Who?"

"An actor friend. Roy Dickerson. Very strange."

"How so?"

I told Lenny that Dickerson was Jack Callahan's cousin and related how he'd been surprised when I'd asked him if his cousin was gay. "I just find it odd to see him in this neighborhood."

"Maybe he's looking for his cousin."

"Could be."

"Either that or he's also gay. And here I thought I was your only gay friend, Eddie."

"Sorry to disappoint. I've been an actor for too many years. And I don't think Roy Dickerson fits the bill."

"Looks are deceiving, honey," he said.

He turned onto a side street, lucked out and found a space. He shut off the car, turned to me and said, "You ready, sailor?"

"As ready as I'll ever be," I said.

"Now listen, if you start to feel uncomfortable let me know, okay? Some of these guys can get a bit ridiculous."

We locked the doors of the Volkswagen and walked back to Santa Monica. There was no sign of Dickerson. Colored lights hung from trees along the boulevard and several young men stood at the curb, smoking. They gave both of us the eye as we walked past them. We came to the front door of a club called Rage. To the left was an outdoor patio with tables full of patrons.

When we stepped inside, the first impression I got was the sound of deafening rock music generated by a DJ at the far side of the room on an elevated platform and behind a fiberglass barricade. He was bare-chested and had a red derby on his head. Sunglasses covered his eyes and he bounced with the music, dreadlocks flying from underneath the brim of the hat. If woofers and tweeters are the two types of loudspeakers, Rage never heard of the latter.

I could feel the bass through the soles of my shoes. Strobe lights in sync with the music pulsed over a full dance floor and faint traces of synthetic smoke wafted through the shafts of light. I noticed a few pairs of female dancers gyrating among the men.

The walls of the club displayed a myriad of posters. Liza Minnelli shared space with Marilyn, Andy Warhol and David Bowie. On a small platform to my left four male dancers in nothing but leather boots and speedos were doing their best to imitate the Village People. Not with lyrics, mind you, but with clothing. Any attempt at singing in this cacophony was hopeless.

As we started toward the bar, two young men with blond hair started gyrating in front of us in time to the music. They were both dressed in black, with gothic-style makeup. Their hairstyles were fashioned in the form of a guillotine blade running down the middle of their heads. If they were sleeping together I couldn't help but wonder if they risked inflicting bodily harm on each other. One of them did a bump and grind in front of me, but quickly moved on when he caught sight of my look of indifference.

Lenny ushered me up to the bar and a young bartender wearing a black wife-beater that showed off two muscular arms full of tattoos ambled over to us. A gold chain was around his neck and a tuft of black chest hair poked over the top of the tank top. The obligatory Hollywood stubble covered his face.

"Oh, my God, Lenny!" he screamed. "I haven't seen you in ages!" He slapped two napkins in front of us. "Where have you been, darling?"

"Staying out of trouble, Tony," Lenny shouted, then leaned over the bar and the two men kissed. He turned to me and put an arm across my shoulders. "This is my friend Eddie."

"Hey, Eddie," Tony said, as he extended a hand across the bar.

"Eddie isn't one of us, Tony, so please be kind."

Tony clapped his hands, and threw his head back in laughter. "I shall be on my best behavior. What can I get you guys?"

"Do you still remember how to make a Between The Sheets?" Lenny said.

"Oh, you devil," Tony replied. "Of course I do. The same for you, Eddie?"

"Just a double bourbon on the rocks," I said.

Looking disappointed, he pursed his lips in my direction and moved off. I turned to Lenny. "What the hell is in a Between The Sheets?"

"Rum, brandy, triple sec, and I forget what else."

"Am I going to have to drive home?"

"One of those is all I can handle, Eddie. Tony makes them special for me." I raised my eyebrows, asking a question with the look. "Okay, okay," he said. "We went out a few times. I left when he started to get interested in NASCAR."

He shook his head and I looked around the room. The dress code was eclectic, to say the least. The night could have been Halloween, with plenty of competition as to who was the trick and who was the treat. There were dozens of bare chests with glitter sprinkled over many of them. A city ordinance obviously prevented women from going the same route, but several of the ladies came damn close.

Tony skipped down the bar and set our drinks in front of us. "Here you go, Lenny. This'll bring back memories." He laughed, picked up the credit card I'd put on the bar and walked off. Lenny's Between The Sheets was amber in color and filled a martini glass. A twist of lemon hung from the lip. He sipped and said, "Delicious. You want a taste?"

"Sorry, pal. Between the sheets has another connotation for me."

He slapped me on the arm. "Well, don't rub it in, for God's sake. I'm glad somebody's getting laid." He pulled the picture of Callahan from his shirt pocket as I took a pull on the bourbon. Tony came with the tab he'd started. A glance at it proved I was in some damn expensive atmosphere.

The DJ's playlist suddenly changed and the bass jungle beat increased. I could swear I saw my drink's ice cubes start to dance. Lenny had to shout as he handed the picture to the bartender. "Tony, does this guy look familiar?"

He looked closely at Callahan's photo. "Yeah, kind of. The hair's different, though."

"Has he been in here?" I said.

"I've seen him a time or two."

"Tonight?" I said.

"Can't say. Pouring booze gets all my attention." He swiped at a patch of liquid with a bar rag. "Why are you looking?"

"His family wants him located," I said."

"What's his name?" Tony asked.

"Jack Callahan."

He stopped what he was doing and looked at me. "Hey, wait a minute. Somebody asked me earlier about a Jack Callahan."

"Big guy?" I said. "Pretty much bald?"

"No, it was a woman. African American. A real princess."

"How do you mean?" I said.

"Big. Not someone I'd mess with," he said.

Lenny and I exchanged a look and I said, "Is she still in here?"

Tony looked around the bar and pointed to a table. "I don't see her, but earlier she was talking to those two black guys. The ones in the tee shirts."

"Thanks," I said.

Tony patted Lenny on the cheek. "Don't be a stranger, sweetheart," he said and walked off.

"So who's the woman, Eddie?" Lenny said.

"I'm not sure, but it could be somebody who knows Callahan."

"Should I start asking around?"

"Yeah, go ahead." I picked up my drink and the tab and walked over to the table Tony had pointed out. The two guys looked to be in their twenties. One sported closely-cropped hair and had a glass sitting in front of him with what looked to be half an orchard dangling from the edge. The other guy's head was shaved. He wore rimless glasses and held a glass of white wine. They were leaning into each other and looked up as I slid into a chair.

"Hi, guys. My name's Eddie." I stuck out my hand to the bald guy.

"Mark," he said, and I extended my hand to his companion.

"I'm Vinnie," said the guy as he shook my hand. "Haven't seen you in here before."

"No, afraid not. I'm..." I left the sentence hanging.

"You're straight," Vinnie said. "Go ahead, you can say it." All three of us laughed. The ice had been broken.

"That obvious, huh?"

"Sort of," Mark said.

I pulled the picture out and showed it to them. "I'm looking for this guy. His name's Jack Callahan. He look familiar?"

Vinnie took the photo and held it up to what little light there was. "What's he done?" he said.

"What makes you think he's done something wrong?"

"You've got cop written all over you," Vinnie said.

"Obvious again?" I asked. Vinnie nodded and sipped from his orchard. "Okay. I'm a private eye. The guy hasn't done anything. His family wants to find him. Have you seen him or do you know him?" They looked at each other and shook their heads. I took a taste of the bourbon. "Tony the bartender over there told me a large African American woman asked him about this guy in the picture. Then he saw her talking to you guys. Sure you don't know him?"

"We're sure," said Vinnie.

"But you know the woman I'm talking about?"

"Yeah," he said, and glanced around. "But look, man, we don't want any trouble."

"No trouble, guys. Just tell me her name."

"Tabatha. Tabatha Preston," Vinnie said.

"Thanks." I stood up and looked around for Lenny. He was across the room at a table with three other guys. I walked back to the bar and ordered another drink.

Another piece of the puzzle had slid into place. Tabatha Preston was the woman arrested at Punch Productions and tried for murder, the same murder for which Jack Callahan had had cuffs slapped on him.

CHAPTER NINE

——— ◆ ———

WE CONTINUED TO CIRCULATE CALLAHAN'S PICTURE around the interior of Rage, but didn't come up with anything more helpful than what I'd learned from Vinnie and Mark. I watched Lenny say farewells to some friends of his, a process that included many hugs and kisses. We finally stood on the sidewalk in front of the club, the sound of traffic on Santa Monica Boulevard a welcome relief.

"Well, what now?" he said.

"Good question. Another place? Or is that spice rack calling?"

"Salt, pepper and garlic powder, Eddie. That's about it."

We headed down the block to another club called Micky's and walked inside. The place was packed and equally as loud as Rage. A gold-plated sphere hung from the ceiling, rotating and shooting out laser beams of various colors. Against the back wall, more lasers shot out from pockets embedded in what looked like a piece of blue sheetrock. In keeping with the light show, someone costumed as Darth Vader was the club's DJ.

A male dancer on a platform near the bar did his best to bring on an early need for back surgery. No speedo for this guy. A jockstrap and high-top work boots. That was it. Several women at the edge of the stage stuffed bills into his jockstrap. At one point he got a friendly grope that provoked a huge smile from him and shrieks from the crowd watching him.

We began to jostle our way through the mob toward the bar. Three men wearing floppy hats that looked like lily pads stood in our way. They had clown-white makeup on their faces, making me think they were rejects from the rock band Kiss. We finally reached the bar, behind which stood three glowing glass pyramids that had bottles of every liquor known to man perched on their shelves. A bartender with a necklace of fake teeth and wearing a leather loincloth leaned over the bar and took our orders. I shouted out another double bourbon and Lenny asked for a glass of white wine.

"No more Between The Sheets'?" I said.

"I'll be three sheets to the wind if I have another one of those things."

"Is it always so damned loud in these places?"

"Loud and proud, Eddie."

"And deaf," I said, as I pointed to Tarzan pouring our drinks. "Do you think he's looking for Jane?"

Lenny doubled over in laughter. "That ring on his finger tells me he's already found him."

Tarzan set our drinks in front of us and I again surrendered my credit card and asked to run a tab. The dancer with the jockstrap was replaced by a drag queen dressed as a cross between Lady Gaga and Mae West. After a couple of minutes Lenny recognized some people he knew and wormed his way down the bar. I sipped on my drink and gazed around, secretly pining for a sweaty Los Angeles Laker locker room. The profession I still consider myself to be a part of is totally indifferent to one's sexual orientation. That's never bothered me, but I had to confess that being in this environment, while I didn't feel threatened or uncomfortable, made me glad I had Carla in my life.

I picked up my drink and stuffed the tab in my shirt pocket, then pulled Callahan's photo out and started making the rounds. The occupants of the first table basically told me to get lost. The next three or four displayed more courtesy, but didn't reveal any valuable information.

I ambled over to a long high-top table and straddled a stool. At one end to my right were two young women with eyes for nobody but themselves. To my left two men sat across from each other. One was a little closer to my age, a fact that gave me an odd twinge of camaraderie. His hair was gray and thinning. Soft wrinkles surrounded his eyes. He looked at me, nodded and smiled. His companion sitting across from him was younger and wore a black tank top. He had floral tattoos on his arms and a spider web on the side of his neck. A small red earring dangled from his right lobe. A black bandana surrounded his head. I nodded at the two of them and sipped on my drink. After a few minutes Darth Vader took a break and I pulled out Callahan's photo and slid over to a stool next to the guy with the bandana.

"Excuse me," I said. "Wonder if I could ask you fellas a couple of questions."

"As long as they don't involve Republicans or the NFL," the younger man said. "Well, maybe tight ends," he added. His companion chuckled and shook his head.

"No right-wingers or tight ends," I said. "I'm looking for the guy in this photo. Either of you by any chance know him, or have seen him?"

The older guy looked at the photo, shook his head and handed it across the table to his companion, then looked at me. "Doesn't ring a bell."

Bandana looked at the picture closely and finally said, "Hmmm, I'm not sure. Maybe." He kept looking at the photo and finally handed it back to me. "Nope. Sorry."

"You look familiar, though," the older man said, addressing me.

"The name's Eddie," I said, as I extended my hand.

"Chris," he said and we shook. He pointed to Bandana next to me. "This Ninja spiderman here is Walt," he continued. Walt laid the picture down and gave me a little martial arts pose with his hands before shaking.

"How do I look familiar, Chris?" I said.

"You wouldn't be an actor, would you?"

"Sometimes," I replied.

"A few years back I worked on a film called *Big Trouble*. You were on it also, weren't you?"

I sipped some bourbon and thought back through my checkered resume. "Yeah, I was. On the Fox lot." I paused for a moment and pointed at him. "You were—"

"The crooked DA," he said.

"Right. The one that got away with it."

"And he's still getting away with it," Walt added.

We laughed and shared a tidbit or two about the film. A waiter came by and I handed him my tab and told him to bring another round.

"You ever see any residuals on that thing?" I said.

Chris scoffed. "Shiiiiit. Might have bought me some cat food now and then. I think that turkey went straight to video." He sipped from his drink. "So, Eddie, I didn't know you'd..." He paused, leaving the sentence hanging.

"I haven't," I said. "I'm also a PI and I've been hired to find this guy in the photo. His name's Jack Callahan."

Walt picked up the picture. "Okay, hold the phone, Alice. I have met this dude."

"When?"

"Earlier tonight."

"In here?" I said.

"Yeah. He was right over—." He pointed to a far corner of the room. "Oh, crap, he's gone."

"Does he hang out here a lot, Walt?"

"I've seen him a few times."

"With the same people?"

"Not always." The waiter showed up with the drinks I'd ordered. Walt finished the old one and we clinked the new glasses. He picked up his drink and the photo and crawled off his stool. "Don't start anything without me. I'll be right back."

I watched him walk away and turned back to Chris. "Am I going to get that picture back?"

"Oh, yeah, no problem," he replied. "Walt hangs out here more than I do. As you can see, his flamboyance is a better fit than mine. Or lack of it, I should say. He knows everybody."

I watched Walt sit down at a table with three other men. He had the picture in his hand and started showing it around.

"So, Eddie, a PI? You give up the acting career?"

"No, not entirely. Still waiting to become a household name. How about you?"

Chris tasted his drink and dabbed at his mouth with a napkin. "Still hangin' in there, even though sometimes I think my agent forgets my name."

"I know the feeling," I said.

"You want to know the latest, craziest thing happening?"

"I'm afraid to ask."

"Now some of these snot-nosed casting directors won't even take a look at you unless your Twitter feed is at a certain level."

I almost choked on my drink. "You have got to be kidding me."

"No lie. Happened to me last month."

"So you've got a Twitter feed?"

"I do now. But I'm not sure I'm keen on letting everyone know what I'm reading when I'm sitting on the can."

"Yeah, I hear you," I said.

The two young women at the other end of the high-top got off their stools and wandered off. Chris and I swapped a few war stories about the biz and he told me he'd come out a few years back. I asked him if he felt it had been a detriment to his career, and he said it hadn't.

"I'm all right as long as I keep tweeting," he said, and we both laughed and raised our glasses.

Walt bounced back to his stool and laid the picture down, along with a slip of paper. He folded his arms across his chest and let out a huge sigh. "Well!" he said, with a look of expectancy on his face.

The two of us glanced at each other, then at Walt and the huge smile on his face. We waited for more, but it wasn't forthcoming.

"Well, for God's sake, what?" Chris finally said.

Walt unfolded the scrap of paper and deliberately placed it in front of me. "Jack Callahan was indeed in here and the guys over there told me they know where he lives. On Cynthia Street between Doheny and San Vicente. They don't know the house number, but it's a corner lot with a white picket fence around the yard."

"They're sure?" I said.

"Absolutely."

I stuffed the piece of paper in my shirt pocket and finished my drink. "Thanks, Walt. I really appreciate it."

"Is this Callahan in trouble?" Chris said.

"No. His dad's trying to locate him."

"Good luck," Walt said, as he stuck out his hand.

"Take care, guys. And Chris, keep on tweeting," I said.

He laughed, shook my hand and I slid off my stool. I looked around for Lenny and spotted him leaning against the bar, talking to two men. I settled up with Tarzan the bartender, caught Lenny's eye through the din and motioned that I'd be outside. As I negotiated the crowd and pushed the door open I felt my cellphone buzz. I fished it out and saw it was a text from Carla, asking me to call her when I could. Lenny came up behind me.

"Any luck?" he said.

I showed him the scrap of paper. "This is where Callahan lives."

"That's right around the corner. You want to knock on his door?"

"Not now," I said. "A stranger showing up on his doorstep at night might spook him."

"You're right. So have you had enough fun for one night?"

"I'm afraid so. You?"

"If I smell any more Hermes cologne I'm going to start baying at the moon."

I clapped him on the shoulder and we walked to his VW. On the way back to my building Lenny told me he'd gotten reacquainted with a former boyfriend. He said he didn't have high hopes for the flame being reignited, since the guy was in a relationship.

He pulled into his parking space and I stuck out my hand. "Thanks for your help, Lenny. I owe you one."

"Oh, stop. It felt good to kick up my heels a little. I'll see you around the ranch."

"Yes, you will."

"You going to drop in on Callahan tomorrow?"

"That's my plan."

"Well, good luck," he said, and put the VW in gear as I extricated myself from the front seat. He chugged off to his house in the Los Feliz district while I opened the door to my building and endured another groaning ascent in the elevator. The cockamamie pattern of the carpet only added to the sensory overload I'd experienced during the last few hours. There were no messages on the answering machine. I battened down the hatch, pawed through the beaded curtain and flopped down in my easy chair. After the assault on my senses for the last couple of hours, the silence in my lair above Hollywood Boulevard was deafening.

I didn't know if Carla was working at the club, but figured I'd chance it. Fortunately she picked up after one ring. "Hi there," I said. "Are you cooling your heels?"

"By that if you mean am I between sets, yes, I am."

"Making any money?"

"A delightful little gentleman slipped me a twenty."

"Wow. He obviously took a liking to that gorgeous leg with the rose tattoo. Or was he drunk?"

"On his way, but thanks for the compliment. One of the girls thought maybe he was a Catholic and wanted to atone for his indiscretions." She laughed and made my night brighter. "And what have you been up to?"

I told her where I'd been and what I'd learned. I could hear her giggling on the other end of the line. "I wish I'd been a fly on the wall."

"Believe me, you'd have fit right in."

"So you're going to surprise him in the morning?"

"Yeah."

"I'd invite myself over, but it sounds like you need to decompress."

"I couldn't think of a better term. My head feels like a drum."

"Let me know how it goes."

"I will." We said our good nights and I hung up. After a couple of minutes I punched the remote for the television. What greeted me was a rerun of the Beatles movie *Help!* I gave up, turned off the set and pulled down Mr. Murphy's bed.

CHAPTER TEN

---◆---

THROUGH TRIAL AND ERROR, ALONG WITH coaxing from my intrepid secretary, I've become relatively proficient in the use of my cellphone and its various uses. Maps, however, baffle the hell out of me, causing me to continue to use *The Thomas Guide* mapbook. I was at my desk with a magnifying glass zeroed in on the page showing where Cynthia, Jack Callahan's street, was located. It was literally around the corner from where Lenny and I had been last night. I put the page number on a Post-It and stuck it in my shirt pocket. Before I could take a sip of coffee, the phone rang.

"Collins Investigations."

"Aha, my favorite gumshoe! This is your favorite agent."

That would be Morrie Howard. "What's up?" I said. "Are you the bearer of good news?"

"No word on that commercial, but I've got you an audition at Universal tomorrow morning. Ten o'clock."

"For what?"

"That *Shades of Blue* thing on NBC. You know? The one with JLo?"

"What's the part?"

"An Internal Affairs cop. Turn on your charm and maybe they'll keep you hanging around."

"Hold that thought, Morrie."

"I'll email you the material and the location. Go get it, gumshoe."

He broke the connection and I hung up the phone. My calendar had just become a little more crowded: a search for a missing person, meeting a daughter I'd never seen, and now trying to get the always-illusive acting job.

Hopefully, the trifecta would be successful on all fronts.

The office door opened announcing the arrival of Mavis. She poked her head around the corner. "Good morning, Eddie."

"Mornin'. How you doin'?"

"I'm sick of this heat." I heard her start up her coffee machine. After a couple of minutes she came into my office and laid a copy of the *Hollywood Reporter* on my desk. "Well, you don't look the worse for wear," she said, as she sat down. "How did it go with Lenny?"

"We were witnesses to a collision between Mardi Gras and Halloween."

"That bad, huh?"

"With a dash of Alice in Wonderland."

"But did you find out anything?"

"I think I know where Jack Callahan lives."

"I'm glad. Because, you know, I got to thinking how you're going to deal with a case when your daughter is coming to town."

"Wait a minute. You're the one who brought up the term multitasking." She looked at me like she'd just been caught with her hand in the cookie jar.

"Hmmmm. So I did," she said. "And do you think you're up to it?"

"Absolutely. And just to show you how much, I just got off the phone with Morrie. I've got an audition for that Jennifer Lopez show."

"Yeah, *Shades of Blue*. She's good in that. When is it?"

"Tomorrow morning. Ten o'clock."

"Well, multitask away, Boss Man."

"Maybe I'll get lucky and Jack Callahan will magically appear."

"So you haven't talked to him?"

"Hoping to do so this morning."

"Robinson said they're coming tomorrow, right?"

"Sometime in the afternoon."

"Good. Then it's going to work out." She got up from her chair and proceeded to tell me that her husband Fritz, a bus driver, had been involved in an accident with some fool trying to cut in front of his bus. No damage, except to the guy's pride and his new Beemer. She booted up her computer and when I came out of my office I saw that she was already on the eBay site to begin her daily selling and swapping of geegaws and tchotchkes.

"Check in with you later, Kiddo."

"Good luck," she said.

WHEN THE ELEVATOR HIT THE GROUND floor, it opened to reveal my neighbor, the Russian doctor. He nodded curtly and mumbled something incoherent as we jockeyed for position in the door's opening. He pushed the button to our floor and stared straight ahead as the door creaked close. As talkative as he is, someday I'm not going to be surprised to find out his practice is a fraud and is actually a front for the Russian mob.

A trash truck was parked in the alley behind our parking spaces. Nobody was behind the wheel. I walked to the rear and saw two garbage men leaned against a dumpster talking to a young woman who definitely wasn't from the League of Women Voters. They had their backs to me and when the woman saw me she said something to one of them and they turned around. I asked them if I was interrupting something and how long they were going to be. With sheepish looks on their faces, they scurried into the cab of the truck. As the truck lurched down the alley, I fired up my car, backed out, made a right on Hollywood Boulevard and headed for Cynthia Street, where I hoped to find Jack Callahan. If ninja spiderman Walt's information wasn't accurate, I didn't have a plan B. Callahan's answering the door would put my fears to rest. Otherwise, I'd have to wing it.

At Melrose and La Brea I caught a red light and pulled up behind a pickup belching black smoke. My cell went off and I looked at the screen. Roy Dickerson. "I'm in my car, Roy, let me pull over." The light changed and a cloud of black smoke erupted from the pickup as we moved into the intersection. I turned right on Melrose to save my lungs, slid next to a curb and put the phone to my ear.

"Hey, Santa, how you doin'?"

"Ho, ho, ho," he replied, then laughed. "I've been practicing. You find my cousin yet?"

"Workin' on it. I might know where he lives."

"Where?"

"On Cynthia, maybe. I don't have a house number. But I'll let you know when I find out for sure."

"Gotcha," he replied.

"Hey, I saw you last night, but you got away before I could give you a shout-out."

After a pause he said, "Last night? Where?"

"On Santa Monica, walking by that club Rage."

There was another short silence. "Oh, yeah, I popped into Barney's, but couldn't find a goddamn parking place. Had to walk back a few blocks." The place he referred to was Barney's Beanery, near the intersection of Santa Monica and La Cienega, one in a chain of very popular gastropubs in the greater LA area.

"Love Barney's," I said.

"Can't argue with you." I caught sight of a bus pulling in behind me. "Well, listen," Roy continued. "I was just checkin' in with you. Thought I'd give Ben a call to see how he's doin'. Maybe if you had some info, I could pass it along."

"I'll let him know if I find out anything, Roy."

"Okay," he said. He broke the connection and I pulled away from the curb.

Cynthia Street consisted mostly of apartment buildings. I drove the length of it between San Vicente and Doheny and found only one house matching the description I'd gotten last night in Micky's. It was a corner lot and had a white picket fence surrounding it, just like Walt had described. I found a parking space a few doors down and walked back to the house. It was painted in pale blue, with white trim around the windows. A small front porch held several potted plants and a wooden glider was suspended on chains from the ceiling. There was a mature apple tree planted in the manicured front lawn. A circular bench surrounded the trunk, and several birds dined on fruit that had fallen to the ground.

I spotted a doorbell next to an aluminum screen door and pushed it. After a few moments the front door swung open. The person standing in the opening definitely wasn't Jack Callahan. He was big, he was black, he was dressed in black, and the scowl on his face made it very clear I was unwelcome on his turf.

"Help you?" he said.

"Does Jack Callahan live here?"

"Who's asking?"

I fished out my PI ticket and handed it to him. He looked at it, then me.

"Got a photo ID?"

Once again, I dug and handed him my driver's license. He eyed it and handed back the IDs. I slipped them into my shirt pocket and he stepped back.

"Come on in."

The room in front of me was small and had glass doors on the far side looking out onto a patio and backyard with a small swimming pool. Two white leather sofas with magazines and newspapers spread over them sat at right angles facing a flat-screen television set in one corner. A hallway to my left led to what I assumed were bedrooms. A dining room was on the right. Other details eluded me because the black guy poked me in the chest and pushed me until I collided with a wall. Two pictures crashed to the floor.

"I saw you in Micky's last night," he rasped. "What the hell do you want?"

I slapped his hand away. "I need to talk to Jack Callahan."

"Why?"

"That's none of your goddamn business." I shoved him backward. He started toward me again, one fist cocked and bound for my head, but he stopped when we both heard a voice from the hallway. I turned to my left and saw Jack Callahan standing underneath an archway.

"Alex! What the hell is going on?"

"This is the guy I told you about. The one who was snooping around Micky's last night," Alex said. "He says he's a private eye."

"Okay, so he's a private eye. You don't need to hit him, for crying out loud."

"Crissakes, guys," I said. "Why don't you invest in a welcome mat?"

Alex picked up the two pictures and rehung them. Callahan walked over to me. He wore sandals, cut-off denim shorts and a white polo shirt. He didn't look too different from his photo, although there was less hair, and what was left was cut short.

"Are you all right?" Callahan said.

"I'll live."

"I'm Jack Callahan," he said, as he extended his hand. "I see you've already met Alex."

"Wish I could say it was a pleasure," I said and handed him my IDs.

Alex scowled at me and said, "Sorry, man, but the word last night was you were getting pretty nosy." I returned his scowl and he walked into what appeared to be a kitchen off to my right.

Callahan handed back my licenses. "Why are you looking for me, Mr. Collins?"

"Your father hired me to find you."

My response caused his eyes to widen and he stared at me for a moment. "My father? What the hell for?"

"He didn't exactly tell me, but it sounded like he might want to make amends." Callahan gestured for me to take a seat. We settled onto the ends of the two white leather sofas. "He basically disowned you a few years ago, right?" I said.

"That's putting it politely."

"He said something about you investing some of his money on a film?"

He let out a huge sigh and shook his head. "Man, is he still obsessing over that?"

"Well, your cousin Roy Dickerson—"

"Oh, my God, crazy cousin Roy? Does he still smoke those foul cigarettes?"

"He does," I said.

Alex came out of the kitchen with a set of keys in one hand. "I'm off to Ralph's. You need anything, Jack?"

"I'm good."

He leaned over and the two men kissed. Alex stuck his hand out to me and we shook. "No hard feelings?" he said.

"You better work on that hair trigger."

"I'll think about," he said, and went out the front door.

"Can I get you anything, Mr. Collins?" Callahan said.

"A bottle of water?"

He jumped up and went into the kitchen and came back with two plastic bottles. He laid a magazine on the glass-topped coffee table in front of me and set one of the bottles on it, then did the same with his.

"I'm sorry about Alex," he said. "He's the alpha dog around here, and he tends to be a little over-protective."

He sat down, twisted off the top of his bottle and sipped. A pack of cigarettes lay on the coffee table next to an overflowing ashtray. He lit one with a lighter, leaned back and said, "Okay, back to my obsessive father."

"Well, Roy and I talked to him the day before yesterday. He gave me the background of your relationship, but I sensed there was something else that your dad didn't share with us. Any idea what it could be?"

"That should be pretty obvious by now, shouldn't it?" he said, with a smile.

"That you're gay?"

He nodded.

"And he didn't approve?"

"To put it mildly."

"So he turned his back on you?"

"Big time," Callahan said. "I haven't talked to him since."

"Why were you arrested?"

He took a drag from his cigarette and exhaled a cloud of smoke. "Did the old man tell you that?"

"No, but he told me about Punch Productions. A dry cleaner on Moorpark told me there was a shooting there. Then I saw the police report."

He took a swallow from the bottle and screwed the top back on. "Well, well, it seems the private eye's been earning his fee."

"Punch Productions moved up to San Fernando. Your name there doesn't exactly meet with approval."

"No, I don't suppose it does."

"What happened?"

Callahan uncrossed his legs and leaned forward. "I asked my father to loan me some money so I could invest in a film I had written."

"A gay film?"

"That's right," he said, "but that doesn't make a damn bit of difference."

"No, you're right. Sorry. Did your dad know what kind of a film it was?"

"Not at first. He found out when I was arrested."

"Tell me what happened."

And he did. Punch Productions had agreed to make his film, with him also attached as director. Two weeks into the shoot, the inevitable "creative differences" reared its ugly head. Tabatha Preston, who was working as crew on the film, got into it with the victim, Jeremy Tipton, and Bart Helms, the other performer. Pushing and shoving started. Callahan attempted to intervene and Tipton lit into him. A gun appeared in Preston's hand. She cold-cocked Callahan with it and he lost consciousness. When he came to, Tipton was dead and both Helms and Preston had disappeared. Callahan called the cops and he was led away in cuffs.

"So they arrested Preston and she was tried, but acquitted, right?"

"Correct." Callahan said. He leaned forward and set his bottle of water back on the magazine.

"Did you know this Tabatha Preston was also looking for you last night?"

"Alex told me a black woman was nosing around. From his description, I assumed it was her. She's probably still got it in for me."

"Even though she was acquitted?"

"She couldn't post bail, so she had to do some time. I don't imagine she's forgotten. Tabatha isn't exactly a shrinking violet."

I made a couple of notes in my book and took a sip of water. "All right, Jack, here's the big question. How do you want to proceed from here? What do you want me to tell your dad?"

He again leaned back in the sofa, covered his face with his hands and uttered a deep sigh. "Oh, Christ, I don't know."

"He seemed pretty sincere about wanting to find you."

"How's his health? I mean, how did he look?"

"Not bad. For a guy in his nineties. He did kind of hint that he might not have that much time left."

He sat upright and said, "I don't mean to sound like a mercenary, but did he mention anything about a will?"

"No. Is there one?"

"There was at one time."

"And you were in it?"

"Yeah, but that doesn't mean I am now." He extinguished his cigarette, stood up and walked over to the glass doors and looked into the backyard. After a few minutes he stuck his fingers into the potting soil of a plant next to one of the windows, checking for moisture. He then turned back, sat down again and pulled a wallet from his hip pocket. "All right," he said, as he pulled out a business card and handed it to me. "Give him my card and tell him if he wants, he can call me. All my contact details are there."

"I'll drive out there now."

"He's still at that place in Woodland Hills?"

"Yup." I took a pull off the water bottle and stood up.

"Well, I don't mean to sound like an asshole, Collins, but he's the one who kicked me out, so the ball's in his court. He's going to have to come to me."

"Fair enough. I might need to reach you. Have you got another card?"

"Sure thing." He pulled out the wallet and slipped me a second one. "Tell the old man I'll wait for his call."

"For real?"

He shrugged his shoulders and said, "If he wants to bury the hatchet, who am I to say no."

"Good thinking," I said. He opened the front door and I walked back to my car. I crawled in and dialed the phone number I had for Ben Roth. There was no answer after seven rings. It was the only number I had for him, so he must be wandering the premises. The news that his son had been found was going to have to be sprung on him. I hoped it would be received favorably.

CHAPTER ELEVEN

———◆———

I DON'T NORMALLY CONSIDER MYSELF A lucky person. I've never even gotten close to hitting the lottery. And believe me when I say I can't count the number of times I've thought I'd landed a film job, only to see it disappear at the whim of some director who wouldn't know talent if it rose up on its haunches and slapped him upside the head. So, after ending my call to Ben Roth, I couldn't help but think fortune had smiled on me. I've tackled missing persons cases before over the years, but had never gotten results as quickly as I had with Jack Callahan. Considering what I was facing with an introduction to a daughter I'd never seen and the possibility of a shot at a TV show, I was glad for the hopefully swift completion of this case.

I pulled away from the curb and took Doheny up to Sunset, hung a left and headed toward the 405 and the Motion Picture Country Home. As I wound through the flats of Beverly Hills I looked up at the palms swaying in the breeze. They looked like giant feather dusters trying to whisk away the haze hanging over the affluence. I had to give them an A for effort.

The parking lot had ample empty spaces, even one under a small tree. I cracked two car windows and started strolling toward the palace of Hollywood's past. Given the roster of Tinseltown's former luminaries who have lived here, I couldn't help but reflect on what it must be like to wind up here at the end of a decades-long career. After years of being pampered and preened, it had to be a challenge to realize that now your existence is defined only by glossy publicity photos on a wall and yellowed, tattered pages in a scrapbook. Film sets have a term called the "martini shot." It refers to the last camera setup, the last scene being filmed for the day. As I walked toward Ben

Roth's room, it occurred to me that these residents all have had their martini shots and for them, this is the final reel.

Two knocks on the door of his apartment didn't raise him. It seemed to be too early in the day for a nap. But then, I'm not in my nineties. I tried once more. Nothing. I walked down the hall, turned a corner and encountered two elderly ladies, both with nicely styled white hair, wearing modest dresses and having reading glasses hanging from strings around their necks. One pushed a walker. The other leaned on a cane as she came toward me. Her other hand gripped a handrail, one of two fastened to the walls of the corridor.

"Good morning, ladies," I said. "Have you happened to see Mr. Roth this morning?"

They stopped and looked at one another. The lady with the cane said, "What did he say, Mabel?"

"He wants to know if we've seen Ben this morning."

"Ben? Who's Ben?"

"Ben Roth, June. You know. We worked with him at Metro."

Mabel thought for a moment and finally nodded her head. "Oh, yes. Goodness, does he still live here? I thought he died."

"No, dear," June said, as she turned to me. "Mabel gets things mixed up once in a while, young man. You must forgive her."

"No problem," I said.

Mabel shuffled a couple steps forward and peered up at me. "You look like Paul Newman. Did you ever work at Metro?"

"Afraid not, ma'am."

"Well, you should have," she said. "You're good-looking. All the good-looking ones worked at Metro."

June reached out and squeezed Mabel's upper arm. "Come, dear, Wanda's waiting for us." Mabel nodded, grabbed the handrail again and shuffled off. June stuck her right hand out to me and I shook it. "Wanda is her daughter."

"I see," I said.

She gestured to the hallway behind her. "I saw Ben in the Frances Goldwyn Lounge earlier. Do you know where that is?"

"I'll find it."

"Follow the arrows on the walls. Can't miss it. He's got a gaggle of coots he hangs out with. Tall tales and lies." She looked at my feet. "You should have worn your boots. It might get pretty deep in there."

"Thanks for the info," I said. "You have a good day."

"They're all good when you get to be my age."

June moved off behind her walker and caught up with Mabel. I watched them slowly move down the corridor and turn the corner. Former queens of Metro, living on memories.

I continued down the hallway, whose walls were covered with publicity stills of long-forgotten legends and bygone eras. I stopped when I caught sight of a photo of Paul Newman. I stared at it for a moment or two, not really seeing the resemblance, but nevertheless flattered being compared to Cool Hand Luke. When I turned a corner I saw an arrow pointing the way. The Frances Goldwyn Lounge was no doubt named for the wife of the legendary producer Sam Goldwyn, who, among many famous quotes, once said, "Give me a couple of years, and I'll make that actress an overnight success."

The lounge was bathed in sunlight from large windows in each of the four walls. Beige and tan were the dominant colors. Sturdy, cubed-shaped end and coffee tables complimented deep chairs and sofas with high armrests, all the better to assist elderly occupants to their feet.

Ben Roth sat at the end of one of the sofas in the middle of the room. An elderly gent sat next to him and two more occupied another sofa across from them. As I approached, a burst of laughter erupted from the men. Ben turned and saw me walking up. His grin disappeared and I stuck out my hand.

"How you doing, Ben?"

"Without," he replied, generating another burst of laughter from the old-timers. I had a feeling it was a coded response, prompting the same laughter every time it was used. "You got some news for me?" he continued.

"I do," I said.

He scooted to the edge of the sofa, propped one elbow on the armrest and started to push himself to his feet. His pal sitting next to him put a hand on his butt and gave him a shove.

"Watch where you're putting that hand, Jerry," he said.

"Gimme a break," Jerry replied. "When's the last time you had a hand on your ass?"

"Two thousand and one," Ben said. "And she was better looking than you." More laughter erupted as Ben finally struggled to his feet. "Come on, Collins, let's find someplace else. These guys are full of hot air."

We found a table in one corner of the room and sat across from each other. "So did you find him?" he said.

"He lives on Cynthia. Just north of Santa Monica, between San Vicente and Doheny."

Ben nodded and looked off to his right. "And what did he say?"

"He agreed to meet with you, but he doesn't want to come out here."

"Why not?"

"He didn't really say. I think he wants you to come to him."

Ben pulled a handkerchief from his shirt pocket and wiped at his nose. "Yeah, well, I suppose that makes sense. Since I kicked his ass out. I can't drive, though. The DMV took my license."

"We'll work something out." He nodded and replaced the handkerchief in his pocket. "Let me ask you something," I said. "Why didn't you tell Roy and me the other day that Jack was gay?"

He closed his eyes for a minute and then looked at me and leaned on the table with his elbows. "I've been in this town and this business going on seventy-five years, Collins. We always knew there were those guys at the studios. Rumors. Randy Scott and Cary Grant. Olivier. Christ, even Brando. Arranged marriages? Hell, we all knew Hudson was gay. But they went their way, and we—" he gestured to the men sitting on the sofas. "We went ours." He stopped and traced a pattern embedded in the table top with his finger. "But when Jack was arrested and I found out he was gay, I wasn't equipped to handle it. It was too close."

"What caused you to change your mind?"

After a moment he said, "Well, that guy Dylan said it, didn't he? The times. They're a-changin', right? California says they can marry now. I'm not totally on board with that, but what the hell do I know? I'll be taking a dirt nap before long, and it doesn't seem like a good idea to take a grudge with me."

He looked at me and among the wrinkles in his weathered face I could sense the struggle he'd had to come to make this decision. I pulled out my cell and Jack's card and slid them across the table.

"There's his phone number and address. He's waiting for your call."

He picked up the card, but slid the phone back to me. "Let's go back to my cell. I've gotta hit the pisser. Third time already. Something you've got to look forward to, Collins." He stood up and shouted to his buddies. "I'll see you guys at dinner. I hear there's a surprise."

"What is it?" Jerry said.

"Not sure. It's classified." His reply prompted more laughter as we started for the door.

"You don't need me, Ben. I might as well shove off."

"No, come on. I don't know how the kid's going to react. I need some moral support. Besides, what the hell else you got to do? You can add it to my bill."

"Whatever works," I said, and we headed toward his apartment.

WHILE BEN WAS IN THE BATHROOM, I looked at the photos that hung on the walls of his apartment. In one he stood with several men clustered around John Wayne. They were all dressed in western gear. I couldn't tell what the picture would have been, but besides Wayne I did recognize another face or two. The bathroom door opened and Ben emerged, the sound of a flushing toilet behind him.

"I see you worked with the Duke," I said.

He leaned in and peered at the picture. "Yeah. Not sure which that one was. Might have been *North to Alaska*. With Stewart Granger. And Capucine. Now there was a hot tomato. Woo hoo. She had a fling with Bill Holden. But then, who the hell didn't." He moved away from the picture and sank into his recliner. "Too bad about her, though. She took a header out of her eighth floor apartment. Damn shame."

I took a seat on the sofa and he picked up the cordless phone, then looked at Jack's card in his hand. "All right, here goes nothing." He punched in the number. "I'll put it on speaker, so you can help me out if I need it. Okay?" I nodded and Jack picked up after three rings.

"Hello?"

"Hi Jack, it's dad."

After a silence Jack replied, "Hi, Pop. I guess you saw Collins?"

"He's right here," Ben said. "I've got you on speaker. All right?"

"Yeah, no problem." There was another pause and Ben laid the phone on the table. "So, what's on your mind, Pop?'

Ben cleared his throat. "Well, it's been a long time. We need to talk about things."

"Like what?"

Ben shook his head and gestured to the phone with a frustrated look on his face. "Come on, Jackie, this isn't easy for me, as you can probably guess. We had a falling out. I said and did some things I shouldn't have. I want to make things right. Simple as that."

There was a long pause on the other end of the line. Ben took his handkerchief out of his shirt pocket and wiped the corners of his eyes, then put it away.

"When do you want to do this?" Jack said.

"How about tomorrow?"

"All right, but I told Collins you've got to come to me."

"I know that, for crissakes. I can't drive anymore, but I'll get there. What time?"

"Two o'clock?"

"Sounds good," Ben said.

"All right, Pop, I'll see you then," Jack replied and broke the connection.

Ben turned the phone off and replaced it on its pedestal. He leaned back in his chair and took a swipe at his nose with the handkerchief. "Christ, the kid sounds like he's still got a chip on his shoulder."

"Maybe, but when I talked to him he gave me the impression he wanted to see you."

"Yeah, well, let's hope so." He lifted himself to his feet and briefly lost his balance, then righted himself. For the first time since I'd met him, I detected a moment of helplessness in the old man. "Can you run me down there tomorrow?"

"I've got an audition at ten o'clock, but I should be through in plenty of time."

"What's it for?"

"That Jennifer Lopez show, *Shades of Blue*. On NBC."

"Speaking of hot tomatoes," he said. "Where's it at?"

"Universal."

"Aw, hell, yeah, you'll have plenty of time to get out here."

"But you're on your own after that, Ben. I don't feel comfortable sitting in on the conversation between the two of you."

"Yeah, I know that, dammit. I may be old as dirt, but I can still stand on my own two feet."

"Okay, you got it. I'll be here about one."

"Come earlier and have mystery meat with me. It'll give you an idea how they feed us here." He chuckled and waved his hand in dismissal. "Aw, hell, I'm just kiddin'. The chow is actually pretty damn good. How's about noon?"

"See you then," I said, and shook his hand. His grip was firm, and he clasped his other hand over mine.

"Thanks, Collins. I appreciate it."

I clapped him on the shoulder and started for my car. The gulf between Ben Roth and his son had narrowed a bit. I was glad for that. And that feeling gave rise to thoughts about a similar gap between myself and a young girl in Cincinnati. I hoped I was in for the same success.

CHAPTER TWELVE

———◆———

BEFORE I GOT BACK ON THE freeway I pulled into a Subway sandwich shop and ordered a six-inch cold cut combo. No mystery meat here, just reliable hoagies. I found a table in the corner and dialed Roy Dickerson's number. He picked up after three rings.

"Hey, Roy, Eddie here. I found your cousin."

"Terrific," he said. "Where was he?"

I gave him Jack Callahan's address and phone number, and also told him about Ben's call to his son and their meeting tomorrow.

"Does he want me to give him a ride down there?"

"I got it covered," I said. "Ben kind of hinted that I was still working for him, so I agreed to drive him."

"Hang on a minute," he said, and took the phone away from his ear. In the background I could hear a fit of coughing. After a moment, he came on the line. "Okay, I'm back."

"You need to quit those damn things, Roy."

"Tell me something I don't know."

"Matter of fact, Jack asked if you were still smoking those foul cigarettes."

"Yeah, he's always been on my case," he said, and cleared his throat. "How is he? He doing all right?"

"He seems to be fine," I said. "Hey, you know when I asked you earlier if you thought he was gay?"

"Yeah." There was a pause and then, "You telling me he is?"

"Yup. His partner's name is Alex."

Another pause and in the background I could hear tobacco and cigarette paper burning as he took another drag. "I'll be damned. I had no idea."

"Never gave you any indication?"

"Nope. It's a complete surprise."

"Well, anyway, just thought I'd check in with you and give you an update."

"Appreciate it, Eddie."

"When are you putting on the fake beard?"

"Next week."

"Good. Hope you get arthritis endorsing those residual checks."

"Couldn't happen to a nicer guy," he said.

I hung up and took a bite out of my cold cut combo. As I chewed, I watched two young guys across the restaurant coming on to a woman texting with her phone. While they were making assholes of themselves, I got to thinking about my cousins. I've got several I haven't seen for years and don't ever remember being that close to them, but at the same time I thought it a little odd that two cousins living in the same city wouldn't be close enough for one to know that the other was a homosexual. None of my business, I decided, but curious nonetheless.

I gnawed on the sandwich and watched the young woman with the phone suddenly stand up and toss the remainder of her drink at one of the young guys before she stomped out. He dabbed at his shirt with a napkin and glanced at his companion with a blank look. A Lothario struck down in his prime. Then the two of them cracked up and jostled each other through the front door. As I watched them start off after the woman, my cell went off. It was Mavis.

"Hey, Kiddo, what's up?"

"Morrie emailed the sides for your audition tomorrow."

"Great. How many pages?"

"Six. I glanced through them. Looks like it's a pretty good scene. They should be on your phone."

"No need to go blind trying to read them. I'm on my way back to the office."

"What's new on the Ben Roth front?"

"I'm taking him to see Callahan tomorrow."

"Terrific. That should wrap it up, right?"

"Don't see why not."

"Where are you now?"

"At a Subway finishing off a delicious cold cut combo. Depending on the traffic, I should be there soon."

"Okay. See you then."

She hung up and I took another bite of the sandwich. Getting Ben back together with his son tomorrow was going to dovetail nicely with the arrival of this daughter I'd never seen, and whose visit, I must confess, was giving me

butterflies the closer the event approached. I finished off the cold cut combo
and climbed into my car, waited behind three cars before I merged onto the
Ventura Freeway and joined the customary free-for-all, otherwise known as
the commute.

THE FIRST THING I HEARD WHEN I stepped out of the creaking elevator was
a scream. Not of panic, but of delight. What greeted me was Lenny and two
long and lean models from the Elite Talent Agency engaged in an improvised
version of Twister on the psychedelic carpet. The ladies were posed in postures
that looked like an audition for Cirque Du Soleil. Lenny laughed his head off
and spun the needle, then called out a direction. One of the models made an
attempt, but fell on a rear end encased in a pair of red shorts. All three of them
burst out in shrieks and Lenny looked up as I walked down the hall.

"Oh, my God, Eddie, we've got a new toy. We now love this carpet!"

The owner of the red shorts picked herself off the floor and tried to wipe
the foolish grin from her face. "Mr. Collins, you have got to try this."

"I'll take a rain check," I said, and pushed open the door to my office.
Mavis stuck her head out from her personal cubbyhole.

"Hi, Eddie."

"Did you see what's going on out there?"

"Yeah. Lenny said he wants to start a tournament with everyone on the
floor."

"Right. Tell that to Travnikov," I said, referring to the Russian doctor,
another one of the neighbors, whose stoic face and grunts masquerading as
conversation made him an unlikely participant in Twister.

"Good point," she said. "The audition pages and the mail are on your desk."

My circular plastic file wound up taking care of most of it. However,
amidst the chaff there was one residual containing a net amount less than the
cost of the stamp. I've often voiced the opinion that with a hundred and sixty
thousand members, the actors' union could put these piddly residuals into
a fund and make a sizable dent in world hunger. With that noble thought in
mind, I made a visit to the loo, then plopped down behind my desk and leafed
through the audition pages. It was indeed a nice scene with some good back
and forth with one of the leads in the show. Mavis came in a few minutes later
and told me she was leaving for the day.

"See you tomorrow," I said. I heard the front door close and listened to the
silence for a moment. Twister had obviously ended. I spent a half hour or so
going over the audition material, but couldn't seem to concentrate because I
kept thinking about this meeting with the Robinsons tomorrow. I decided a
few dishes in the sink needed washing. That done, I made up Mr. Murphy's
bed and replaced some DVDs in their cases. A couple of shelves got a swipe

with a dust cloth. I stopped and came to the realization that I was beginning to feel like a caged animal. I opened the French doors, stood on my mini-balcony and looked down on Hollywood Boulevard, essentially my front yard. The usual mob of tourists with cameras and shorts, Hawaiian shirts and sunglasses swarmed over the sidewalks in search of a slice of glitz and glamor to share with the folks at home.

Squatting down on one of the stars on the Walk of Fame was a little girl with a floppy straw hat on her head. She mugged for the camera as her mother took several pictures of her. When mom was done, the girl bounced over and looked at the digital image that had just been captured. She squealed with delight and then skipped along the sidewalk and looked at the next concrete chunk with the name of another Hollywood luminary embedded in it.

As I watched her from my overhead perch, my mind started to wander and I thought back to twelve years ago. The murder of my ex-wife. A daughter unknown to me, who was now on the verge of meeting me, her birth father. Being an actor for as many years as I have, I've never experienced a lack of self-confidence. But as I looked down at the Boulevard, a feeling of uncertainty washed over me. It unnerved me and I shut the doors and picked up the phone. I needed some ballast.

"My favorite gumshoe," Carla said when she answered her phone.

"A gumshoe without a case."

"You found your guy?"

"I did. I'm re-uniting him with his old man tomorrow."

"That's great, Eddie."

"And just in time," I said. "My daughter flies in sometime in the afternoon."

"Perfect."

"Yeah. Worked out fine, I guess."

It must have been something in the tone of my voice because she said, "Are you still nervous about meeting her?"

"Truth be told, I'd rather be doing a monologue at the Hollywood Bowl."

She took the phone away from her ear as she burst into a guffaw of laughter. "Then you could put her in the front row."

"You're a lot of help."

"I try."

"Are you tantalizing vulnerable men today?" I said.

"Now that's an interesting way of putting it. I assume you're asking me if I'm working."

"Yes."

"I go in at four for three hours. Why, do you need some tantalizing?"

"Could be. Turns out I also landed an audition for *Shades of Blue* in the morning. Besides tantalization, I might need some help with lines. You still have that Weber grill in your backyard?"

"I do. Are you inviting yourself over?"

"Me and a couple of steaks."

"I'll be there when I can. You know where the key is." She planted a kiss on her end of the line and hung up.

Ballast.

In the guise of Velvet La Rose.

CHAPTER THIRTEEN

———————•◆•———————

T HE HUNDREDS OF AUDITIONS I'VE GONE to over the years have all had their own particular quirks, some good, some not so good. I've been in casting situations where I've had the impression I was a rude interruption in their day. Other times I've been upstaged by a pastrami sandwich slathered with inspired indifference. On other occasions, I've left the room to glowing comments, only to get the call from my agent telling me they "went another way." I've always been puzzled as to where that "other way" is. In any case, it's never contributed to my bank account.

The *Shades of Blue* audition, however, felt good. I arrived at Universal at nine forty-five, fifteen minutes early, plenty of time to look over the material one last time and size up the competition. I knew one other hopeful, and we nodded to each other and exchanged pleasantries. The "suits" consisted of the casting director and the director of the episode. They seemed genuinely interested in what I brought into the room. I left feeling confident, which flies in the face of my usual attitude of leaving it at the door and hoping for the best.

After sending Carla a text as to how it went, I hit the freeway an hour before I was due at my lunch date with Ben Roth, and thought I had plenty of time. Not so fast, Collins. I swore by all that's holy I didn't know where everybody in Los Angeles was going at eleven o'clock on a Friday morning. However, if the destination involved the intersection of the 405 and 134 freeways, the answer was nowhere. I sat on the westbound ramp to the latter, under the overpass of the former and tried to find a radio station that would give me some information about what the hell was causing the holdup. No such luck.

I dialed Ben Roth's number. After the fourth ring I was about to hang up when he growled into his end of the line. "Yeah, hello."

"It's Eddie Collins, Ben."

"You're early. You miss me that much, huh?"

"I've run into some traffic."

"Hell of a chauffeur you turned out to be. Where are you?"

"The 405 and the 134."

"Ah, Christ, the Bermuda Triangle. Well, keep me updated."

"Do you have a cell, Ben?"

"Hell no. I'll wait here. The Dodgers are on."

"All right. I'll call you back."

I hung up, inched forward two car lengths and stuck a CD of Dry Branch Fire Squad into the player. As the band worked its way through "Rollin' on Rubber Wheels," I tapped my fingers on the steering wheel in time to the music and thought back to last evening with Carla. Like Mavis, she'd done her utmost to lessen my anxiety about the Robinson meeting later today. She finally convinced me to lighten up. I was an adult, for crissakes, she basically told me. And she was right. I was being foolish. I could talk myself into feeling otherwise, but at the moment I was optimistic, despite sitting in a traffic jam that gave new meaning to the word frustration. After about fifteen minutes, cars began moving and eventually I was in the right-hand lane of the 134 westbound. I risked breaking the law, dialed Ben's number again and gave him an anticipated time of arrival as twenty minutes. That's the standard for LA and environs. Pasadena to Venice? Twenty minutes. No problem.

It was closer to thirty when I finally pulled into the Motion Picture Country Home parking lot. Ben hollered to come in when I knocked on his door. He wore a pressed pair of gray trousers, a checkered red shirt and a navy blazer.

"Lookin' sharp, Ben."

"Yeah, well, figured I'd lay it on thick for the kid," he said, as he clicked off the remote.

"The Dodgers winning?"

"Crap. They should have stayed in Brooklyn." He struggled to his feet, paused for a minute to get his bearings and then started for the door. "Come on. Let's get some chow. You can meet my fellow inmates. They commandeered a table."

Ben's good-natured belittling of the dining hall certainly wasn't warranted. Pictures of Hollywood legends adorned the walls and looked down on tables covered with pale yellow tablecloths and white napkins. Deuces and four-tops were scattered throughout the room, along with some tables that sat six. Soft music filtered down from speakers in the ceiling. Ben led me to a table where three of his pals from yesterday sat munching salads. Introductions were made, and I shook hands with Jerry Daniels, Paul Baker, and George

Higgins. Being the movie junkie I am, their faces were vaguely familiar, but from what specifically I couldn't say. When I asked, both George and Paul mentioned several of the old western TV shows, like *Bonanza* and *Wagon Train*. They remembered the episodes and the characters they played as if it were yesterday.

A waitress filled our water glasses and Ben led me to a salad bar where a picture of Charlie Chaplin looked down on the display of greens. Of course, I immediately thought of his film *Gold Rush*, where he did his can-can dance with two forks and two dinner rolls and then later on ate his own shoe, which I've subsequently learned was made of licorice.

Plates filled with salad, we came back to the table and for the next fifteen or twenty minutes I was regaled with stories of a Hollywood where guys like these four could count on enjoying a steady diet of work. Martini shots and last reels be damned. Ben and his pals spoke with reverence about their time at the studios and I didn't doubt for a minute that, if given a call, they'd chomp at the bit to be on the set tomorrow morning. As I dug into a delicious rib eye and listened, I couldn't help but be envious of that era, where character actors like me could go from project to project year round. The studio gate guards would know your face. Directors knew you by your first name. Grips and makeup people remembered the names of your kids. It was a far cry from needing a Twitter feed to put food on the table.

I finally glanced at my watch and then looked at Ben.

"Time to go?" he asked.

"Yeah, we better saddle up."

"All right, let's do it." He took his napkin off his lap and I helped him to his feet.

"Where the hell you going, Benny?" Jerry said.

"Eddie here's taking me to see my son."

"Jack?" George added.

"Yup," he said. The three men were silent and glanced at each other with surprised looks on their faces. "Yeah, yeah, I know. The prodigal son has been found, guys."

"Hey, that's great, Ben," Jerry said.

"Give him our best," Paul added.

"Great to meet you guys," I said, as I extended my hand to the three of them.

"Likewise," George said. "See that he behaves. We don't let him out too often."

Ben snorted and shook his head and we walked to the door of the dining hall. He greeted several women as we made our way through the tables. He obviously was known by everyone.

"You're quite the ladies' man, Ben."

"Yeah, right. They probably all want my money."

I DON'T CONSIDER MYSELF TO BE a particularly fast driver, but looking at Ben as we headed eastbound, I had the feeling he thought he was riding with Mario Andretti.

"Your buddies hinted that you don't get out often," I said. "That true?"

"Aw, they herd us into a van now and then and take us to museums, malls, shopping and shit. Not exactly my cup of tea. Roy comes out and takes me on a road trip now and then."

"Good for him," I said.

"Yeah, he's been kind of a substitute son for a while. Ever since Jack and I had our falling out. Matter of fact, he took me out for pizza the other night. Domino's. Three-cheese special with pepperoni and sausage. Jesus, thought I was in Heaven."

"They don't feed you pizza, huh?"

"Oh, Christ no! Gluten-free, low-sodium, no-taste for the inmates." He scoffed and waved his hand in dismissal, and I couldn't hold back a chuckle. After a moment he said, "What about your old man, Collins? Still alive?"

"Yeah. My mother passed away a few years ago. Dad's retired. He worked in a grain elevator back in Kansas."

"Plenty of that back there. He treat you right when you were a kid?"

"No complaints."

"Good," he said. He was silent as we approached what Ben had earlier referred to as the Bermuda Triangle. There was no obstruction at the intersection of the two freeways and we sailed onto the 405 south.

"You're a good driver, Collins."

"Been doing it long enough, I guess."

"So you're not a California boy?"

"Nope. Midwesterner through and through."

"How long you been out here?"

"Going on twenty-eight years."

"Hah! A veteran," he said.

"How about you?"

"I came down here from Montana. The Depression had set in. A buddy told me they were looking for cowboys. So I put on my chaps and started making the rounds. Metro, Warners, Universal. Most of those guys kept falling out of the saddle. Not me." He laughed and pulled his handkerchief out of his pocket and blew his nose. "Didn't take long for me get kind of a reputation."

"Must have been a hell of a time," I said.

"Yeah, it was. I miss it." He lapsed into silence as we made our way through the Sepulveda Pass.

"You nervous about seeing Jack?" I said.

He turned and looked at me. "Obvious, huh?"

"A little bit."

"Not easy saying you're sorry sometimes, you know?"

"It's going to be okay, Ben."

"Yeah." After a moment he said, "You got kids?"

I thought about his question for a couple of minutes, debating whether or not I should share with him what I was facing later today. I found myself developing a kind of a bond with the old guy and decided it might help to relieve his apprehension about meeting his son.

"Jesus, what the hell do I have to be nervous about?" he said after I told him. We shared a laugh. "I hope it goes well."

"Thanks," I said. I exited at Sunset and we started making our way through Pacific Palisades. I turned onto Cynthia and parked across the street from Jack's house.

"Nice place," he said.

"You've got my cell number, right?"

"Ah, shit, I forgot to take your card."

I dug out another one and handed it to him. "Call me when you're ready to go back."

"Right," he said, and got out of the car.

I slid my window down and watched him shuffle across the street, open the gate and start up the sidewalk. Halfway there, the front door opened and Jack stepped onto the porch. I heard them greet each other. Ben climbed the stairs and after a moment, the two men embraced and Jack ushered his father into the house. Before he closed the door he turned and gave me a wave of recognition.

I returned the gesture, put the car in gear and pulled away from the curb with the hope that this meeting between father and son would bode well for the upcoming meeting between father and daughter.

THE ADAGE IS DON'T SIT AND wait for a pot of water to boil; the same sort of anticipation could apply to waiting for a phone to ring. That thought crossed my mind as I awaited Ben's call and sipped on my second cup of Starbuck's regular coffee, no soy, no mocha or frappucino or any other froo froos, just basic coffee, although I did concede to some cream. I breezed through the *Los Angeles Times* crossword, and after glancing at my watch, called Mavis.

"Hey, Kiddo, any word from James Robinson?"

"No. Where are you?"

"Waiting for Ben Roth's call to see if he needs a ride back to Woodland

Hills."

"Robinson has your cell number, doesn't he?"

"Yeah, but I thought maybe he'd call the office."

"Did he say what time they were getting in?"

"No," I said, and took a sip of coffee. "Just checking if you'd heard anything."

"If he calls here, I'll tell him you're waiting for his call."

"Okay."

"You're looking forward to this, aren't you?"

"Absolutely," I replied, mentally trying to put conviction in my statement.

"Chin up, Boss Man, it's going to be okay."

And with that, she broke the connection and I went back to my coffee and newspaper. Fifteen minutes later the cell rang, revealing an unfamiliar number.

"Mr. Collins?"

"Yes?"

"It's Jack Callahan. I just wanted to give you a heads-up that you don't need to give my dad a ride back to Woodland Hills. Alex and I have got it covered."

"All right. How did your meeting go?"

"Very well." He paused and I could hear a voice in the background. "Just a minute," he continued. "Dad wants to talk to you."

After a moment, Ben came on the line. "Collins?

"Yeah, Ben, everything all right?"

"It's all good. Sorry to keep you hangin'. The boys and Roy are taking me out to dinner tonight. Kind of a reunion thing."

"That's great."

"Thanks for your help, Collins. You're a mensch."

"My pleasure. Great to meet you, and let me know if there's anything else I can do for you."

"You got it. And I hope meeting that daughter of yours is the best thing to happen to you in a long time."

"Thanks, Ben," I said, and ended the call. I left the *Times* for someone else, finished off the coffee and headed for my office.

MAVIS WAS BUSY AT HER COMPUTER, and after a quick shower with my cell close enough to hear it ring, I got dressed and sank into one of the chairs in front of her desk. After a moment, she looked at me and said, "What?"

"Do you think I should bring a gift or something?"

"Hmm. Good question. What's your gut tell you?"

"Not to. I mean, I don't know these people."

"True. You're maybe better off trying them on for size. They'll want to do the same thing." The office phone rang and she picked it up, then handed it to me. "False alarm. It's your agent."

"Put him on speaker," I said, and she punched a button.

"You better be the bearer of good news, Morrie," I said.

"I have good news and bad news. Which would you prefer first?"

"The bad."

"The *Shades of Blue* casting director called. She told me they really liked you, and want to use you..." He paused and I heard him cough in the background.

"But?" I said, expecting the worst.

"The producers sat down with the director and the writers, and she said the episode is being rewritten. But she assured me they liked you, and most likely will bring you in for another show."

"'Most likely'? Ah, Christ, Morrie, how many goddamn times have we heard that before?"

"I know, bubbele, I know. But I think this time is different."

"Yeah, and I think Trump will wind up on Mount Rushmore."

He laughed, which provoked another fit of coughing. "But all is not lost. Are you ready for the good news?"

"Hit me."

"You remember that commercial you did for Ace Hardware last year?"

"Yeah."

"Well, they want to re-instate it and need your approval."

"Hell, yes, if it means more money."

"Thought you'd say that. I'm gonna ask them for two and a half times over scale. I won't go less than double scale. You up for that?"

"Absolutely. How long do they want to use it?"

"Well, they're gonna have to guarantee at least thirteen weeks."

"Go for it."

"Atta boy. I'll keep you posted. Have a good weekend." He hung up and Mavis disconnected.

"All right, Boss Man. Good for you. Money in the bank."

"Maybe. But I suppose that means you're going to ask for a raise again, right?"

"Hmmmm," she purred, and batted her eyelashes at me. I shuddered to think what that utterance meant, so I retreated to my office and picked up a Dennis Lehane paperback I'd been trying to get through. However, I couldn't concentrate. I don't suffer from claustrophobia, but for the next few minutes I felt like a caged animal with a severe case of cabin fever. Waiting. At times I felt like Gary Cooper in *High Noon*, looking at the clock on the wall and the pocket watch in his vest, waiting for Frank Miller to show up. The watch on my wrist said it was approaching three-thirty. When it was three-fifty, my cellphone chirped. The caller ID said it was James Robinson. I accepted the call and put the phone to my ear. "Eddie Collins."

"Mr. Collins, this is Jim Robinson."

"Yes, sir. You've arrived?"

"We have. Just getting settled in."

"Any trouble finding the place?"

"None at all." Mavis appeared in the doorway and I heard another voice on the other end of the line. Robinson took the phone away from his ear and came back after a moment. "I thought we'd have a little rest and then meet you for dinner. How does that sound?"

"Just fine," I said. "I can meet you at the Sportsman's Lodge."

I told him I'd be the guy wearing the porkpie hat. We agreed on seven o'clock and ended the conversation. "Okay, we're on for dinner," I said.

"Do you have to wear a porkpie?" Mavis said.

"It's my trademark, Kiddo. Besides, how the hell else is he going to recognize me? I'm not exactly a household name."

Mavis's face broke into a huge grin. "This is exciting, Eddie. I wish I could be a fly on the wall."

THE SPORTSMAN'S LODGE IS NO ORDINARY run-of-the-mill hotel. It sits on six acres in the San Fernando Valley just off Ventura Boulevard, east of Coldwater Canyon. In operation since the 1880s, the place was a favorite gathering place for the luminaries of Old Hollywood back in the day. The now-defunct Republic Studios were nearby and many of the old western stalwarts found it to be a convenient watering hole. Clark Gable frequented the hotel. Bogie and Bacall hung out there, as did Tracy and Hepburn. John Wayne taught his kids how to fish from the trout ponds that dotted the grounds. The fish have since been replaced by swans, but the ponds remain.

Several years ago a wealthy developer bought the real estate and made plans to tear down part of it and build what would amount to a shopping mart. Just what the San Fernando Valley needed, another shopping mecca. I didn't see any signs of construction as I pulled into the parking lot and found a space next to sleek BMW convertible. I was fifteen minutes early. A red and white tour bus occupied one corner of the lot.

I walked under the *porte cochere* and nodded to two elderly gentlemen sitting on a redwood bench next to the front entrance. Glass doors silently slid open as I approached the front door and stepped into a blast of welcome air conditioning. An attractive Hispanic woman stood behind the front desk and flashed me a big smile as she bade me welcome. I told her I was meeting someone and she told me to let her know if I needed any help. I said I would.

The stuffed head of some animal with curved horns hung on one wall of the lobby, in keeping with the "sportsman's" theme, I suppose. But the horned animal didn't look down upon over-stuffed leather furniture, dark wood, and raw beams in the ceiling, décor one would normally associate with a hunting lodge. Rather, the beast looked over sharp angles and sleek lines, more in tune with Art Deco.

I ambled over to four bucket chairs surrounding a modular table with several copies of a local advertising magazine spread out over it. I picked up one of them and took a seat. As I leafed through the pages I watched a bellboy standing in front of a mirror dancing. He was oblivious to anyone watching him. He did a few steps, stopped, then repeated them. He was no John Travolta in *Saturday Night Fever*, but I had to admire his determination.

From behind me a voice said "Mr. Collins?"

I turned. The girl was at my eye level and looked like a miniature version of Elaine Weddington, my ex-wife. A lump formed in my throat. She had to be Kelly Robinson. Standing on either side of the girl were her parents, James and Betty Robinson. I stood up, surprised. The surprise came from the fact that both the Robinsons were black.

Chapter Fourteen

——————◆——————

Ĵames Robinson stood about six feet tall. He was a handsome man who sported a neatly-trimmed mustache in the middle of a narrow face that broke into a broad smile when he saw me. His closely-cropped black hair was speckled with gray. He wore a blue, short-sleeved striped shirt and Bermuda shorts and had sandals on his feet. His arms and torso looked like he was no stranger to a gym. As I stood, he stuck out his hand and gave me a firm handshake.

"Jim Robinson. Pleasure to meet you, Mr. Collins."

"Just Eddie," I said. "How was your flight?"

"Not bad. A little tight going through Denver."

"Well, welcome to Los Angeles."

"Thanks," he replied, and gestured to his wife. "This is my wife, Betty."

Betty Robinson was a tall pretty woman who also flashed a smile as she stuck out her hand. Black hair hung to her shoulders and she wore a floral blouse and a dark blue skirt and had a purse slung over one shoulder.

The top of Kelly's head came up to Betty's shoulders. The girl had dark hair, the same color as her birth mother. She looked up at me with eyes wide open and full of curiosity. I couldn't blame her. The opportunity to meet someone she now knew to be her second father, as it were, would no doubt put a lot of questions in any girl's head. The photo of her that I'd been given over six years ago didn't do her justice. First of all, she was taller than I had anticipated. But then, with my knowledge of twelve-year old girls being practically nil, I didn't know what I was expecting. Puberty had arrived, as evidenced by the trace of budding breasts. Her black hair was shoulder-length and gathered in a ponytail. She wore a yellow blouse over jeans and had tennis shoes on her feet.

"So nice to meet you, Eddie," Betty said. She put her hands on the girl's shoulders and gently moved her so she stood in front of her mother. "And this is Kelly."

I stuck out my hand. "Hello, Kelly. I'm glad to meet you."

After a moment and a gentle nudge from Betty, Kelly offered her hand and I enveloped it in mine. "It's nice to meet you, Mr. Collins," she said.

"Why don't you call me Eddie, too?"

"Okay," she said, as I let go of her hand. She smiled and looked up at her mother.

"Today is only the second time Kelly's been on an airplane," Jim said. "I think she's a bit overwhelmed by it all."

"I feel the same every time I get on one of those things," I said.

He chuckled and said, "It looks like there's a nice restaurant right here. I believe it's called the Patio Cafe. Unless you know some other place you'd rather go?"

"Fine with me. You've probably had enough driving."

"Yes we have," Betty said. "I swear, that 405 freeway has gotten worse in the twelve years since we've been here."

"It's a bear," I said. "Any time of day."

"Shall we?" Jim said. We started to move toward the restaurant and three young boys passed us, towels wrapped around their shoulders, flip-flops on their feet.

Kelly tugged at Betty's hand. "They have a pool, mom, can I go swimming?"

"In the morning, honey. You've had quite a day."

"Will you go, too?"

"For a while," she said. "Then I have to go to the reunion."

"Cool," she said, and we continued on.

The interior of the Patio Cafe was predominately white, with splashes of orange on the plastic chairs. Blowups of some of Hollywood's legends hung on the walls. A waiter showed us to a table for four. Jim and I sat across from Betty and her daughter.

Kelly pointed to the photographs. "Mom, who's the guy in the western hat?" Both Betty and Jim had blank looks on their faces and Jim turned to me.

"I'm not sure. Eddie?"

"That's Gene Autry," I said. "They called him the Singing Cowboy. Kelly, you've heard *Rudolph, the Red-Nosed Reindeer*, haven't you?" She nodded and I said, "That was one of his biggest hits."

"Cool," she said, as a young woman promptly appeared and filled water glasses and placed menus in front of each of us. There were only a half dozen tables occupied. We looked at our menus for a moment until the waiter walked up.

"Good evening, folks, my name is Bryan. I'll be your server. Can I bring you something else to drink besides water?"

"I'll have a glass of Chardonnay," Betty said.

"Same for me," Jim said.

"And for you, sir?" the waiter asked, looking at me.

"A glass of beer," I replied. He rattled off my choices and I settled on Heineken.

He was standing next to Kelly and bent over slightly. "And for the young lady?"

"I'd like a Shirley Temple, please," she said, without the slightest hesitation. She glanced at the grownups sitting around her, almost as if she was seeking approval. The smiles on Jim and Betty's faces validated her display of sophistication.

The waiter disappeared and we went back to our menus for a few moments until he came back with the beverages. Jim ordered chicken, Betty settled on a shrimp dish and I chose a pasta entree with a salad. Kelly decided on a hamburger and fries. Betty suggested some salad as well, and offered to share one with her. Kelly thought that was just fine and sipped on the straw sticking out of her Shirley Temple. As I looked at her, she caught my glance and smiled at me over the lip of her glass. I was amazed at her striking resemblance to her birth mother, Elaine, the woman who would never experience the delight of watching her daughter sitting with adults, on the verge of becoming a teenager.

Jim proposed a toast. We raised our glasses and he said, "To Kelly, for being such a good traveler today and for wanting to meet you, Eddie." The four of us clinked glasses and I choked back a lump in my throat for being fortunate enough to be a part of this foursome.

We sipped on our drinks and the Robinsons told me about themselves and what they did in Cincinnati. Jim taught high school English, and Betty was the co-owner of a real estate firm. Her high school class reunion took place tomorrow and Sunday, and they were flying back on Monday afternoon.

The salads arrived and we began munching. I took a sip from my glass of beer and turned to Kelly. "So, Kelly, what grade are you in school?"

"I'll be in the seventh when we start in the fall," she said.

"And do you like school?"

"I do," she said. "My dad makes sure of that." Her parents and I shared a laugh and Jim nodded his head in agreement as she continued. "I'm going to a new school next year."

"Oh, boy. So you'll have to make new friends, right?" I said.

"Yeah. But two of my girlfriends, Mary and Chloe are also going, so there'll be someone I know." I nodded and she put a piece of lettuce into her mouth and chewed for a moment. "Eddie, can I ask you a question?"

"Shoot," I replied.

"Mom and Dad said you're an actor. Is that right?"

"It is."

"Are you famous?"

Betty put her fork down and laid her hand on Kelly's forearm. "Honey, you shouldn't put him on the spot like that."

"No, it's okay, Betty." I leaned across the table and said, "Well, let's put it this way. I'm not famous, except in my own mind."

She thought about that for a moment, looked at her parents and when she saw that they were smiling, her face broke into a huge grin. Our waiter appeared with a huge tray and a collapsible stand, which he unfolded and then set down the tray and began distributing the orders.

Kelly dipped a fry into a little container of ketchup and said, "Well, I saw you in a movie, so I think you're famous."

"Why, thank you," I said.

She told me what the name of it was and I recalled the film as being a silly comedy I made several years ago about a fading soap opera star. Another in a long line of obscure credits, which now made me feel rather proud, knowing Kelly had seen it.

"Did your mom and dad tell you that I'm also a private eye?"

This was new information that prompted more curiosity in her eyes as she slowly chewed on a bite of hamburger. "Like Sherlock Holmes?"

I laughed and wiped my mouth with my napkin. "Yes, like him, but Sherlock was more successful than me."

Satisfied, she took another bite of the burger and the four of us ate in silence for a few minutes. I asked her some more questions about her school and she told me that she was in gymnastics and also played soccer.

"I'll bet you're pretty good," I said.

"I'm getting better."

"She's being modest, Eddie," Jim said. "This spring she led her team with most goals scored."

"All right!" I said, and put out my palm to her. She slapped it with hers and her eyes lit up. I had a feeling we were getting to know each other pretty well. We continued with our meal, making small talk. Jim said they had been Los Angeles Dodgers fans when they lived here, and now took in several Cincinnati Reds games during the season. They told me they'd lived in Culver City before moving to Ohio. I asked Jim what they planned on showing Kelly while they were here. He replied that the trip was too short to do much, but since it was close, the Universal Studio Tour might be a good idea. Betty would be at her reunion tomorrow, but asked me if I'd like to accompany him and Kelly in the afternoon. I said I'd like that very much.

Jim sipped from his glass of wine and turned to me. "Then maybe Sunday morning we could take her to see Elaine's grave site. That a possibility?"

"Absolutely," I said.

"That okay with you, Kelly?" he asked.

She glanced at me for a moment, then said, "Yes, I'd like that." Betty put her arm around her shoulders and gave the girl a hug.

We went back to our food for several minutes. At one point a cellphone buzzed and Kelly pulled one from her pocket and looked at the screen.

"Kelly," Betty said. "Later, okay? We're in the middle of dinner."

"It's Julie. Can I just text her back?"

"Okay, but then put it away, all right?"

She nodded and her thumbs started to fly. I turned to her parents. "I don't know how they do it," I said.

"You mean with the thumbs?" Betty asked, and I nodded. "Me neither."

Kelly uttered a little giggle and put the phone back in her pocket. "Eddie, do you know what the nickname for Cincinnati is?"

"Ummmm, you got me there."

"It's called the Queen City," she said.

"Really?"

She nodded and slurped on the remnants of her Shirley Temple. "Yes. We had to write an essay about it for Mrs. Tompkins' class. There was this poet …" She paused and glanced at Jim.

"Henry Wadsworth Longfellow," he prompted.

"Yeah, that guy," she continued. "He wrote a poem where he called it the Queen of the West. And the name stuck."

"I'm glad to know that," I said. "Thanks."

"You're welcome." She bit off a piece of fry. "And there's like—"

"Kelly," Jim interrupted. "Like?"

"Oops, my bad," she said, and put her fingers over her mouth.

Jim turned to me. "The most over-used word in the lexicon. We try to discourage the use of it."

"I hear you," I said, and glanced at Kelly, then gave her a little wink, which prompted a smile.

"There's seven hills in Cincinnati," she said. "The same as Rome, Italy. We learned about that too."

I thanked her again for the information and after more conversation the waiter came back, cleared our plates and asked if we'd like dessert. We passed, and Jim wrestled the check away from me. Kelly and I sneaked glances at each other and I could tell she was fascinated by this actor-cum PI guy.

Betty folded her napkin and said, "Jim, it's been a long day. I'm starting to fade, and I think our daughter might be too. Why don't Kelly and I go up to the room and you and Eddie can carry on."

"Good idea," he said.

"I'm not tired, Mom," Kelly said.

"Let's you and I see if we can find a movie while your dad and Eddie have some man talk, okay?"

Kelly glanced at me with a serious look and whispered, "Oooh, man talk." She winked at me and I broke into a huge grin.

We pushed our chairs back and stood. Kelly placed herself in front of me and looked up. "So I'll see you tomorrow, Eddie, right?"

"You bet. I want to see how good a swimmer you are."

She smiled, offered me her small hand and we shook.

"Sorry to cop out," Betty said, as she also stuck out her hand. "But I'll catch up with you sometime tomorrow. Come join us for a swim."

"Thanks. I'll think about that," I said, as I shook her hand. She and her daughter walked off. Kelly turned at one point and glanced back at me. Both Carla and Mavis were right: the meeting went off without a hitch.

"You want to get a drink?" Jim said.

"I'd like that."

The bar in the hotel's lounge snaked around the center of the room like a huge golden reptile. We found a small circular table with a lit candle in the center of it. A waitress brought a scotch for Jim and bourbon for me. We again clinked glasses and were silent for a moment.

"Kelly's a wonderful girl, Jim. You must be very proud of her."

"We are. Sometimes she and her brother are a handful, but they're both good kids."

"So she has a brother?"

"Troy. A ten-year old. He's at a Y camp."

I sipped on my drink and was silent for a moment, hesitant to ask the obvious question.

"Is he a white child also?"

"No, he's black," Jim replied. "But he's also adopted." He sampled some Scotch and after a moment continued. "I couldn't help but notice a little surprise on your face when we shook hands."

"I'd be lying if I denied it," I said. "Can I ask you why you made the choices you did?"

"Sure." He wiped a spot of liquid off the table with his napkin and told me the story behind their adoption of mixed-race children. Betty had had a younger sister, who, along with two of her friends, were attacked outside a mall in Compton by three hoodlums, all of them white. Betty's sister didn't survive the assault, but her companions did. They went on to testify that the attack was racially motivated.

"Losing her sister was really tough on Betty," he said. "After we married, we learned that she couldn't conceive. She was adamant about adopting a white child. I guess we both considered it sort of a challenge. We both felt that if Kelly grew up witnessing that there was no difference between us and her, it would be a positive influence on how she looked at the world. Then when we adopted Troy it sort of reinforced our decision."

"Kelly's never had a problem with it?"

"Not at all," he replied. "Obviously, when Troy came along, she started asking some questions, so we told her that both she and her brother were adopted. Initially she exhibited a little disappointment, but that dissipated as time went on.

"We had many long discussions with both of them about adoption and some of the reasons why it happens. Obviously, we told them about the fact that Betty couldn't have children. As Kelly grew older, it finally came to the point where she wanted to know about her birth parents. That's when we took steps to find out about Elaine Weddington, your ex-wife. It took a little bit of investigating on our part, but it finally led to us reaching out to you."

"What did you find out about Elaine?"

"That she was an actress. We're not sure of all the particulars surrounding her death. But she was murdered? Is that right?"

"Yes," I said. "Truth be told, she was poisoned."

"Oh, my God," Jim said. He paused and sipped on his drink. After a moment, he continued. "It's none of my business, but what happened?"

I swirled the ice cubes around in my glass of bourbon and thought for a moment. On the surface, I wasn't too keen on digging up the past, but given who I was talking to, and what the relationship between Elaine and Kelly had been, I figured Jim and his wife should know the details. They could decide how much they wanted to share with their daughter. "She was working on a picture with another actress," I said, and went on to describe all the seedy circumstances leading to the murder of my ex.

When I finished, Jim shook his head and picked up his glass. "Man, that almost sounds like something out of those old movies from the forties. Film noir, isn't that what they called them?"

"Yeah, you're right," I said. "Real tawdry stuff."

"What happened to the producer?"

"He went to prison. They discovered him one morning, dead from a heart attack."

"Good riddance, huh?"

"To say the least," I said, and took a pull off the bourbon. "But before they threw his ass in jail, he told me about Kelly's birth. It was the first I'd heard of it. Elaine had kicked me out when she got pregnant."

"Wow, talk about surprises," he said. "Must have come as quite a shock to find out about her existence."

"Yeah, big time. Elaine's pregnancy came at a period in our lives that wasn't pleasant, and my behavior contributed to it, I'm afraid. I wasn't in a good place, career-wise, and did some stupid crap I'm not proud of." I paused and sipped from my glass. "But that was then, this is now. So let me ask you this, Jim. Do you think this is a conversation I should have with Kelly?"

After a moment he said, "I don't know if she needs to know all the details, but she'll probably want to know what happened to Elaine. Are you okay with that?"

"Absolutely. I just hope she doesn't feel anger about being given up for adoption."

"I don't think that will happen. Our discussions have pretty well covered all the bases, except for what you've just told me. Kelly's curious, and as I mentioned in my letter, she was initially upset to learn about Elaine's death. I think we've smoothed that out, and she seems to have taken to you in a big way."

"I'm glad," I said. "I didn't know what to expect."

Jim sipped on his drink and we were silent for a moment. "Look, Eddie, I don't want this to come out the wrong way, but I wouldn't want there to be any ... I don't know ... sense of competition between us."

I put my hand on his forearm and said, "No, no, Jim, not in the least. I can't tell you how relieved I am to see that she's in a nurturing environment."

"That doesn't mean that we want to shut you out," he said. "She looks like she'll want to stay in touch with you."

"I hope so," I said, and took a sip from my glass. "What about your son, Troy? Did he want the same questions answered?"

"Not so much. I suppose the color issue is less of a concern for him."

"I'm amazed, in a way, how Kelly has accepted..." I let the thought hang in the air, trying to find the right words.

"The whole race issue?" Jim said.

"Yeah."

"I guess it has to start with children," he said. "Betty and I many times have caught ourselves looking at each other with pride when we see how Kelly and her brother relate to each other. Kind of gives our choice some validation."

"That it does," I replied, and took a sip from my glass.

Our attention was drawn to some boisterous patrons who had just come into the bar. We finished our drinks and walked out into the lobby. I shook his hand and told him again how impressed I was with his daughter. Jim bowled me over when he told me that I should consider myself being part of the result. We agreed to meet up around ten the next morning and I walked back to my car, filled with a good feeling about my past yielding something positive for a change.

CHAPTER FIFTEEN

———— ◆ ————

MY MORNING RITUAL OF LOOKING OUT over Hollywood Boulevard from my mini-balcony never ceases to present me with strange and wonderful episodes of street theater. Right below my building a young man wearing a sandwich sign that read "the wicked shall be turned into hell" was deep into conversation with Captain Jack Sparrow. I couldn't catch the gist of what they were discussing, but the Johnny Depp look-alike had obviously had enough because he pulled from his belt what I hoped was a rubber cutlass, swatted the sandwich board a couple of times and then loped off down the sidewalk. The evangelist shouted after him, and getting no response from the pirate, threw his head back in frustration and saw me.

"You, sir," he shouted, pointing at me. "Have you been saved?"

"By the bell," I responded.

A bus lumbered past and he put his hand to his ear, then again shouted, "I said, have you been saved, sir?"

I leaned over the railing and shouted, "Yes. In the nick of time."

After processing my response, he flipped me the bird and sauntered off in pursuit of the pirate. I chuckled, sipped my Starbucks and stepped back into my apartment.

"Eddie, who the heck are you talking to?"

The voice was Carla's and it came from the bathroom. "Some guy on the street," I said.

"I need a clean towel. I don't suppose you have such a thing?"

"At your service, madam," I said.

After I'd returned from dinner with the Robinsons last night, Carla had called, and when I filled her in on the events of the evening, we decided that she'd spend the night after her shift at the club and then join me in meeting them this morning. I pulled a fresh towel from a closet, and entered the bathroom with it and a cup of coffee in a cardboard container.

Carla stood in the shower, wringing water from her hair, a sight which I'm sure would cause that sidewalk evangelist to throw off his sandwich board and seek the pleasures of the flesh. I gave her the towel and set her coffee on the sink. She dried off and took the hand I extended as she stepped out of the shower. She pressed herself against me and kissed me.

"You could have joined me, you know," she said, as she reached for the coffee.

"Then you wouldn't have your grande, double caffe-latte soy, or whatever the hell that is."

"And the lady is ever so grateful," she said. She took a sip and kissed me again. "I'll be decent in a couple of minutes." I was about to pick up on the double entendre when she said, "Keep it, sailor. Now scoot." I grinned and turned to go, but she grabbed my elbow. "You're sure it's all right if I tag along with you today?"

"Absolutely," I said. "You're going to like Kelly. She's adorable."

"Considering who her real father is, that's not surprising."

"Flattery will get you everywhere."

"I'm counting on it," she said.

WE GOT TO THE SPORTSMAN'S LODGE fifteen minutes after ten, and were given directions to the hotel's swimming pool. Deck chairs canted at a forty-five degree angle surrounded the concrete lip, like sentries awaiting their entrance into an Esther Williams aquatic ballet. Towels were draped over several of them, and flip-flops were scattered underneath. On the far side of the pool two elderly ladies reclined, floppy straw hats on their heads. A young boy did a cannonball into the pool right in front of them, causing them to give up their chairs and seek refuge at a table under an umbrella. Even at this hour the Olympic-sized pool was brimming with kids and adults, a concession, I suppose to the oppressive heat. I spotted Jim and Kelly at the far end horsing around with a rubber ball. He playfully pushed her head under water. She spluttered to the surface, squealed, then grabbed him around his neck from behind and pulled him under.

As we watched them, I couldn't help but reflect on the fact that it wasn't too many years ago the sight of a black man and a white girl carrying on like this would be grounds for swift and severe punishment. Then I had the thought that some of that prejudice might still exist, but a glance around the pool didn't seem to bear that out. Small black and brown bodies dotted the surface of the pool. Progress. Small steps though they may be.

From our right Betty entered the pool area, a towel wrapped around her like a sarong. She was talking on her phone and when she saw us, she waved and discontinued the call as she walked up to us.

"Good morning, Eddie," she said.

"Morning. Betty Robinson, this is my friend Carla Rizzoli."

"Hello, Carla. So nice to meet you." She extended her hand and the two of them shook. She turned to look at the far end of the pool. "Well, my two water sprites are going to have to get out of there pretty soon or they'll turn into prunes. Let me tell them you're here." She walked to the other end of the pool and Carla put her arm through mine as we followed her.

Betty caught Jim's attention and pointed in our direction as we walked up. When he saw us I gave him a wave. Kelly turned, saw Carla and me and tossed the ball in my direction. I caught it on the bounce and lobbed it back to her. They waded to the stairs in the shallow end and climbed out of the pool. Betty picked up two towels from a table and handed them to the two swimmers. Introductions were made and Carla turned to Kelly.

"Eddie told me you were pretty, Kelly, but my goodness, I had no idea."

Kelly smiled and wiped her hands, then stuck one of them out and shook with Carla. "Pleased to meet you." She regarded Carla with a look of fascination, immediately zeroing in her like she had done with me last evening. It was evident she took to people right off the bat, something I remembered her birth mother doing.

Betty took the towel from Kelly and began to tousle her hair. "Time to get changed if you're going to Universal." She draped the towel around Kelly's shoulders.

"You're not coming with us, Betty?" I said.

"No, you're going to have to carry on without me. My class is having its first get-together this afternoon. You guys have fun."

We walked out of the pool area and Betty apologized for not being able to go with us. When we got to the lobby, Carla and Betty exchanged goodbyes and the three of them entered the elevator. Carla and I sat on a leather bench to wait for them. She pulled out her phone and discovered we could make a one-thirty departure for the tour, giving us time for some lunch at the Universal City Walk. She put her phone back in her purse and put her arm through mine.

"Kelly is simply adorable, Eddie," she said.

"I know. It's eerie how much she reminds me of Elaine."

"Were you surprised when you saw that Jim and Betty were black?"

"Completely. But you know, it's amazing how it doesn't seem to make a difference to her."

"A tribute to what they've taught her. Don't you think?"

"Absolutely," I said.

"I did see something weird by the pool, though."

"What?"

"Those two women with the straw hats on? I saw them pointing in the direction of Jim and Kelly when they were in the pool. Whispering to each other, with scowls on their faces. Made me want to go over and get into it with them."

"Different generation, I guess."

She let out a huge sigh that pretty much expressed the negative opinion both of us felt about the attitude of the two ladies. Twenty minutes or so later father and daughter stepped out of the elevator. Jim was in cargo shorts and wore a pale yellow polo shirt. Kelly also had on a pair of shorts, a tee shirt, and sneakers on her feet.

"Ready?" I said.

"Ready, Eddie," Kelly replied, and followed it with a little giggle.

"Carla checked the tour schedule, and it looks like we can make a one-thirty. What say we grab some lunch at City Walk before?"

"Sounds good," Jim said. "We have to pick Betty up later this afternoon, so why don't Kelly and I meet you?"

"You remember how to get there?" I said.

"Been a while, but I think so."

"All right, let's hit the road," I said. Kelly did a small bounce on her feet and grabbed Jim's hand as we headed for the parking lot.

COMMERCIALISM RUNS AMOK ON THE CITY Walk. Somebody in the Universal hierarchy hit the nail on the head when they decided to augment their highly successful studio tour with this paean to entertainment and retail. A huge guitar sits outside a Hard Rock Cafe franchise. A neon King Kong dangles from the side of a building. Anything you want to eat you can find. You can catch a movie in a multiplex, and during the course of an afternoon, one can put a sizable dent in one's wallet.

Carla and I found a bench in a central plaza and watched the parade of humanity in front of us. I'm a great lover of people watching and this was paradise. A little shaver stopped in front of us and offered to share his ice cream cone with us. His mother quickly apologized, wiped his face and led him off.

At one point I glanced to my left and saw a familiar face. It was Alex Foster, Jack Callahan's husband, who had gotten in my face when I'd shown up at their house. My curiosity was immediately piqued because he was with a young white man who wore a straw hat and they looked like they were more than just friends. With an arm around each other, they walked in front of a clothing store. I reached for my cellphone and snapped some pictures of the pair. They stopped and looked through the front window, then pointed to something and burst out laughing. Carla noticed where my attention was focused and nudged me in the ribs.

"Who are you taking pictures of?"

"Remember Ben Roth? And his son Jack Callahan?"

"Yeah, what about them?"

I gestured to where the two men were standing. "See the black man next to the guy in the straw hat?"

"Yeah. That's Callahan?"

"No. It's his husband," I said.

"So who's the guy in the straw hat?"

"I don't know."

Carla looked at the two men as they stood in front of the store. "What's the big deal?"

"They look pretty friendly," I said.

"So they're friendly," she said "What's wrong with that?"

"Nothing. Just kind of curious, that's all. Callahan and this Alex guy are married. To me, that means a committed relationship." As we watched them, the two men embraced and Alex kissed the man wearing the straw hat. I took a couple more pictures and turned to Carla. "Does that look like a committed relationship to you?"

"You ever heard of *ménage a trois*?"

"Yeah, but someone who almost bashed my face in doesn't sound to me like he'd be a candidate for that kind of arrangement."

"Hey, Shamus, don't go making up scenarios," she said, as she put her arm through mine. "They could just be friends."

I watched the two men disappear down the sidewalk. Carla was right. It wasn't a big deal, but I still couldn't deny my curiosity. "Yeah, you're right," I said, and gave her a squeeze. Let it go, I told myself.

A few minutes later I got a text from Jim saying they were on the way. Shortly after, I spotted the two of them coming toward us. Kelly had her phone out and was taking pictures of her surroundings.

We debated where we should have lunch. Bubba Gump Shrimp was an option, but consensus favored the Hard Rock Cafe. We found a table and ordered. Cellphones came out and the two girls had to have selfies of themselves with each other. It quickly became obvious that they had taken to each other right off the bat. As our drinks came and I watched them together, I was filled with a sense of wistfulness, confronted with what I had missed for the last twelve years without Kelly in my life. Granted, there are aspects of my past that didn't exactly lend themselves to raising a daughter, but since I hadn't known of this girl's existence until she was six years old, I wondered if I could have risen to the challenge. As I watched her with Carla, the huge smile on the girl's face made me think I could have given it a good shot.

Jim's cellphone went off and he put it to his ear. After a moment he said, "Kelly, it's your brother. I'm going to take it outside. I'll get a better signal. Excuse me, guys," he said, and pushed himself away from the table. Kelly was curious about my hat, so I gave her a brief background on the porkpie. She picked it up and put it on her head. It came down around her ears, which prompted a goofy face and pictures from both Carla's and my cellphone.

After a moment I said, "Now can I ask you a question?"

She grinned and said, "Shoot."

"What did you think when you found out about me?"

The question caught her by surprise. "You mean about you being my biological father?"

"Yeah."

She stirred her soda with a straw and then sipped. "I guess I was, like, curious more than anything. I mean, when I saw that my brother Troy was different, I couldn't quite figure it out at first."

"When you say 'different,' you mean because Troy was black and you aren't?"

"Yeah."

"Did that bother you?"

"Not really." She sipped some soda and continued. "When I got a little older, mom and dad explained it to me."

"That you were both adopted?"

"Yes."

"And that's when they told you about Elaine?"

She nodded and said, "She your was wife, right?"

"She was."

"And she was killed?"

"Yes," I said.

A little frown appeared on her forehead. "What happened?"

I gave her the abbreviated version of Elaine's death. She listened quietly as she processed the information.

"So you didn't know that I was born?"

"Not until you were six," I replied.

"Wow," she said very softly. Her simple reply spoke volumes.

Carla reached out and squeezed my hand. She had a smile on her face. "When I found out that you wanted to meet me," I said. "I wasn't sure if you'd be angry with me and Elaine."

She shook her head. "I can't be angry with people I didn't know."

I nodded, relieved at what I heard and impressed with a comment that seemed far beyond her years. "Your dad and I talked about you seeing where Elaine is buried. Is that something you'd want to do?"

After a moment she said, "I think that's a good idea."

"I agree."

"Great." She sipped from her soda and we both turned as Jim walked up to the table.

"Is he okay?" Kelly said.

"He's having a blast. Said to give you a kiss from him." Jim leaned over and did just that.

The waitress arrived with our food. It met all expectations and while we chowed down on burgers, corned beef sandwiches and soup, Carla gave Jim and Kelly her background as an actress, prudently leaving out her other career as Velvet La Rose. She told them all about *Three on a Beat*, the pilot she had just landed, which would start shooting on Monday morning. Kelly wanted to know every detail, and after she heard that she would be playing a character called Billie Guardino, she decided that Carla was also going to be famous. When the waitress laid the check on the table Carla grabbed it before Jim could get his hands on it. He protested, but it didn't do any good and she pulled out a credit card.

"She's going to be rolling in dough soon, Jim," I said. "She can afford it."

Carla made a silly face at me that prompted a giggle from Kelly. We finished up and while Carla settled the bill and the Robinsons went to the restrooms, I stepped outside and immediately stopped in my tracks when I saw my second familiar face of the day. Walking toward the parking structure was Roy Dickerson. I hadn't given it a second thought when I'd spotted him outside the gay nightclubs the other night. His explanation for being unable to find parking at Barney's Beanery seemed logical enough.

On the face of it, seeing him here now was coincidental enough, but it was almost spooky. I remembered Ben Roth telling me over the phone yesterday that he was going to have dinner with Jack, Alex, and Roy last evening. So the two guys obviously knew each other. What were they doing in the same locale at roughly the same time? The private investigator in me latched onto it like a junkyard dog. Something else to just let go? I wasn't sure. Jim, Kelly, and Carla came out from the restaurant and we started making our way to the studio tour.

We walked past a clothing store and Jim stopped, leaned over and whispered something in Kelly's ear. She nodded and went inside.

"Give us five minutes, guys," Jim said. "Are we good on time?"

"We're fine," Carla said, and Jim ducked into the store. "You know, Eddie," she continued, "the way Kelly talked about her brother gave me the impression she's wise beyond her years. You think so?"

"Yeah," I replied, my noncommittal answer drawing a puzzled look on her face.

"What's the matter?"

"Are you a big believer in coincidences?" I said.

"Sometimes. Why?"

"Jack Callahan has a cousin by the name of Roy Dickerson. He's an actor."

"Yeah, so?"

"I just saw him walking into the parking structure."

She looked at me with the trace of a grin on her face. "Coincidence, Eddie."

"Wait a minute. Almost four million people in this town and I see two faces I know within the space of a couple of hours?"

"You said he's an actor. Maybe he had an audition."

"On a Saturday?" I muttered. She shrugged. "I think it's weird, though. Just like seeing Callahan's partner with someone else."

She laughed and kissed me on the cheek as the Robinsons came out of the store. Kelly had a huge grin on her face and a pale yellow straw porkpie hat on her head.

"Well, all right!" I said. "It's perfect."

"Do I wear it with the brim up or down?" she said.

"Whatever suits you."

"Brim down." She made the adjustment and we set out for the tour.

For the better part of the next two hours we got the best of the back lot. The shark from *Jaws* erupted from a creek as we crossed it. Shrieks filled the tram as it sank back into the water. We rode through a western street where we did indeed see some cowpokes simulate a shootout. The hero got a round of applause and took a bow. At one point the tram stopped and the tour guide pointed out the house where Norman Bates and his mummified mother lived in Hitchcock's film *Psycho*.

The tram returned us to the starting point and we piled out and watched another load of sightseers clamber aboard. A snack shop was nearby and we all got cool drinks and found a round table. Our conversation turned to our plans to view Elaine's grave the following morning. I told Jim I'd call him with directions to the cemetery.

At one point Kelly turned to me. "So, Eddie, where's Hollywood?"

I pointed to the hill separating Universal City from the Basin. "On the other side of that."

"Julie sent me a text asking me if we were going to Hollywood. What's the Walk of Fame?"

"All kinds of famous people have their name engraved on stars along Hollywood Boulevard," I said.

She turned to Jim. "Can we go there? Julie asked me to send her a picture of me on the Walk of Fame."

He looked at her for a long moment and finally said, "Tell you what. We can swing down there tomorrow after you see Elaine's grave. How's that?"

"Great," Kelly said.

The four of us finished our drinks and walked to the parking structure. We were on different levels and when the elevator stopped on their floor, the Robinsons and Carla said their goodbyes, with hugs all around and wishes for success on her television show.

"Your daughter is quite the charmer," Carla said, as we headed south on Lankershim.

"Yeah, isn't she?" I replied. "I feel a little weird, though, thinking of her as my daughter."

"Why?"

"Ah, I don't know. All the years that have gone by. And me not being around."

"But that certainly wasn't your fault."

"Yeah, I know, but I sometimes wonder if maybe I should have done more to find out about her."

She squeezed my shoulder and said, "How could you possibly have done that if Elaine didn't tell you about her?"

"I don't know," I said, as I turned left onto Cahuenga and started over the hill into Hollywood. "I start to think about that and then I get pissed off at her for keeping me in the dark."

"Water under the bridge, Eddie."

"I know." I slowed behind a Fedex truck that looked like it was searching for an address. "Which makes this whole introduction to the girl a little strange."

"Strange, how?"

The left lane cleared and I signaled and moved the car over. "I'm not sure how things proceed from here. Do we just go our separate ways? How much am I expected to be in her life?"

Carla stroked the back of my neck and was silent for a moment. "Well, from what I can tell after being around her, I think she'll let you know. And certainly Jim and Betty will. Have they said anything to you about that?"

"Jim sort of gave me the impression that they hoped I wouldn't just turn my back on her."

"Well, there you go," Carla said. "Whose idea was it for her to see where Elaine is buried?"

"Jim said he and Betty had talked about it. When I brought it up, they said it would be a good idea."

"And Kelly agrees, so that looks to me like she's interested in staying in touch with you."

"I suppose," I replied, as we drove past the Hollywood Bowl. I made my way to my building and Carla's car. She was scheduled to do a shift at the club that evening, probably the last for a while before she started her television stint as Billie Guardino. I pulled to a stop in the alley and she gathered up her things and turned to me before getting out of the car.

"Trust me, Shamus, you and Kelly have made an impression on each other. It's all good. Let me know how it goes tomorrow morning." She leaned over for a kiss and opened the door. "I think it'll be even better when she learns about Elaine."

"I hope so," I said. "Good luck with all those dirty old men tonight."

She laughed, closed the door and backed her Honda Fit into the alley and headed for Glendale and her other life as Velvet La Rose. I parked, rode the antique elevator up to Collins Investigations, thoughts swirling around in my head about suddenly becoming an ersatz father and the implications that came with it.

CHAPTER SIXTEEN

———— ◆ ————

SUNDAY DAWNED SUNNY AND WARM. A good day to visit a grave, if such a qualification is ever possible. I put a call into Jim Robinson and we arranged to meet up at Forest Lawn Hollywood Hills at ten o'clock. On the way I stopped at a florist and picked up some jonquils in a small plastic pot. They'd been Elaine's favorite flower. The cemetery had installed metal benches at intervals along the curbs. I found one at the top of a slope that dropped down to Elaine's grave, set the blooms beside me and gazed out over the bustling Ventura Freeway at the Disney and Warner Bros. studios. I, and of course Elaine, had worked at both of them.

I hadn't been a regular visitor at this gravesite over the years, but from time to time I'd remembered a birthday or an anniversary and found my way here. Vince Ferraro, Elaine's boyfriend at the time of her murder, kept tabs on the site. I'd offered to split whatever maintenance and upkeep fees there were, but he'd insisted in taking on the responsibility himself. The arrangements for Elaine's funeral had been made by Sam Goldberg, the producer, who, in a broad stroke of irony, was the person ultimately responsible for her death. The mere thought of him welled up unpleasant memories.

The warmth from the sun was pleasant. Marshmallow clouds drifted over Burbank, borne by soft breezes that ruffled the leaves of a nearby tree where two squirrels played tag. There didn't seem to be an apparent winner. I started thinking about the events of the last couple of days. The more I did, the more the thoughts took on an almost surreal turn when put into the context of a daughter's visit to the gravesite of a birth mother she'd never seen. And yet, a birth mother whose ghost could conceivably be prowling cavernous sound stages only a few hundred yards away.

Where the hell those thoughts came from, I couldn't say, and was glad when they were interrupted by a call from Jim Robinson. He said they'd just come through the main entrance of the cemetery. I gave him directions and told him to look for me standing at the curb. I stood, and after a few minutes, spotted the rental and signaled my location with a wave. They pulled up behind my car and the doors opened.

"How were my directions?" I said.

"Perfect," Jim replied. He stuck out his hand and we all exchanged greetings. Kelly still wore her new porkpie hat and gave me a very grown-up handshake.

I gestured to the grave. "It's right down here."

"Why don't you and Kelly go, Eddie?" Betty said.

"Are you sure?" I replied.

"It should be a moment you share with each other. Okay, Kelly?"

She looked up at her dad and Jim concurred. She nodded and we walked down the slope to the grave. The site was marked by a simple bronze plaque set in the earth, inscribed with Elaine's name and the dates of her birth and death.

I handed Kelly the pot with the jonquils. "Why don't you set them down?"

"Okay. Where?"

"How about next to the plaque?"

She knelt and carefully set the flowers on the grass just above the edge of the marker. "How will they get any water?"

"There are probably sprinklers that come on periodically. When they wilt, the groundskeepers will take them away."

I knelt beside her and we were silent for a few moments as we looked at the inscription. She reached out and ran her fingers over the embossed letters. "How come she had a different name than yours, Eddie?"

"Weddington was her stage name," I said. "When she first got to Hollywood she took that name because her agents figured it was more...oh, I don't know... theatrical, I guess."

"So what was her real name?"

"Schultz." Off her look, I added, "Probably a good idea, huh?"

"Where did she grow up?"

"Montana. She came to Hollywood when she was in her twenties."

"How did you meet her?"

"We did an educational film together. She played my secretary."

Kelly plucked a couple of stray blades of grass from the edge of the plaque. "My mom and dad watched one of her movies with me."

She told me the name of it and I pointed across the freeway. "See where that water tower is?" She nodded. "That's Warner Bros., where she filmed most of it."

She then pointed to the Disney lot a little further east. "Is that another studio?"

"Yup. That's Disney. Sometimes it's called the Mouse House."

A slight look of puzzlement disappeared after a moment and she said, "Oh, I get it. Mickey, right?"

I nodded and shifted myself so I was sitting on the grass. "What did you think of the movie?"

"I didn't think it was all that good. But I liked her. She was very pretty."

"Yes, she was." Kelly turned to look at her parents sitting on the bench and gave them a little wave with her fingers. "You remind me of her," I said.

"Really? How so?"

"Well, she was outgoing. She had a great sense of humor and a wonderful laugh. I think everybody that met her liked her immediately."

Kelly looked at me and smiled, and after a moment said, "I don't understand."

"What?"

"If she was all that, why would someone want to kill her?"

She caught me off guard and I had to think for a moment. "Well, that's a good question, Kelly. She was a very competitive woman, and at one point got associated with some people who were jealous of her and her talent."

"Enough to kill her?"

"I'm afraid so." I took off my hat and laid it on the grass next to me. Kelly's question rekindled for a moment the emotions that I've lived with ever since Elaine's murder and the morbid events surrounding it. I bit my lip, trying not to choke up. Kelly caught my reaction and squeezed my hand.

"Did you love her, Eddie?"

"Very much."

"Then can I ask you a question?"

"Shoot."

"Why didn't you stay together?"

Again, she put me on the spot, and I took a minute to formulate my thoughts. "We were two actors with competing careers. Elaine's started to take off more than mine did, and I didn't handle it all that well. I did a lot of things I'm not very proud of."

"Like what?"

"I was angry. I drank too much. It finally got to the point where she told me to leave. But had I known that you were on the way, I would have cleaned up my act, repaired the damage I'd done and been in your life."

She took all this in for a couple of moments. "Why did she give me up for adoption? Why didn't she want me?"

The abruptness of her question had an edge of hostility to it and I took one of her hands in mine as she dropped her head and looked down at the ground. "I don't know that I have a good answer for you, Kelly. I've thought about that a lot over the years, and I suppose she took out her frustration with me on you. That was totally unfair, and I wish it hadn't happened." Kelly looked up as a helicopter came over the hill behind us and veered off to the east, following the freeway. "Does that make any sense?"

"Yeah, I guess," she said.

"But you know what?"

"What?"

"I am so glad your mom and dad found you. I can tell that they love you very much, and that they want you. They want you a lot. You know that, don't you?"

"Yes," she said, and reached over to right one of the jonquils that had come loose from its mooring. "It's like, kind of weird, though, you know?"

"How so?"

"Finding out about Elaine, and now, you."

"You think I'm weird?"

She laughed and playfully slapped me on the arm. "No, silly. Just that I, like, finally meet you after all these years."

"Yeah, I know." We were silent for a moment or two, lost in our thoughts. "But what do you think? Maybe I can be sort of a second dad. A long-distance dad?"

"Yeah, that'd be cool," she said. "And maybe sometime I can come and visit again."

"I'd like that." She leaned over and again ran her fingers over the embossed letters of Elaine's name. "Ready to go?" I said.

"Yeah. Thanks for bringing me here."

"You're welcome," I said, and lumbered to my feet. Before standing up, she pulled out her cellphone and took a picture of Elaine's marker with the jonquils adding a splash of color. Then she handed me her phone and had me take one of her sitting by the plaque. I also took one with mine, after which we turned and walked up the slope to where Jim and Betty sat. Kelly went around to the back of the bench between her parents, put her arms around each of their shoulders and gave them a hug.

"Ready for Hollywood, honey?" Betty said.

"Yes! And I'm getting hungry."

"That's our girl," Jim said. We laughed and I gave Jim the best way to get into Hollywood, telling him where my office was and the location of a nearby parking lot. Kelly said she'd like to see where a real-life private eye hung out his shingle.

I pulled away from the curb and the Robinsons followed me out of the cemetery. I lost sight of their car for a moment going over the hill on Cahuenga, but picked them up again as we came down Highland. When I turned left, I saw them pulling into the lot I'd told them about. Jim called me as I stood in front of my building and as we talked, I saw them round a corner and walk toward me. Kelly was busy looking at the stars on the Walk of Fame. When they reached me I asked her who her favorite movie star was.

"Besides you?" she said.

I chuckled and said, "Besides me."

She thought for a minute and finally said, "Julie Andrews. She played Mary Poppins, right?"

"Right," I replied. "I've got a map in the office. We'll find where her star is. Come on." I opened the door to the building and we headed for the antique elevator. As we rode up, I told them to beware of the new carpet. Finding the map in my desk, I located Julie Andrews and then pointed out my apartment through the beaded curtain.

"I told my friends you're a private eye," Kelly said. "Can you sit behind your desk and look like one and let me take a picture?"

"For goodness sake, Kelly," Betty said. "He's not your personal photographic subject." "Happy to oblige," I said, and sat down, grabbed a magnifying glass from one of the drawers, tilted my porkpie down and looked at her through the glass. She giggled at the distortion and snapped a couple of pictures.

"Time to hit the Boulevard," Jim said. "I'm getting hungry too."

After some food at the Hollywood and Highland complex, we strolled along the Boulevard, dodging tourists. At one point, we stood on a corner that had a good view of the Hollywood sign. I positioned the three of them with the sign in the background and took pictures.

Eventually, the heat coming up from all the concrete began to wear on us, and Jim and Betty indicated that, since they had another class reunion event that evening, they had better head for the hotel. I walked them back to their car and since their flight tomorrow didn't leave until mid-afternoon, we made plans for brunch at the Sportsman's Lodge

"Thank you so much for today, Eddie," Betty said. "It meant a lot to Kelly."

"My pleasure," I said.

I turned to Kelly. She had a smile on her face as she stepped up to me and enveloped me in a hug. A lump formed in my throat, and I got a little overwhelmed.

She stepped back and looked up at me. "My friends are going to be so jealous of me for knowing a real-life actor and a private eye."

"Well, I hope I live up to their expectations," I said.

We said more goodbyes. They climbed in their car, cracked the windows to cool it off, then pulled out of the lot and headed for Highland and the Cahuenga Pass, leaving me a tad melancholy about this soon-to-be-teenager who had nudged herself into my life.

My melancholia dissipated when I hit Hollywood Boulevard and headed for my building. Street theater provides a daily potpourri in Hollywood, even on Sunday. At the corner of Hollywood and Wilcox Superman and Batman circled The Joker—Heath Ledger's version, not Jack Nicholson's. A small crowd had gathered, some cheering on the superheroes, others offering support to the villain. As I attempted to edge my way around the onlookers, the Joker suddenly grabbed my arm and used me for a shield while he backed down the street.

"Come on, man," I said. "I live here. Cut me some slack."

"Just tryin' to make a buck, buddy."

"I'm gonna call Nicholson. He'll kick your ass."

The guy burst into laughter, let me go and sidled behind a young woman. He grabbed her by the upper arms and spewed threats to his superhero foes as I kept on walking.

When I stepped off the elevator, one of the models from the Elite Talent Agency I'd gotten to know was just about to open the office door. She had a package under one arm.

"Hi, Eddie."

"What brings you here on a Sunday, Allison?"

She held up the package. "Dropping off pictures. Peggy gave me the key." Peggy Stafford ran the talent agency. Allison turned the knob and looked down at the psychedelic carpet.

"Your first viewing?" I said.

"Yeah. Whoever designed this had some really wacky tobacky."

"It'll probably grow on you."

"Either that or I change agencies," she said, as she stepped inside.

Another ringing endorsement of Lenny Daye's Twister game.

CHAPTER SEVENTEEN

———◆———

I HAVE ONE OF THOSE PAGE-A-DAY calendars sitting on my desk. Each date has a funny quote on it, or at least someone's idea of funny. I sipped some coffee that desperately tried to live up to its name and ripped off pages from the last three days. The quote for today—Monday—was from a guy who didn't get any respect, Rodney Dangerfield. A gag attributed to him is "I haven't spoken to my wife in years, I didn't want to interrupt her." I grinned and looked at the page. Only a week ago Roy Dickerson had told me about Ben Roth and his need for a private eye. I still found it amazing and perhaps lucky that I had been able to locate his son in so short a time. Even more amazing to me was that at the end of the week I'd met Kelly Robinson and her adoptive parents. The girl had far outweighed my initial angst about meeting her, and now, faced with having to say goodbye to her later this morning, I found myself saddened.

A buzz from my cellphone interrupted my reverie. It was a text from Carla: *Wahoo! A trailer with fridge, microwave, bathroom one can turn around in. I could get used to this!*

I responded by texting, *Ride the wave, m'dear. Hope your first day goes well.* After a couple of moments, she replied with one of those emojis of a pair of kissable lips. Last night I'd given her the run-down on the visit to Elaine's grave and our brief foray into Hollywood. She told me she'd already received a text from Kelly saying how she knew *Three on a Beat* was going to make her famous.

Admittedly feeling a bit envious of Carla's landing a pilot, I took the offensive cup of coffee back to my apartment and deposited the dregs of it into the sink and rinsed the cup. The sound of the front door opening announced the arrival of Mavis.

"Eddie?"

"Yeah, back here." I parted the beaded curtain and saw her standing in the doorway to my office. "Good morning," I said.

She deposited herself in a chair in front of my desk, and after a moment, said, "Well, how did it go? Tell me everything."

I started out by handing her my phone showing the pictures I'd taken of Kelly and the Robinsons over the weekend. She started scrolling and after a moment looked up at me and said, "Wow, that must have caught you by surprise."

"That her parents are black?" She nodded and I said, "Completely. But the interesting thing is that it doesn't make any difference to Kelly. They've also adopted a black boy. He's ten, and she's oblivious to the racial difference."

"That's terrific," she said. "Fritz and I have some friends with mixed-race children and to them it's the most natural thing in the world." She continued scrolling through the photos. "That is one cute kid."

"Tell me about it."

"I've only seen pictures of Elaine, but she looks so much like her. Don't you think?"

"Definitely. Sometimes it was almost eerie. A miniature Elaine. She's outgoing, precocious, funny. When she laughs I almost think I'm hearing her mother."

"Was she glad to meet you?"

"She was a little wary at first, which is understandable. But we warmed up to each other pretty quick. She was fascinated to hear that I was both an actor and a private eye. We took her to see Elaine's grave and at one point I asked her if it was okay for me to be sort of a second dad, long distance. She said that was fine." When Mavis heard that, she reached over and yanked a tissue from a dispenser on the corner of my desk and dabbed at the corner of one eye.

"Oh, Eddie, that's great. I assume her parents didn't have any objections?"

"Not that I was aware of," I said.

"Remember how uneasy you were about meeting her?"

"Yeah, I was kind of a nervous Nellie, wasn't I?"

"And now you're glad it happened, right?"

"More than I would have thought, I guess. I mean, she did bring back a lot of memories that I'd just as soon leave buried, but I'm damn glad she turned out to be who she is."

"Me too," Mavis said.

"Meeting her and her parents kind of makes up for all the times I was such a butt-hole."

"Oh, phooey, you're not a butt-hole, Eddie." She stood and took a couple of steps toward her office, but then stopped and said over her shoulder, "Most of the time, anyway." She still had my phone in her hand as she entered her office. "I'm going to put these pictures in my computer so we can print them out and you can have them in an album. Okay?"

"Good idea," I said.

"When are they going back?"

"This afternoon. I'm meeting them for brunch in an hour or so."

"All right, this will only take a few minutes. There may be a couple they might want."

"Yeah, there's one of the three of them with the Hollywood sign in the background. While you're doing that I'm going to hit the shower."

Ablutions finished and wearing a fresh set of togs, I donned the porkpie *du jour* and went into Mavis's office. She finished cropping one of the photos and laid it on top of several others. I picked out a couple and put them in my shirt pocket.

"Ben Roth called while you were in the shower," she said.

"Did he say what he wanted?"

"No. Just to call him back."

I found his number in my cellphone, dialed, and put it on speaker. It rang three times and Ben answered.

"Hey, Ben, it's Eddie Collins."

"Oh, yeah, thanks for calling me back."

"How you doin'?"

"Not so good."

"What's up?"

"It's Jack. Somebody killed him, Collins."

BEN ROTH HADN'T GIVEN ME MUCH in the way of specifics. He'd sounded pretty broken up over the phone, so I told him I'd drive out there after my brunch with the Robinsons. And of course I was running behind, due to an accident in the Cahuenga Pass. Some asshole had started weaving in and out of traffic by the Hollywood Bowl, and now as I was about to transition to the Ventura westbound, I saw his car straddling the concrete median and him arguing with someone on his cellphone. I couldn't resist, and gave him the proverbial middle finger salute as I glided past him.

I sent Jim a text as I climbed out of the car and headed into the Sportsman's Lodge. I met them in the Patio Café, and try as I might, I couldn't disguise the bad vibes I was feeling in the wake of Ben Roth's call. I told them about it and they all expressed their shock at the news.

"When did it happen, Eddie?" Jim said.

"Apparently early this morning. I haven't been able to get all the details yet."

"That's terrible," Betty added. "And you said you'd just reunited him with his father?"

"Yeah, last Friday. From what I could gather, both of them seemed genuinely pleased to be back together. And now this. I'm real sorry to dump this bad news on you guys before you travel."

"No need to apologize," Jim said. "It has to be tough for a father to lose a son. How old a man is he?"

"He's in his nineties." They both shook their heads and I sipped on some coffee and looked over at Kelly. She was still wearing her new porkpie and had a slight frown on her face as she poked at her scrambled eggs with a fork.

"Will you try and find whoever did this?" she said.

"I don't know how much I can do, Kelly. I'm not allowed to become involved in a murder investigation."

"How come?"

"My PI license prevents me. State law. About all I can do is offer support for Ben. The police will find whoever's responsible."

Satisfied, she ate some eggs and I suddenly remembered the pictures in my pocket.

"Oh, I almost forgot," I said, handing them to Kelly. "Here's a couple of shots you might want to have." One of the photos was the three of them silhouetted against the backdrop of the Hollywood sign. The other was the one I'd taken of her with her new porkpie hat.

"Wow, these are great," Kelly said. "My friends are going to be sooooo jealous."

After looking at them, Jim said that he'd taken a couple that he would email to me. Our conversation turned to what the rest of the summer had in store for them. Kelly's soccer was in full swing, plus it wouldn't be long before she'd start getting ready for a new school in the fall. Jim said they had a couple of Cincinnati Reds ballgames on the schedule. I did my best to wrestle the check from him, but he wouldn't hear of it, and we made our way to the front of the lodge. At one point Kelly reached out and grabbed my hand and gave it a squeeze. I glanced at her and she flashed me a smile.

We were met with a surge of hot air as we walked through the front doors. Jim stuck out his hand and said, "Eddie, it's been a real pleasure meeting you. Thanks for spending some time with us and getting to know our girl."

"I've enjoyed every minute of it," I said.

Betty put out her arms and gave me a hug. "Yes, thank you so much, Eddie. I'm glad we sought you out," she said. "And I know Kelly has really enjoyed getting to know you."

I nodded and turned to Kelly. She had a smile on her face as she stepped up to me and enveloped me in a hug. A lump formed in my throat, and I fought back some tears. She stepped back and said, "Am I ever going to see you again?"

"Well, I sure hope so," I replied. "Maybe you'll come out and visit again."

"That'd be cool. Do you text, Eddie?"

"Not as good as you, I'm afraid."

"I want to send you a text now and then. Is that okay?"

"Not only okay, but required," I said. "And I promise I'll text you back."

"Great. You have to tell me when you become even more famous than you are now."

I chuckled and said, "I'll do that." She gave me another hug, this one a little longer. I wished them a safe flight and we said more goodbyes. I walked to my car, climbed in and looked back to see them watching me. They waved. I did the same, then pulled out of the parking lot and headed for the Ventura westbound and Ben Roth, a man who had just lost a son. Juxtaposed with the pleasure I felt after having met my own daughter, I couldn't begin to imagine the profound loss the old man was experiencing.

During the brief times I'd spent with Ben, I'd gotten to like him a lot. He was a survivor in a tough business in a tough town. The fact that he had acknowledged his mistake in dealing with his son had made a huge impression on me. And after making attempts to rectify it, to now see his efforts explode in front of him made me angry.

Woodland Hills finally appeared and I glided down the off-ramp and parked in the lot of the Motion Picture Country Home. The door to Ben's apartment was ajar. I knocked.

"Come on in," he said.

I pushed the door open. He sat in his easy chair, had slippers on his feet and wore another Hawaiian shirt, this one with floral combat as a pattern. A tall glass of what looked to be iced tea was at his elbow. His three buddies, Jerry Foster, Paul Baker and George Higgins, whom I'd met the other day, were on the sofa, somber looks on their faces.

"Hey, Collins," Ben said. "Thanks for driving all the way out here. Traffic must have been a pisser."

"I made it. No problem," I replied.

The three pals pushed themselves off the sofa. "We'll let you two talk," George said. He grabbed Ben's hand, squeezed it, and walked to the door. "Come on, guys." Jerry also took Ben's hand in his, and Paul bent down and gave the old man a hug, then pulled the door shut behind them.

"Get you anything?" Ben asked.

"I'm fine."

"Good. I don't know if I've got the energy to drag my ass out of this chair."

He pulled a handkerchief from his shirt pocket and blew his nose. I sat on the sofa and put my hat next to me. "How did that meeting with your daughter go?" he said.

"Terrific." I pulled up a picture on my phone and showed it to him.

"Hey, she's a doll." He handed the phone back to me. "Don't lose touch with her, Collins. Believe me, you'll regret it if you do." He teared up and choked back a sob, then dried his eyes. "Sorry. Been a tough morning."

"Yeah," I said, and let some silence sit with us for a moment or two. "Sorry to hear about your loss, Ben."

"Thanks."

"What the hell happened?"

He reached for his glass of iced tea and raised it to his mouth. His hand trembled, but he sipped, then set the glass down and heaved a huge sigh.

"Jack's husband..." He paused, searching for the name. "Aw, what the hell's the guy's name?"

"Alex," I said.

"Alex, yeah. Alex Foster. Well anyway, he called me a few hours ago. Jack's body was found about four o'clock this morning in an alley. Beat to death, for crissakes." His voice cracked and he brought one hand to his mouth. I could see tears welling up.

"Who found him?"

"Apparently some guy walking his dog."

"At four o'clock in the morning?"

Ben chortled and took another swipe at his nose. "Yeah, can you imagine? A goddamn dog with insomnia? The cops found Jack's address on the body and woke Alex up."

"What was he doing there at that time of the night?"

"Damned if I know. Alex didn't say."

His hand still trembling, Ben picked up his glass of tea and took a swallow. He used both hands to set the drink down, then leaned his head back. Another audible sigh came from him.

"Ah, Christ, Collins, what the hell's wrong with this world? The kid seemed to be happy with this partner of his. Who the hell would want to do something like that? It don't make any fuckin' sense."

I didn't have an answer for him, but putting on my nosy PI hat for a minute, I couldn't help but recall seeing Alex with the guy in the straw hat at City Walk, the two of them planting a lip-lock on each other. Then the guy he's married to is roaming around in the middle of the night and winds up dead. Something wrong with that picture.

"Did you get that check I sent you?" Ben said.

"I did. Thanks for the extra. That wasn't necessary, you know."

"Yeah, well, hell, it's only money." He scooted to the edge of his chair and pushed himself to his feet, then shuffled over to his desk and pulled a checkbook and a pen from one of the drawers. "I wanna give you some more."

"Why?"

"What else? I hired you to find him. Now I'll hire you to find out who the hell killed him." He collapsed back into his chair and wiped his nose with the handkerchief.

"I don't know if I can be of any help, Ben. LAPD isn't going to let me get involved in a homicide."

"Why not?"

"Rules. It comes with the license."

"Well, that's bullshit."

"Maybe so, but there's nothing I can do about it."

He looked at me for a long moment. "For crissakes, you can poke around, can't you? You must have some cop friends."

"I do, but that doesn't carry a lot of weight."

"Yeah, well, I don't know how much weight the murder of a gay man is going to carry with the LAPD either."

I could hear the cynicism in his voice, and as I thought back on the reputation the Los Angeles Police Department has had over the decades, Ben's statement was not without merit.

"You might be surprised, Ben. Different times. Jack's murder most likely is a hate crime. They'll probably pounce on that pretty good."

"Well, let's hope so." He reached down between his chair and table and pulled up a rectangular piece of particle board, put it in his lap and proceeded to write a check.

I had been involved in a murder investigation in the past, specifically the one where Elaine was the victim. But in that case I'd been hired by a motion picture completion bond company, therefore giving me the legal authority to work with the police. Looking into the murder of Ben's son was different. However, my friendship with Charlie Rivers usually resulted in unofficial cooperation, provided I bribed him with enough meals, drinks and tickets to sporting events. As I watched Ben scribbling out the check, I came to the realization that after losing the *Shades of Blue* gig at Universal, I could stand to have something to occupy my time.

He tore the check off and handed it to me.

"Tell you what, Ben. You keep that. I'll poke around, and if I produce any results, I'll take it. In the meantime, I'm just asking questions out of curiosity as a friend. Okay?"

"All right. If that's the way you want it."

He put the check back in the book, laid it and the pen on the table next to his chair, then replaced the particle board and trembled some more tea up to his lips.

I took out my notebook and made a notation of Alex's last name, which I hadn't known up to this point. "I know you and Jack weren't in each other's company for a number of years, but can you think of anyone who would want him dead?"

He shook his head. "Nah, I don't have any idea who the hell he was hanging out with."

"What about that movie he was making? When he got arrested?"

"I didn't know any of those people." He paused for a moment and leaned forward to scratch his back. "And given my shitty attitude back then, when I found out about that crowd he was involved with, I didn't give a damn about them."

That pretty much sealed off that avenue of inquiry. Fortunately, I had names of the parties involved and could do some digging. "Did Alex give you any more information over the phone?"

"Nope. He was pretty shook up."

"How long had he and Jack been married?"

He thought for a moment and said, "When I had dinner with them and Roy, they said it had been seven or eight years, if memory serves me correctly. And sometimes it doesn't."

I jotted some notes, and debated whether or not what I was about to ask him was appropriate. If he didn't want to tell me, he damn sure wouldn't. "Let me ask you this, Ben. When Roy first talked to me about you possibly wanting a PI, he kind of suggested that you might have wanted to find Jack to give him some money. Any truth to that?"

He looked at me like he was about ready to throw his glass of tea at me. "Getting awful damn personal, aren't you, Collins?"

"Yeah, but if I'm going to work for you, you've got to level with me."

"I don't know why the hell that makes any difference."

"Motive, Ben. Did you give Jack some money?"

He glared at me and picked up the tea and sipped. Some liquid dropped on his shirt and he took a swipe at it with his handkerchief. "Yeah, I gave him some so he could finance another goddamn movie."

"How much?"

He threw another serious glare at me. "Five hundred grand. But that's not for publication, got it?"

"Client confidentiality, Ben." I was a little taken aback to hear the size of the figure, and momentarily wondered if he had that kind of money. But then, considering how long he'd been in Hollywood and the amount of work he'd done over the years, I had no reason to disbelieve Ben was worth that kind of money. "Who knew about it?" I said.

"We talked about it at dinner. So I guess Alex and Roy."

"Anybody else?"

"No." I made some more notes and he continued. "Collins, you don't honestly think Alex or Roy had anything to do with this, do you?"

"I don't know, Ben."

"That's batshit crazy! Jack was married to one of them, and the other one is his cousin, for crissakes."

"I know that. But you also know the cops are most likely going to talk to both of them."

"Yeah, well, good luck with that."

There was a moment of silence, and I took the opportunity to jot down some more notes. Ben pushed himself out of his chair and took his glass into the kitchen, muttering under his breath. He dumped the ice in the sink and when he turned back into the room someone knocked on the door.

"Enter," Ben called out.

It slid open and a woman stuck her head in the opening. She had an identification badge pinned to her blouse that indicated she was an employee of the facility.

"Are you okay, Mr. Roth?" the woman said.

"I'm fine, Harriet. What time's chow?"

"In about half an hour."

He gestured to me. "This young fella is practically homeless and looks like he needs a decent meal. Can we make room for him?"

"Absolutely." She smiled at me and continued. "I just wanted to see if you're doing all right, Ben, considering all that you've gone through today."

"You're a princess, darlin'. Why don't we run away together?"

Harriet laughed and shut the door behind her as Ben collapsed into his chair. "Stay for lunch if you want, Collins. Those three amigos that were here took a liking to you."

"Thanks, Ben, but I better hit the road."

"Yeah, okay. Rain check. Hey, by the way, did you get that show with the Lopez gal?"

"No, they wrote the part out, but I was told they still want to use me. Sound familiar?"

"Ah, those bastards! In the old days, when Lew Wasserman ran the place, they wouldn't dare dangle a carrot like that in front of an actor. He was a mensch. Nowadays?" He snorted and made a dismissive wave with his hand. "Don't get me started, for crissakes!"

Despite what Ben had learned today, I had to admire the fact that he hadn't seemed to lose his characteristic crustiness.

"Do you have Jack's telephone number?"

He pointed to the desk. "There's an address book in there somewhere. I think I wrote it down on a slip of paper."

I pulled open a drawer, saw the number on a scrap of paper in the front of the book and jotted it down in my notebook. "Is this his cell, or a landline?"

"Damned if I know. You'll find out when you call it."

Couldn't argue with that logic. I put the notebook and pen back in my shirt pocket and picked up my hat off the sofa. "Okay, Ben, I'll see what I can find out."

"And I'll put the check on ice."

I stuck out my hand. He reached up and gave me a firm shake. "I'm sorry about Jack, Ben. Fathers aren't supposed to bury their children."

"Yeah, well, I got a different script. His martini shot came before mine."

"I'll be in touch," I said, and opened the door and walked back to my car. I'd just been shown another facet of the old man's toughness, even faced with the prospect of burying his only son.

CHAPTER EIGHTEEN

———◆———

I'VE NEVER BEEN TOO DILIGENT WHEN it comes to looking at labels on food products. That fact was reinforced when I took my first spoonful of Cheerios, spit it out and looked at the expiration date on the milk carton. Definitely a health hazard, confirmed by the smell test. I drained the milk from the bowl, threw the cereal in the trash, and poured the soon-to-be sour cream down the drain. As I rummaged around in the cupboards and found a solitary granola bar, I rationalized that after all, a mini-fridge doesn't allow for a large store of perishable grub, so a person can forget, right? Made sense to me, but I didn't think there was a chance in hell that feeble excuse would find favor with either Mavis or Carla.

I'd talked with Carla last night, once again touching on the possibility of the two of us moving in together. Given my attempt at breakfast this morning, the idea loomed more appealing than ever. Her first day of shooting had gone well, and she had the impression that the company was going to be a good bunch of folks to work with. My news of Jack Callahan's murder, however, put a damper on her enthusiasm. She agreed that doing some sleuthing on Ben Roth's behalf would be good for me.

The microwave went off and I rescued a cup of sinister-looking coffee. I grabbed it and my granola bar and shouldered my way through the beaded curtain as Mavis came through the front door.

"Good morning," she called out, and appeared in the doorway wearing a blue skirt and matching blouse with a busy paisley pattern. "How was Ben Roth? Taking it pretty hard?"

"Yeah, but he's a tough old bird. He wants me to poke around and see if I can find out anything."

"You better stay out of the way of LAPD, you know."

"I know. Been there before." She cocked her head and gave me a look as if telling me I was walking on eggshells. "Just sayin'," she said, and went into her office.

When I'd gotten home after talking to Ben yesterday, I'd taken another look at the Jack Callahan arrest report Charlie Rivers had given me. Tabatha Preston and a Bart Helms were also arrested. Helms was released, due to lack of evidence. Preston had been arrested, tried, and acquitted. Since she had spent some time in jail before her acquittal, it seemed to me that she might have an axe to grind. Also, given the fact that she had been spotted at one of the gay nightclubs Lenny Daye and I had visited and was looking for Callahan certainly made her a person of interest, as the saying goes.

Money and sex are always sure-fire motives for violent crime. With Ben's revelation that he'd given five hundred grand to his son, one motive had reared its ugly head, and sex—even between two gay men—had also surfaced, especially because I'd seen Callahan's husband with another man. Ben was probably right when he said that Alex Foster and Roy Dickerson didn't figure into the equation, but that didn't mean they could be ignored.

I picked up the report and entered Mavis's office. "Can you find phone numbers for these two people?" I said, handing her the file. "Tabatha Preston and Bart Helms. I don't know if those addresses are current, but see what you can find, okay?"

"Sure thing," she said. "I can't imagine experiencing the murder of a son. Roth must be absolutely devastated."

"Yeah, it hit him pretty hard, but you'd be amazed at his toughness."

"But still. You have any ideas?"

I shared with her what I had seen at Universal City Walk on Saturday. Besides basically running my office, Mavis has proved to be an invaluable sounding-board in the cases I've handled. Despite Ben Roth's request that the gift of money remain confidential, I considered Mavis to be part of my business, so I told her about the five hundred grand he'd given to Callahan.

"That's a pretty good chunk of money," she said, "but I mean, enough to cause someone to beat a person to death? What do you know about this Alex Foster?"

"Only that he tried to bash my face in the other day." I bit off a corner of the granola bar. It could now be classified as a fossil. "I gotta tell you, though, it surprised the hell out of me to see him with that other guy at City Walk."

"Could just have been a friend, Eddie."

"Yeah, I know, but that doesn't take away from the fact that he seemed very protective of Callahan. When he answered the front door, he was ready to put some serious hurt on me."

I took the coffee cup and the fossil back to my apartment, disposed of them, grabbed a hat and started for the front door. Mavis already had her computer booted up.

"I'll call you if I come up with anything," she said. "Where you off to?"

"I'm going to see if another bribe works with Charlie Rivers."

"One of these days he's going to tell you to forget it."

"Let's hope it's not today," I said, as I doffed my hat and left the office.

FIGURING ONE BITE OF A FOSSILIZED granola bar wasn't going to cut it, I popped into a Denny's, pulled a *Los Angeles Times* from a dispenser, then grabbed a booth in the corner and ordered a Grand Slamwich and real coffee. A few years back I'd helped a friend of mine, Donny Briscoe, with an ugly divorce case. He worked in the front office of the Los Angeles Rams. It was mid-morning and I took a chance on him being at his desk. He was.

"Eddie Collins, Hollywood gumshoe, how you doin'?"

"Hangin' in there, Donny. Glad to see the Rams are back where they belong."

"You and me both, man. I got nothing against St. Louis, but my God, there's other beers besides Budweiser."

"I can vouch for that, my friend. Say listen, do you think you can hook me up with a couple of good seats for a home game? Doesn't matter which one. I've got a friend I'm trying to impress. Seats close enough to hear the grunts would do it."

"Lemme check." I could hear computer keys clicking. "How about the 49ers? Third game."

"Sweet." I gave him a credit card number and asked if he could email me the receipt so I had physical proof of the tickets. He said no problem, and went on to tell me that he'd leave the tickets at will-call. I gave him my email address, told him I owed him one and broke the connection.

The Grand Slamwich came and I dug in and watched two little elderly ladies gently arguing over who was going to pay for their breakfast. They finally decided to go Dutch and tottered out the front door. As the waitress filled my coffee cup, my cell chirped with an email. The screen was filled with a receipt for the football game. Ten rows up, mid-field. I tried to restrain myself from having boastful thoughts, but I was pretty sure tickets like these were going to impress Lieutenant Rivers.

CHARLIE'S CELL RANG THREE TIMES BEFORE he picked up. "What do you want, Collins?"

"No 'hello,' 'how ya doin', Eddie?'"

After a sigh and a pause I heard, "Good morning, Mr. Collins. I hope you're having a pleasant day. How's that?"

"Spoken like one of LAPD's finest."

"What's up?"

"Do you know what *quid pro quo* means?"

"My Latin's a little rusty, but I've heard the term."

"Jack Callahan. Beat to death early yesterday morning."

"Is that the *quid* or the *quo*?"

"Not sure," I said, "but I'm looking at a receipt for two tickets to a Rams game with the 49ers. Close enough to see 'em sweat."

There was a pause on the other end of the line. "Wasn't Callahan the guy you were looking for a few days ago?"

"One and the same."

"Did you find him?"

"I did. Guess my client wasted his money."

"No kiddin'," he said. There was a pause and I could hear chatter in the background. "So what do you want from me, Collins?"

"A peek at the crime scene report?"

"You don't listen so good, do you? I told you we haven't got a homicide desk here anymore. You're barking up the wrong tree."

"But you could ask around, couldn't you? One cop to another?"

After a pause he let loose with a huge sigh. "Aw, crap. I'll make a call." He broke the connection. I asked the waitress for another cup of coffee and then opened the *Times* to the crossword puzzle. I was on my third cup trying to come up with a nine-letter word for "a secret agreement" when my cellphone went off. The screen said Rivers.

"Have you had your morning coffee?"

"Could always use another cup," I said, even though I was about ready to float. He told me to meet him at a coffee shop on Sunset around the corner from the Hollywood station on Wilcox. Ironically, the word "collusion" fit the puzzle. I filled it in, paid for my Slamwich, hit the loo and found a parking place close by. Charlie hadn't arrived, so I ordered an iced tea and a muffin, rationalizing it was dessert. I sliced it in four parts and watched a young man hunched over his laptop. Another screenplay taking shape. After a few minutes Charlie walked through the door, a folder in his hand. He saw what I had and said he'd have the same. A cute barista filled the order. I sat across from him and showed him the football tickets receipt on my phone.

"You know, Collins, I'm not that far away from my pension. You ever stopped to consider what I'm doing may be putting that in jeopardy?"

"Then why do you do it?"

He nibbled on his muffin and looked at me. "I like football." We both chuckled and he shoved the report across the table to me. "This goes out the door with me."

"Understood." I opened the folder and scanned the computer printouts. Callahan's body had been found by an Albert Tisdale at approximately three-fifty yesterday morning. The guy was an Uber driver whose shift started at six, therefore the early dog walk. In the report was a photo of Callahan that made me forget about my muffin. His face was almost unrecognizable. Both eyes were swollen shut. One side of his head was caved in and the ear dangled by a thread of flesh. His nose had been broken. Whoever killed him hadn't held back. The body was clad in a yellow polo shirt saturated with blood. He had cargo shorts on, and one of his legs was bent at an unnatural angle.

I asked Charlie if I could take a picture of the photos. He scrunched up his face for a moment, weighing the request.

"Go ahead, but they don't leave your phone and they're deleted when the case is solved. You got me?"

"I got you." I snapped photos of the pictures and made some notes of the details in the report. A preliminary canvass of the neighborhood had revealed nothing. No witnesses. Callahan's ID was on the body, giving his address. Detectives notified Alex Foster at five-fifteen.

I closed the folder and slid it back to Charlie. "Who's the lead on this?"

"Rudy Hawkins. Lieutenant, West Bureau. I wouldn't go asking him for any more details, Eddie."

"I don't plan on it."

"Why are you interested? I assume you satisfied your client?"

"He wants me to poke around. I guess he trusts me."

"And not the LAPD?"

"I don't know, Charlie. The guy's in his nineties. He's been in this town for decades. He probably remembers things."

Charlie took a swallow of his tea and deliberately set the glass down. His eyes narrowed and he leaned across the table. "By that I suppose you mean Watts and Rodney King? And Rampart? While he's at it, I suppose he remembers all the way back to the chokehold and the Chief Parker days?"

The things he referred to were instances that had cast an unfavorable light on the LAPD. I put up my hands in a gesture of self-defense. "I didn't mean anything, Charlie. I think the old guy feels pretty helpless. Callahan was his only son."

"The Department will solve this, Eddie. You can take that to the bank."

"I don't doubt it for a minute. I'm not going to get in your way."

He stared at me for a long moment, slowly chewing a bit of his muffin. I wasn't sure if he believed me, but he finally nodded and said, "If I hear anything I'll give you a call."

"I'd appreciate it."

We made small talk as we finished our muffins and then parted ways. I cracked the car windows, waited for the inside to cool off, then pulled up the crime scene photo and looked at it again. Inflicting that kind of damage to another human being was inexplicable. If Callahan's beating was prompted by him being a gay man, it was impossible for me to have any regard whatsoever for someone exhibiting that kind of hatred. Callahan's lifestyle was not mine, but that didn't make it any less relevant. Certainly not enough for him to wind up in an alley in the middle of the night, essentially butchered. If Ben Roth were to view this picture, I was sure it would destroy him. I resolved to keep the image on my cellphone, only to be erased when the animal responsible for this carnage was removed from polite society.

Before my finger closed out the photos on the phone, and out of force of habit, I guess, I touched the "collections" link and the pictures I'd taken of the Robinsons' visit popped up. I scrolled through the images, stared at them, unable to reconcile the innocence of this young girl with the savagery and hate inflicted on Jack Callahan.

It was a depressing thought, but dwelling on it wasn't going to prove anything. Ben Roth needed more than that.

CHAPTER NINETEEN

———————◆———————

I CLOSED THE WINDOWS ON THE car, shut the photos app and was about to pull away from the curb when the cell went off. Mavis.

"Hey, Eddie. Did the bribe work?"

"For the most part, but he pretty much told me to keep my nose clean."

"Well, I found a number for this Tabatha Preston. Looks like it's a landline. It matches the address in Glendale. Couldn't raise anything for Bart Helms, though."

She gave me the number for Preston and rang off. I punched the number into the cell and waited as the call went to a robotic voice telling me to leave a message at the sound of the tone. I declined, put the car in gear and set out to see if Tabatha Preston did indeed have an axe to grind against Jack Callahan.

The address for Preston was on Elk Street, a stone's throw from the Glendale Galleria and also not far from Chez Cherie, where hopefully Carla had danced her last shift. The house was a squat white duplex on a street with stunted trees providing little shade. The building had a flat roof and a small patio jutted out from the front wall. It was covered with red adobe tiles. A sparse lawn whose grass had long ago been forgotten by a sprinkler was flanked on one side by a sidewalk and on the other by a narrow driveway.

I parked across the street and reached into the glove compartment where I keep an assortment of dummy business cards. I selected one of them, refreshed myself with the spiel to go along with it and slipped it into my shirt pocket. I grabbed a zippered attaché case off the back seat. Mavis has worked her magic and created several letters with official-looking letterheads. I found the one that matched the business card and walked up the sidewalk that had tufts of weeds sticking out from cracks in the concrete. Metal mailboxes hung on the wall next to each door, neither of which had screens.

I pushed a doorbell, waited a few minutes and pushed it again. From inside I heard music stop and after a moment the door opened as far as a chain allowed and the gaunt face of a black woman appeared in the opening. She had close-cropped gray hair and her eyes were heavy-lidded. The air that came through the opening smelled of marijuana and food cooked in grease. The woman cleared her throat.

"He'p you?" she said.

"I'm looking for Tabatha Preston."

"Who're you?"

I handed my fake card to her. "Tony Baldwin. Rainbow Holdings."

She looked at the card and said, "What you want wit' her?"

"We recently settled a class action suit and Ms. Preston is listed as one of the beneficiaries."

"That mean she got some money comin' to her?"

"Possibly, yes. Is she here?"

"No, she ain't."

"Do you know when she'll be back?"

"Not fer sure. She workin'."

"I see," I said, and looked to my left as two kids on skateboards came barreling down the street. "Could you tell me where she works?"

"Pit Stop. On Colorado. She tends bar."

"Where on Colorado?"

"Head on toward Eagle Rock. It's on your left."

"Thank you, ma'am," I said, and turned to go.

"How much money?" she said.

"That's still to be determined. Thanks for your time."

She closed the door and I walked back to my car.

THE PIT STOP SAT ON A corner next to a record store called Tunes 4 U. Across the side street a two-story building was under construction. I pulled the bar's door open and was met with a welcome rush of cool air. The place was dimly-lit and smelled of stale beer and sweeping compound. Five booths ran along the wall to my left, two of them occupied. The L-shaped bar was on the right. An array of liquor bottles occupied shelves behind it. Television sets dangled from the ceiling in each corner. Two different baseball games filled the screens. In the rear sat a pool table where two young men were in the middle of a game.

Three guys wearing baseball caps and grease-stained flannel shirts and jeans hunched over glasses of beer with whiskey chasers. They turned to look at me when I came in. The looks on their faces told me they were getting a head start on happy hour.

I straddled a stool that had duct tape covering cracks in the vinyl and laid the attaché case on the bar next to me. The bartender ambled toward me. He was a big man with thinning gray hair and a look on his face that said he'd rather be at the beach. A slight paunch hung over his belt and his nose had enough blue veins to suggest that he didn't shy away from sampling his wares. He picked up a napkin from a pile and set it in front of me.

"What'll it be?" he said.

"What do you have on tap?"

"Bud and Coors. That's it."

"Bud's fine."

He walked off and I pulled a double sawbuck from my money clip. A crack of pool balls came from the rear and two women in one of the booths let loose with a burst of laughter. The Pit Stop was obviously a comfortable oasis for locals seeking refuge from the July heat. The bartender picked up a wooden stick one would use to stir a can of paint and used it to shave off the head of foam on the beer glass. Satisfied, he carried it down to me, drops of Budweiser falling to the floor. He set the beer on the napkin, picked up the twenty, made change and laid it on the bar in front of me.

"I'm looking for Tabatha Preston," I said. "I was told she works here."

"She's on a break."

"You suppose I could talk to her?"

"Depends on whether or not she wants to talk to you."

"You suppose you could ask her?"

He looked at me like I'd just asked to marry his daughter, then finally picked up a phone on the back-bar and hit a couple of keys. "Someone here to see you, Tabbie." He listened a moment, hung up the phone and turned to me. "She'll be out in a minute," he said, and moved off down the bar.

I sipped from the glass of beer and looked around the room. One of the grease monkeys at the bar continued to give me the evil eye laced with attitude, implying that I was on his turf and he didn't like it. He finally decided I wasn't worth any more attention and turned back to his buddies. A door opened in the rear and a tall black woman appeared. The bartender said something to her and pointed in my direction. She caught my eye and started toward me.

If women were ever to play in the NFL, Tabatha Preston would be a first round draft choice. She was dressed in skin-tight jeans and a black tank top with the logo of the rock band AC/DC on it. Describing her as being well-endowed would be an understatement. Her head was shaved on the sides, leaving a Mohawk that morphed into a long ponytail hanging past her shoulders. Tattoos covered both arms. Silver chains were draped around her neck and metal studs ran along the outer edges of both ears. She didn't walk the length of the bar; she strutted. Despite all the trappings, she was an attractive woman, in a take-no-prisoners sort of way.

She stopped in front of me, leaned on the bar with arms spread and said in a voice that could restore the head of foam on my glass of beer, "I don't know who the hell you are, pal, and I've never heard of Rainbow Holdings."

"So you got a phone call?"

"Fuckin' A. Now who is Tony Baldwin?"

She had me. I reached in my pocket and pulled out my PI ticket and showed it to her.

She looked at it and tossed it on the bar. "A private dick? What do you want with me?"

I reached in another pocket, pulled out my cell and brought up the photo of Jack Callahan. "Let me show you something," I said, and held up the photo so she could see it. "Recognize him?"

She looked at the photo and displayed a grimace before pushing it aside. "Christ, who the hell is that?"

"Jack Callahan," I said. "Remember him?"

The mention of the name caught her by surprise. Her brow furrowed and she glanced at the photo again. "Good God, who did that to him?"

"That's what I'm trying to find out. You knew him, right?"

"Yeah. When did that happen?"

"Monday morning, about three thirty." I sipped some beer as she grabbed a stool to her right, fished a bottle of beer out of a cooler and sat down. "Mind telling me where you were then?" I said.

She twisted the top off the bottle, glared at me while she tipped it up and swallowed. "Oh, I see how this plays. I get busted, can't make bail and have to do some time while Jack Callahan skates. Now he gets bumped off and that makes me a suspect. That about right?"

"Not what I said." I closed the photo and laid the phone on the bar. "So tell me where you were Sunday morning."

"I was with my partner, Georgia Hall. I'm a dyke..." She paused and looked at my card again. "...Eddie Collins. We were bumpin' titties, and that's exactly what she'll tell you."

"After you call her, I suppose."

Tabatha picked up my cell and punched in a phone number. Someone answered and she said, "Hi, Hon. There's a guy here wants to talk to you. Hang on."

She handed the phone to me and I spoke with Georgia Hall on the other end of the line. I asked the question and she confirmed that she was with Tabatha all night on Sunday. I thanked her and broke the connection.

"Satisfied?" Tabatha said.

I nodded and took a swallow of the Budweiser. "Can you tell me why you were looking for Callahan at Rage in West Hollywood a few nights ago?"

"When?"

I gave her the date and she sampled some of her beer as she stared at me. "Why the hell were you there, Mr. Private Dick? You don't impress me as being a guy who walks on that side of the fence."

"I was hired to locate him."

"Looks like somebody beat you to it."

"No, I found him before this happened. My client rehired me."

"Who's your client?"

"Can't tell you that. But you can tell me why you were looking for Callahan."

The bartender called out for her to hold down the fort for a few minutes. She climbed off her stool and asked the grease monkeys at the bar if they needed anything else. They said they did, and she served them, then came back down the bar, wiping her hands on a bar rag.

"Okay, look, Collins, I get the scenario here. You probably know the situation surrounding my arrest. Thanks to a good lawyer, I beat the rap. While you may think I wanted some payback, the fact is I was looking for Jack because I'd heard he was trying to get another movie financed. I thought he might have some work for me."

"As an actress?" I said.

She almost choked on a swallow of beer and laughed. "Look at me, for crissakes! You think anybody wants to pay money to see me bare-assed naked? You gotta be dreamin'."

I shrugged and said, "You might be surprised. Did you make contact with Callahan that night?"

"No, I didn't."

"Can you think of anyone else who might have wanted to do something like this?"

She shook her head. "Not to that extent. Jesus, that's a fuckin' execution." A lady from one of the booths walked up to the bar and called to Tabatha. She walked down the bar and drew two glasses of beer, set them on the bar, picked up some bills as the lady tottered back to her booth. Tabatha walked back and sat down on the stool.

"That tribe that Jack ran with back then could be kind of dicey sometimes," she said.

"Dicey? How so?"

"Making gay porno films isn't exactly the Boy Scouts, Collins. It's a rough crowd. Lots of drugs. People who do that sort of thing aren't exactly shy about going off on anyone."

"There was a Bart Helms also arrested. Any idea where I could find him?'

"No idea. Dead, or in rehab would be my guess. Bart could never get high enough. Or care whose bones he jumped."

I took a pull from the glass of beer and glanced to my right as the door opened and two elderly guys came in. One of them came up to the bar and his buddy collapsed into one of the empty booths.

"How you doin', Floyd?" Tabatha said.

"It's hotter'n than a hundred-dollar hooker out there, Tabbie."

"C'mon, you've never even seen a fifty-dollar hooker."

"I can dream, can't I?" They both shared a laugh and Tabatha reached over and slapped the brim of his baseball cap. She filled a pitcher of beer and Floyd walked off with it and two glasses. She came back to where I was sitting.

"Jack was living with a guy by the name of Alex Foster," I said. "You happen to know him? Big black guy."

"Come to think of it, there was a dude who looked like he mighta been playin' house with Jack. Kind of a Denzel wannabe. Wouldn't have minded spreadin' 'em myself if I swung that way. I don't remember his name, though. Been a few years ago now."

The bar's front door burst open and a group of six young men wearing hard hats stumbled into the bar, shouting out greetings to Tabbie and jostling each other as they bellied up to the bar. The bartender with the blue-highways nose walked around the far end of the bar and indicated it was time for her to tend to business.

"Sorry, Collins, it's the crew from across the street. They drink like fish. Duty calls."

I picked my business card up off the bar and handed it to her again. "Stick this in your pocket and give me a call if you think of anything else."

She held up the card. "So forget about Tony Baldwin?"

"Never heard of him," I said. She smiled, stuck the card in a hip pocket of her jeans and walked down the bar to where the hard hats were sitting. I jotted down some notes and sipped on my beer. After a few minutes Tabatha walked up again.

"Hey, Collins, I just thought of something else."

"Yeah?"

"There was this other guy that hung around that film set back then. He was sort of a gaffer, or gofer, I don't know. I remember one time Jack tried to get him to do a part in the film, but he raised holy hell and wouldn't do it."

"Do you recall his name?"

She leaned on the bar and thought for a moment or two. "Roy something."

Her mention of the name caught me up short.

"Mickelson, maybe?" she continued. "Torkelson?"

"Dickerson?" I said. "Roy Dickerson?"

"Yeah, that's it. He was a real asshole. You know him?"

"I might," I said. "Was he around when that murder happened?"

"Nah, I don't think so. Seems to me he was gone by then."

"Thanks," I said.

She tapped the bar with her fingers, picked up my empty glass and strolled back down the bar. I grabbed my attaché case, pushed open the front door and stepped into the heat.

And asked myself why Roy Dickerson, who professed not to know of his cousin's sexual identity, winds up working on a gay porn film made by that same cousin.

CHAPTER TWENTY

———◆———

FORTUNATELY, BEFORE I'D GONE INTO THE Pit Stop I'd parked the car under a tree so the interior wouldn't be the seventh ring of Hell when I opened the door. Nevertheless, the heat was such that I had to slide down all the windows to give the air conditioning a leg up.

The information Tabatha Preston had provided caught me completely by surprise. Roy Dickerson had lied through his teeth when he'd expressed surprise at learning that his cousin was a gay man. If Preston's recollection was correct, not only did Roy know Jack Callahan was gay, but also that he made porno films, one of which Roy himself had been involved with. Did that mean that Roy was also gay? Not necessarily, but I was reminded of the old saying that if you hang around a barber shop long enough, sooner or later you're going to get a haircut. It didn't bother me if Roy was gay, but what did bother the hell out of me was that he'd lied to me.

I pulled out my cell, found Roy's number and made the call. It rang four times and went to voice mail. I left a message telling him that Ben had asked me to look into his cousin's murder and to give me a call when he got a chance.

The car's air conditioner groaned to life as I shut the windows and pulled away from the curb. I drove no more than fifty feet when the cell rang again. The thought of buying one of those high-tech, hands-free phones briefly crossed my mind, but recognizing my inherent tendency to be a Luddite, I thought better of it, pulled over and answered the phone. It was Carla.

"Hey, Shamus."

"Hey yourself, you working actress, you. Are you waiting for your closeup?"

"Already had it, and I was gorgeous."

"I'd expect nothing less."

"We're between set-ups. I've got a few minutes and thought I'd give you a call. Where are you?"

"Glendale." I told her about my meeting with Tabatha Preston.

"Aha! The plot thickens, as the saying goes," she said. "Say listen, I've got an early call in the morning. Can I crash with you tonight?"

"No problem. I'll tell the neighbor girl I have to cancel."

She blew me a raspberry, hung up and I headed back to my office.

ALTHOUGH COLLINS INVESTIGATIONS DOESN'T USE IT much because of all the digital resources at Mavis's disposal, we still do have a white pages telephone book covering the greater Los Angeles area. When I'd walked in the door, my gal Friday was in the midst of a bid on eBay for a set of Rocky and Bulwinkle placemats. Rolling my eyes in disbelief at the inane items people pay good money for, I carried the tome into my office and tossed it on my desk. Another call to Roy's cell produced only a voice mail. I then dialed Ben Roth's phone to see if he could give me his nephew's home phone and address. No answer and no voice mail.

Forced to let my fingers do the walking, I jotted down the listings for Dickerson. Surprisingly, there weren't all that many, with only three for "Roy" and four more for "Dickerson, R." Calls to the "Roy" numbers resulted in one no answer, and when I identified myself to the other two, both parties said they had nothing to do with the movie and TV business and damn sure didn't want to. After I identified myself to the second "Dickerson, R." with no address given, I struck pay dirt.

"Dickerson's," a woman's soft voice said. "This is Amanda."

"Hello, ma'am. My name is Eddie Collins. I have an actor friend by the name of Roy Dickerson. Is this by any chance his home phone?"

"Yes, my husband Roy's an actor."

"Oh, great. All I have for him is a cell, and he doesn't answer. Is he home by any chance?"

"No, he's not," she said. "He's up at Lake Arrowhead. Fishing."

"I see."

"We share a cabin up there with another couple. I can give you the number, if you'd like."

"That would be terrific," I replied.

"Just a moment," she said. I heard rustling in the background and she came back on the line and gave me the number. "If Roy calls, can I give him a message?"

"No, it's nothing that important. I'll try and reach him up there. Thank you very much, Amanda."

I hung up and leaned back in my chair. Would Ben Roth have called his nephew after learning of Jack Callahan's death? My guess is he would have. If he knew his cousin had been brutally murdered, why would Roy not care enough to be in LA, rather than fishing? There was only one way to find out.

I dialed the number Amanda Dickerson had given and listened to it ring twice before it was answered by a woman's voice.

"Hello?"

"May I speak to Roy Dickerson please?"

"I'm sorry, but he's not here."

"Do you know when he'll be back?"

The woman paused a moment before answering. "This is June Palmer. My husband Chuck and I share this cabin with Amanda and Roy Dickerson. But I'm afraid they're not here."

"I just spoke with Amanda, and she told me Roy was up there fishing."

"Well, if he is, I certainly don't know about it. Amanda and Roy were up here in May. My husband and I didn't expect to see them now."

"Thank you very much, ma'am. Sorry to bother you."

I put the phone back on its cradle and stared at it for a long moment. The chance meeting I'd had with Roy Dickerson a few days ago while he was trying to be Santa Claus was innocent enough, but now the man had become an enigma. I thought back to when I'd seen him walking along Santa Monica while Lenny and I were on our way to one of the gay clubs. He said he'd been at Barney's Beanery and was walking back to his car. Okay, fine. But I still found it curious that Jack Callahan and Alex Foster had been in the vicinity, along with Tabatha Preston. Then Roy showed up at City Walk, after I'd seen Alex with another man. Pieces of a jigsaw puzzle floated around in my head, looking for places to fit in.

Mavis stuck her head in the office and said, "Success! Rocky and Bulwinkle have found a new home."

"Terrific," I replied, as I leaned back in my chair and stared at the wall across the office.

"What's with the long face?"

"Questions, and no answers." I leaned forward and closed the telephone book. "Let me ask you something. If you had a cousin and found out he or she was murdered, would you go off on a fishing trip?"

"Well, first of all, the closest I'll get to fish is on a plate with tartar sauce on the side. But if you mean would I leave town, I doubt it."

"That's what I figured," I said. "Roy Dickerson tells his wife he's up at Lake Arrowhead when he's apparently not."

She sat in front of the desk and I shared the pieces of the puzzle with her.

She wasn't much help. I didn't blame her. What Roy Dickerson was up to baffled the hell out of me.

Mavis left for the day and I gave Roy's cell a couple more tries. No success. Then I tried Ben Roth again and this time he answered.

"Ben, it's Eddie Collins. How you holding up?"

"If I could sleep it would help. The three amigos here been hanging around me like vultures. They must think I'm gonna commit suicide or some goddamn thing."

"Don't do that. It won't solve anything."

"Yeah, I know. Speakin' of solving. What's goin' on at your end?"

"I'm poking around. Have you heard anything from Roy?"

"No, dammit. His wife says he's fishing, for crissakes! But he don't answer his cellphone. You know where the hell he is?"

"I can't raise him either."

"I don't know if he even heard about Jack." I heard him cough on the other end of the line before he said, "Well, listen, I don't know whether or not this is your cup of tea, but there's a service for Jack tomorrow. You're welcome to be there. According to Alex, the kid didn't go to synagogue anymore. No skin off my nose, I guess. I haven't exactly been going myself. Besides, he said he wanted Jack to be cremated. Doesn't set too well with me, but I figure it ain't my call."

He gave me the time and where the service was taking place. "Do you need someone to drive you there?"

"I hired a car. The three amigos are going to ride with me."

"Okay. I'll see you there," I said. I'd barely gotten to know Jack Callahan and was surprised that Ben had extended the offer. Kinda made me feel like a member of the family. I moped around the office waiting for Carla. When she arrived, we went out for a pizza. I presented the puzzle pieces to her. She wasn't much help either.

"Come on," I said. "You're a detective now. I need help."

"And I need a script," she replied. When I shook my head, she laughed and put an arm around my shoulders. "I wish I had an idea, Eddie. Maybe this Alex Foster can help. You told me they know each other, right?"

"They do. I'll see if I can talk to him tomorrow."

We finished our pizza, stopped for ice cream and went back to my office. Carla filled me in on her day of shooting, making me green with envy for being in front of a camera. She said she was sure *Shades of Blue* was eventually going to hire me. I hoped she was right.

With Carla's early morning call in mind, we decided to call it a night. When Mr. Murphy's bed emerged, both of us burst into laughter at the absurdity of pulling this contraption out of a wall, like something out of an Edgar Allan Poe story.

We resolved to do something to change that.

CHAPTER TWENTY-ONE

———————◆———————

SELDOM ARE THE TIMES I PUT on a coat and tie, but I did manage to unearth one of each to wear to Jack Callahan's service. Before leaving the office, Mavis offered her usual comments on my wardrobe, all of them favorable for a change. I descended the elevator to the parking lot and was greeted with wind. Strong wind. Unseasonably hot wind. Autumn normally brings the infamous Santa Anas that, according to Raymond Chandler, made meek little housewives check the edges of their knives as they looked at their husbands' necks. I didn't think these were anywhere near that sinister, but I nevertheless had to chase my porkpie as it careened down the alley.

The address Ben Roth had given me yesterday was a funeral parlor in Westwood. Of course, parking was sparse. After nosing the car just beyond a fire hydrant, I left my hat on the front seat and walked back half a block to see Ben, Jerry Daniels, Paul Baker, and George Higgins crawling out of a black limo. Ben spotted me and we shook hands. His three pals offered their greetings and we walked into the mortuary.

Appropriate soft instrumental music filled the air as a somber undertaker ushered us into a small chamber off the main lobby. A couple of large flower arrangements in vases occupied a small raised platform. Off to one side stood a small wooden lectern. Two dozen folding chairs were set up, several of them filled by young men. In the front row sat an elderly gray-haired woman dressed in black. As we walked into the room, she stood and Ben walked up to her and they embraced. I assumed the woman was Jack's mother.

There was no coffin, just a picture of Jack Callahan that sat on an easel between the flowers. The smiling redheaded young man in the photo bore no resemblance whatsoever to the person in the gruesome picture in my cellphone.

Alex Foster rose from his chair and greeted Ben with a tentative hug and murmurs of condolence. Surprise washed over me when I recognized the young man who sat next to Alex. It was the guy in the straw hat I had seen with him at Universal City Walk. Noticeably absent from the gathering, however, was Roy Dickerson.

Alex caught sight of me and registered a look of surprise at my presence. Ben led him over to me.

"Eddie Collins, this is Alex Foster, Jack's partner," Ben said.

"Yes, we've met," I said, as I took the hand Alex offered. "My condolences."

"Thanks. And I'm sorry about the other day."

"No worries."

"I asked Collins to poke around and see if he can find out who did this to Jack," Ben said.

"I see. Good idea." I detected an odd lack of conviction in his voice, but given the fact that he'd just lost his husband, it was understandable.

"Did you ever hear from Roy?" Ben asked.

"No, he's not answering his phone," Alex replied.

"Yeah, I know, fer crissakes," Ben muttered, as he turned and sat down next to Jack's mother.

"I'd like to ask you a few questions about that night, Alex, whenever it's convenient for you," I said.

He gave it some thought and finally said, "Why don't you stop around after we're done here? A few of Jack's friends are dropping by. We can talk after everyone leaves."

"Fine," I said. "And once again, my condolences on your loss."

He nodded and I took a seat in the back row and scanned a small pamphlet about Jack Callahan and his all-too-brief life. Two young women and several more young men entered the room and took seats.

At the top of the hour a tall, bespectacled man wearing a religious collar stepped behind the lectern and read a passage from the Bible, then offered a few generic comments about Jack Callahan. It was obvious he didn't know the deceased, nor did it appear that he showed much remorse for his demise. Several of Jack's friends, however, spoke a few words and described him in more glowing terms. A young man related how Jack used to love Halloween and the opportunity to come up with crazy costumes. One of the women shared the time she and Jack had sat through an entire marathon of *Friends* on television.

Ben stood up to speak and teetered a little until George Higgins grabbed his elbow and steadied him. He shuffled up to the lectern and wiped his nose with his handkerchief before looking at the people in the room. His face registered the sadness and strain he was no doubt feeling.

"I never thought there'd be a day like this," he said. "But I'd like to thank you all for being here." He paused and his lips trembled. "There's a term in the film business called martini shot. It refers to the last scene of the day, before they turn off the camera and everyone heads for the nearest saloon. I always figured I'd have my martini shot before my only child, but whoever pulls those strings didn't see it my way. A few years ago I did a very stupid thing and disowned Jackie." He paused again and dabbed at the corners of his eyes with the handkerchief. "I'm an old man and been known to do some dumb things. That one I really regret. I didn't like his lifestyle. It took me a long time to realize that was none of my goddamn business." He blew his nose and then gripped the lectern before turning to Alex and continuing. "Alex, my apologies. What you and Jackie had together was probably better than anything he had with me. I'm sorry for your loss."

Alex put his fist to his heart and then pointed at Ben. His companion from the day I'd seen him at Universal City Walk draped his arm across Alex's shoulders.

"So now he's gone," Ben continued, "and I'll miss him. That's all I can do." He walked over to the picture on the easel, kissed his fingers and touched Jack's face in the photo. "I love you, Jackie. Rest in peace." He stuffed his handkerchief into his breast pocket and walked back to his seat. Jerry Daniels rose, hugged him and helped him into his seat.

There was silence in the room. Ben's words were brief, but said volumes. I can't imagine anything more difficult than a parent being forced to lay to rest a child. My introduction to my daughter Kelly Robinson had been years in the making, but now, knowing of her existence, the mere thought of her undergoing the same fate as Jack Callahan was inconceivable to me.

Ben's ex-wife stood to speak. Her grief was less palpable than Ben's, but she expressed her wish that she had been closer to her son during the last few years. She went on to admit that it was probably her fault for moving out of Los Angeles up into Ventura County.

Alex was the last to address the small gathering. He briefly described how the two of them had met at a gay pride rally in West Hollywood, and how they'd gotten married when same-sex marriage became legal in California. His comments were heartfelt, and several times he had to choke back tears as he talked.

The proceedings concluded after twenty minutes. Alex provided the address on Cynthia Street, and the mourners slowly filed out of the funeral home, leaving behind two solitary vases of flowers and a picture of a young man whose reconciliation with his father had been nullified by an horrific murder. To me, the few chosen words didn't seem to provide much justification for Callahan's death, but then murder seldom takes responsibility for what it leaves behind.

THE WIND CONTINUED TO CHURN UP scraps of paper and other trash as I drove to Cynthia Street. One of the young women who had been at the service walked ahead of me with two friends. The wind caught her floppy hat and sent it flying down the sidewalk right in front of me. I bent to pick it up and received her thanks, then opened the gate in the picket fence and we entered the house.

Ben and his three amigos were already there, along with a few of those who'd spoken at the service. Alex had provided a table of refreshments. A young lady wearing a catering uniform flitted around it, tidying up and making sure serving plates were full. There were cheeses, crackers, several other finger-foods and wine.

I filled a small paper plate with munchies and poured myself a plastic glass of Chardonnay, then sat down in a canvas director's chair next to Ben and balanced the plate on my lap. "You doin' all right, Ben?"

"Ah, I'll make it," he said, then sipped from a glass of wine and looked around. "I don't know any of these kids. Glad to hear they liked Jack, though."

"Was that his mother you were sitting next to at the service?"

"Yeah. Maureen. She won't be here. Lives way the hell up in Ojai, and wanted to hit the road, I guess. Seems to me she could have paid her respects and stopped by, but that's Maureen. I gave up tryin' to figure her out a long time ago." He uttered a derisive laugh and placed a piece of cheese on a cracker and took a bite. Most of it fell onto his lap and he muttered under his breath as he swept the crumbs off his pants. "You made any progress, Collins?"

"Not much. I'm going to have a talk with Alex in a bit. Hopefully he can tell me what the hell Jack was doing in that alley in the middle of the night."

"Yeah, that don't make a damn bit of sense to me." He turned as Paul Baker and George Higgins started laughing. "What the hell's so funny?" he said.

Paul started to tell of an incident involving Jack from a few years past. Ben joined in the laughter and I took my plate over to a wastepaper container and refilled my wine glass. Alex was in the backyard in the shade of a tree, smoking a cigarette. Next to him stood the guy who was in the straw hat that day at Universal City Walk. I slid open the glass door and stepped onto the patio. Alex put his cigarette out and motioned for me to come over.

"Eddie, right?" he said. I nodded and he gestured to the guy next to him. "Eddie Collins, this is Dennis Abrams. Jack was a friend." I shook hands with him and Alex continued, "Collins is a private investigator. Jack's dad hired him to look into what happened."

"Well, good luck," Dennis said. "I can't imagine who would do something like that to Jack. He wouldn't hurt a fly."

I sipped my wine and made some small talk. A guest stuck his head out the glass door and called for Alex and Abrams to come inside. They excused themselves and I wandered around the backyard that consisted of a swimming pool and a small patch of grass. The pool was tiny by Hollywood standards and littered with leaves from the surrounding trees.

After I'd poured another glass of wine, people gradually started to filter out the front door. Ben came over to me and stuck out his hand.

"Let me know how it's going, Collins."

"I'll be in touch, Ben."

I watched as Alex ushered Ben and his three pals out the front door. Dennis Abrams was next. He and Alex embraced and kissed each other. I found that odd somehow, not because they were men, but that Alex had just lost his husband and had been seen with Abrams looking like the two of them were more than just friends. Then Carla's words of admonition came back to me. *Get over it, Collins! Where is it written that friends can't kiss each other? You've done it yourself, for crying out loud.* Alex shut the front door and came back into the living room. The young girl carried leftovers into the kitchen.

"Thanks, Lois," he said. "Just take care of the perishables and I'll do the rest." He pulled a money clip from his pocket and handed her several bills. She thanked him and carried away what was left of the food.

"I need a smoke," he said. "Let's go outside." He slid open the door and I followed him onto the patio. The wind whipped the fronds of small palm trees at the rear of the property. Alex gestured to one of two white metal garden chairs clustered around a small matching table. I sat and watched him reach in his shirt pocket and take out a pack of cigarettes. "Oh, crap," he muttered, as he realized it was empty and crushed it. He looked around, then tossed the empty pack in a small plastic wastepaper basket. He put his hands on his hips and looked at me. "Do you smoke?" he said.

"Sorry."

He kept glancing around the patio and finally walked over to another small table at the edge of the pool. He picked up something I hadn't noticed before. It was a pack of cigarettes, the same kind of cigarettes Roy Dickerson smoked. Sobranie Black Russians.

"Those are Roy's brand, aren't they?" I said.

"Yeah, he left them. And they're terrible."

"So he's been here?"

"He stopped over last Saturday to see if Jack and I wanted to go fishing," Alex said. He stuck one of the cigarettes in his mouth and put a match to the end of it, but the wind blew it out. He tried again and was successful. He sat in the other garden chair and continued. "I don't know what the hell gave him the idea that Jack and I'd want to sit in a boat for hours on end waiting for some stupid fish to gnaw on something at the end of a hook."

"I tend to agree with you," I said. "Did Roy say where he was going?"

"Lake Arrowhead, I guess. He's got a cabin up there."

"Except he's not there," I said.

"What do you mean?"

"His wife gave me the phone number of the cabin. I talked to a June Palmer. She and her husband share the cabin with the Dickersons. She told me they haven't seen Roy."

Alex took a deep drag on the cigarette and flicked the ashes into a tray sitting next to him. "Well, maybe he's not using the cabin."

"Could be," I said, as I took my notebook out of my coat pocket and opened it. "But you said you've been trying to call him?"

"I've called his cell many times, but he doesn't answer."

"So he doesn't know about Jack's murder?"

"Not as far as I know," Alex said. "Which is a shame, because I think he and Jack were close over the years, until Ben did what he did."

"You mean when he disowned him?"

"Yeah." He took another drag on the cigarette and stubbed it out. "What did you want to know, Mr. Collins?"

"I imagine the police told you where he was found, right?"

"Yes."

"Did they ask you to identify the body?"

He nodded and his face crumbled. He leaned on his knees and hung his head, then heaved a huge sigh and said, "I couldn't believe that someone would do something like that."

"I know. I saw the crime scene photos."

"Christ. I almost didn't recognize him." He shook another cigarette out of the pack and lit it up.

"Why do you suppose Jack was in that alley at that time of the night?" I said.

"I don't know. He was invited to a movie screening Sunday night and a party afterwards."

"And you weren't?"

"I was, but I decided not to go. I had an early morning at work on Monday."

"Where is that?"

"I'm a menswear buyer at Macy's in the Beverly Center."

"What time was the movie screening?"

"I believe it was at eight."

"Do you know where?"

"A little art house on La Cienega. Just north of Melrose. Jack told me the name but I'm afraid I don't remember it."

"No offense, but given the nature of Jack's movie-making, was it a gay film?"

"What the hell difference does that make?"

"None. But if some of the audience went to the party, it might help to know if they were Hell's Angels or card-carrying members of the NRA."

Alex chuckled and pointed at me. "*Touché*," he said. "It's my understanding it was a small documentary film. Something to do with the pharmaceutical industry."

I made some notes and said, "Did Jack call you at all that night?"

"No. He told me he might be late, so I didn't think anything about it. I went to bed around ten thirty, and didn't wake up until the police knocked on the door."

"Can you tell me where the party was? Some of the people who would have been there? Your friend Dennis, for instance? Was he there?"

"Yes, I believe he was." He gave me Abrams' address and cell number, along with the locale of the party and the names of several people that he thought were most likely in attendance. As I began to jot them down in my notebook, a gust of wind caught the ashtray and blew the contents over the table we were sitting at. Alex continued giving me names while he fished a soiled napkin out of the wastebasket and swiped the ashes off the table.

"Would any of these people do something like this?" I said. "Somebody have an axe to grind? A grudge?"

He shook his head. "Aside from Dennis, I'm only acquainted with one or two that were at the screening, so I couldn't say for sure. But I seriously doubt it. Most of them were involved in Jack's movie work. It would have been a friendly group. But frankly, I didn't really have anything to do with that part of his life."

I looked at him for a moment, debating whether or not I should go down this avenue of questioning, but then decided it needed to be broached. "Ben told me he'd given Jack some money to help him with another movie project. Did you know about that?

"Yes," Alex said.

"Do you think anyone else knew about it?"

"Well, Ben broke the news when we were at dinner with him on Friday night, so Roy knew."

That coincided with what Ben had told me over the phone. Alex puffed on the cigarette as I jotted notes in my book. I looked up to see him glaring at me. "I'm a step ahead of you, Collins. Jack and I had a joint bank account. I know that probably makes me a suspect. Money is always a motive, right? Isn't the spouse the first person the police question?"

"Usually," I said. "Is that what they did?"

"Repeatedly. And I'll tell you what I told them. We loved each other, and for anyone to think I'd do harm to him because of money is just disgusting."

"Look, Alex, I know you and I got off on the wrong foot the other day, but I'm not the enemy here. Yes, five hundred grand is a motive, and so naturally you as the spouse arouses suspicion. But that's all. Evidence is something else. And that's something I don't have yet."

"Point taken," he said, as he stubbed the cigarette out, rose and emptied the ashtray, then sat down again.

"I suppose the cops also asked for your whereabouts at the time of the murder, right?"

"Yes. And I don't have an alibi, other than the fact I—"

He stopped and put one hand to his mouth. I could see him fighting back tears and he leaned forward in his chair. "Other than the fact I loved him very much. I could never do him harm. You just have to believe me."

He stood up and took a few steps toward the pool. He stopped, bent over and gripped his knees. His powerful shoulders trembled and I heard him stifling sobs. The emotion seemed genuine. I had given some thought about confronting him with the picture I'd taken at Universal City Walk, but seeing him in obvious agony made me change my mind. It didn't seem wise to invade any more of his privacy. I'd make it a point to talk to Dennis Abrams without Alex's knowledge.

He stood up, took a deep breath and then turned around and came back to his chair. "I'm sorry, man. I'm not handling this as well as I thought I could."

"No apologies necessary, Alex." I handed him a business card and stood up. "Give me a call if you think of anything else, okay?"

"Will do," he said, and plucked another Black Russian out of the pack and lit it up. "Good luck," he said, as he stuck out his hand. "I hope the bastard is found."

"He will be," I said, and started for the front door. "But let me give you some advice."

"What's that?"

"Quit smoking those damn cigarettes. They'll kill you."

A sheepish look washed over his face and he chuckled. "Yeah, I know."

Chapter Twenty-Two

---◆---

I PULLED MY TIE OFF AND waited for the car to once again cool off. It gave me a chance to think about what I'd learned from Alex Foster. While two errant plastic bags took flight with the wind in front of the car I glanced at my notes and made some adjustments. Normal investigation would indeed make Alex Foster a prime suspect. There was money involved. Plus, no one could corroborate his whereabouts at the time of the murder. It was obvious to me that he loved Jack Callahan, so the romantic in me gave him the benefit of the doubt. At the same time I couldn't erase from my mind the scene between him and Dennis Abrams I'd witnessed at Universal City Walk. Despite Carla's admonitions to the contrary, something about that incident still gnawed at me, politically incorrect as it may be.

And then there was the absence of Roy Dickerson. On its face, there's nothing odd about someone turning off a phone and wallowing in the dictates of Izaak Walton and *The Compleat Angler*. More power to him. But Roy was also an actor. Actors are tethered to cellphones. They risk scolding from agents, wives, girlfriends, and secretaries. With that thought in mind, I dialed Roy's cell once more and still got voicemail. I didn't bother to leave a message. Roy wasn't paying attention to anything. Either his phone was dead, or he wasn't paying any attention to it because of all the fish he was catching.

I closed the car windows and pulled away from the curb. In addition to those of Dennis Abrams, Alex had given me the name and address of Randy Tyson, the person who'd hosted the party after the movie screening. He lived on Norwich Drive. The route there took me south on La Cienega. Alex had said the theater where the screening had taken place was just north of Melrose. I kept looking at buildings on both sides of the street. Sure enough, to my right I caught sight of a glass door with a sign above it that said Beaux Arts. I spotted a vacant parking meter and pulled to the curb. Twelve minutes remained. I stuck two bits in it and walked back to the storefront. The door was locked, and a glance through it revealed a hallway with a counter on the right. It had a glass top and beneath it I could see various boxes of candy bars displayed. An antique popcorn machine sat behind the counter. On a table next to it was an espresso machine and a two-burner hotplate. A card was taped to the inside of the door above the lock with a telephone number to call for information about booking the space. Thinking that whoever ran the place could possibly remember something about Jack Callahan at that screening, I jotted down the number and then walked back to the car.

After turning right on Melrose I started looking for Norwich, found it, and turned left onto a one-way going south. The street was lined with old trees on both sides, had neatly manicured lawns and upscale cars parked at the curbs. Any wind seeking paper and trash to scatter was going to be disappointed. Norwich Drive was immaculate.

The address Alex had given me was on my right. I slid in behind a Mercedes convertible with a vanity license plate that said "BENZ4ME." The apartment building consisted of three stories. Ivy climbed up the facade. The entrance was in a recess in the front wall. The door was solid wood with narrow glass panels on each side. I looked through one of them and saw a small lobby on the left. Stairs and an elevator lay straight ahead. Locked mailboxes were embedded in the left wall of the recess and on the right was a directory with the name "Tyson" next to number five. As I pushed Tyson's button I noticed a security camera above in one corner. After a moment "yes?" came out of the speaker.

"Randy Tyson?" I said, looking into the camera.

"Yes. And you are?"

"Eddie Collins. I'm a private investigator looking into the murder of Jack Callahan. Alex Foster gave me your name and address. I'm wondering if I could ask you a few questions about the party you hosted after that movie screening on Sunday night."

There was a pause and the voice said, "Alex gave you my name?"

"That's right. Feel free to call him."

"I will. Hang on a minute."

I pushed my hat back on my head and kept looking into the camera so he could relay a good description of me. A gust of wind knocked some leaves of ivy off the vines and they swirled around my feet. I held onto my hat and after a few minutes Tyson's voice came out of the speaker.

"Okay. I'll come down and meet you in the lobby."

A buzzer sounded, followed by a click and the door opened when I pulled on it. Cool air washed over me. I took my hat off and sank into a beige easy chair with soft cushions and a footstool in front of it. A puffy tan sofa sat on the other side of a glass-topped coffee table. The walls of the lobby were painted a soft yellow and several generic landscape and still-life paintings hung on display. Two arrangements of fresh flowers occupied small tables on either side of a gas fireplace. The faint trace of air freshener tickled my nostrils and I shuddered to think what the rents were in this place. Most likely not in my price range.

I heard footsteps behind and turned to see a young man coming down the stairs. I recognized him as being one of the mourners at Callahan's service. He wore dark brown slacks and a light blue shirt. His hair was jet-black and a thin beard followed the contours of his jawline. Jeweled studs pierced both his ear lobes.

I stood and extended my hand as he stepped off the bottom step. "Eddie Collins. Thanks for agreeing to talk to me."

"I'm Randy," he said, and gave me a firm handshake. "I saw you at the funeral home, right?"

"That's correct."

"I apologize for sounding paranoid on the intercom. Just being careful."

"No worries," I said.

"I never knew Jack all that well, so I didn't think it appropriate to be at the reception." He gestured for me to sit and sank down onto the sofa. "Sorry I didn't invite you up. I've got a schnauzer who's behaving very badly today. He wants to hump anything that moves."

"Might be the Santa Anas," I said. "They tend to drive anybody crazy."

"Hadn't thought of that." He chuckled, leaned back and crossed one leg over the other. "What can I do for you, Mr. Collins?"

"I wonder if you can tell me about the party that night. Who Jack talked to. Did you notice anything that might have been bothering him?"

Randy thought for a moment and then replied. "Well, the only thing that comes to mind is that several people who'd been at the movie were upset by it."

"How so?"

"It was a pretty strong indictment of the pharmaceutical industry and its attitude toward AIDS/HIV medications. As a matter of fact, a couple of arguments broke out."

"Any of them involve Jack?"

"Yeah, at one point he got into it with Dennis."

"Would that be Dennis Abrams?" I said, as I jotted down a note.

"Yes. I know both of them only slightly, so I didn't pay much attention to what they were arguing about."

"What was the outcome?"

At that moment the front door of the building opened and a young woman wearing red shorts and a white T-shirt entered. She was pawing through a handful of mail.

"Hi Audrey," Randy said.

She looked up and said, "Oh, hi Randy. I swear that wind is driving me nuts."

"I know, honey," he replied.

She nodded to me, said "hello" and made her way up the stairs.

"Where were we?" Randy said.

"The argument and its outcome."

"Right. After five minutes or so another one of Jack's friends stepped in and seemed to cool the rhetoric a little. Things settled down. An hour or so later people started filtering out."

"Including Jack?"

"Yes. As a matter of fact, he and Dennis left together."

"Were they still arguing?"

"I wouldn't call it arguing, but they did seem to be discussing something. Intently, I guess one could say."

Randy's cellphone buzzed and he looked at the screen, then held up one finger and answered a text. As he did so I made a few more notes. When he finished, he laid the phone next to him.

"You mentioned that you didn't know Jack and Dennis very well. But did you ever see them together before? At a club, say?"

He gazed to his right for a moment. "I think I might have seen them at one of the clubs on Santa Monica. But with a bunch of people. Jack and Alex were always together."

"So you don't remember ever seeing Dennis with Jack?"

"No."

"How about Dennis with Alex?"

The question seemed to catch him a bit off guard. He uncrossed his legs and leaned forward on the sofa. "I don't know where you're going with this, Mr. Collins, but I sense some sort of implication in your question."

I had to admire Randy's intuition. With the image of the photo I'd taken at Universal in the back of my mind, I was indeed trying to feel him out about whether or not there was anything going on between Alex and Dennis. Now that he'd sensed it, I figured I'd better follow through.

"The only implication is one that leads me to a motive for Jack's murder," I said. "From what I gather, his relationship with Alex was solid, but sometimes what lurks behind the curtain belies the facts."

"As in, Dennis being behind the curtain?"

"Something like that."

"I don't know how familiar you are with the gay community, but—"

"I'm also an actor, Randy," I interrupted, "and I have a lot of gay friends, so I don't need a lecture."

"Maybe not, but you're going to get one anyway. This is a ten-minute town, Mr. Collins. If two men are married, the word gets around damn quick. So if anyone wants to 'lurk' behind a curtain and wait in the wings for someone to go astray, they can forget about it. Promiscuity in the gay community is good fodder for the tabloids, but it's far less common than you may think. From what I've heard, Alex Foster and Jack Callahan were in a marriage that didn't have room for anyone lurking behind a curtain, as you put it."

He finished with a look of defiance on his face, one that he'd previously honed to a fine edge. Randy hadn't told me anything I wasn't aware of, so I didn't feel like I'd been lectured. But it was time to play a hole card, if that's what I had. I took out my cellphone and pulled up the picture from the Universal City Walk.

"Okay," I said. "I get your point. So tell me what you think of this picture." I handed the phone to him and watched his face. His eyes lit up and he pulled the photo closer.

"So who's doing the lurking now, Mr. Collins?"

"I wasn't lurking. I was there with friends."

"And you felt the need to spy on them by taking this picture?"

"Look, Randy, when I took that photo I'd just been instrumental in reuniting Jack with his father. I was pleased to see the guy in a committed relationship with someone, and seeing this display of affection for another man raised my curiosity. That's all. If you want to give it some other definition, it's your problem, not mine."

He looked at me for a long moment before saying, "If it was him with a woman, would you still have been curious?"

"Yes. I'm not here digging up dirt, Randy. I'm trying to find Callahan's killer."

"So you've said," he replied, as handed the phone back to me.

"Does that picture change your opinion of their relationship?"

"Not in the least. As I've told you, I know these guys only slightly. How long they've known each other is something I'm not privy to. Male friends express themselves in ways that may not be to your liking, Mr. Collins, but catching two people displaying affection does not constitute a crime."

I closed the photo app and put the phone back in my pocket. "Fair enough." I stood and reached into my pocket for one of my business cards and handed it to him. "Give me a call if you think of anything else, okay?" He nodded and stuck the card in his shirt pocket, where it would probably remain until he got back upstairs and threw it away. "Not to pry, but what do these apartments rent for?" The amount he relayed to me was more than I had expected. I gestured to the fresh flowers and said, "I suppose that includes those."

"They're changed every week. A nice little lady by the name of Estelle."

I nodded and headed for the front door. "I'll let you get back to your schnauzer before he destroys the place. Maybe those winds will die soon." I left the building and quickly had to grab my hat before a gust sent it flying. So much for my prediction.

CHAPTER TWENTY-THREE

———◆———

As I walked back to my car, the winds that were blowing would by now have made Chandler's meek little housewives do more than just feel the edge of their knives and study their husbands' necks. Danger was in the air.

I crawled into the front seat, waited for the air conditioning to kick in and thought about the interview with Tyson. I hadn't expected to be in the witness box with him as inquisitor, but he had made a point. Two male friends expressing affection for one another wasn't a crime. I was okay with that. However, I still couldn't ignore the fact that Dennis Abrams may have been the last person to see Jack Callahan alive. Not only that, but he was seen arguing with the victim. Carla probably wouldn't agree with me, but Abrams had to be confronted with the picture of him and Alex Foster falling all over each other at Universal City Walk.

Besides Abrams' address, Alex had also given me his cellphone number. I tapped in the digits and after three rings he answered. "This is Dennis."

"Hi, Dennis, it's Eddie Collins calling. We met at the reception earlier?"

"Yeah, right. How did you get this number?"

"Alex Foster."

A slight pause and he said, "I see. What can I do for you?"

"He told me you were at a movie screening the evening of Jack Callahan's murder. I also understand both of you were at a party at Randy Tyson's afterwards. I was wondering if I might follow up with you about the party. Who Jack talked to, anything along those lines?" There was another pause and I could hear people in the background. "I'd be glad to, but I'm at work right now."

"Where would that be?"

"I tend bar at the Sofitel."

The location he mentioned was a luxury hotel at the intersection of La Cienega and Beverly, across from the Beverly Center. I looked at my watch. Early afternoon. "Should be kind of slow there about now, right?"

Yet another slight pause. "Actually, it is," he said. "If you want to swing by, we can probably squeeze in a few minutes, if you don't mind being interrupted."

"No problem. I'll see you in a few."

I broke the connection and pulled away from the curb. I knew I was risking putting him in a sort of "gotcha" moment, but if he was the last person to see Callahan alive, shortly after arguing with him, the risk would be worth it.

MY ONLY ENCOUNTER WITH THE SOFITEL has been of the drive-by variety. A Motel 6 it is not. The parking structure's fees alone would constitute a month's worth of leaving the light on for you, as the pitchman says. The machine burped out the ticket and I squeezed my humble car between a Rolls Royce and a Jaguar. I had the feeling I was wearing tennis shoes to a black tie dinner.

A very chic young lady behind the registration desk pointed me in the right direction. The bar was horseshoe-shaped with cylindrical black light fixtures that threw spotlights along the highly polished hardwood surface. A six-foot rectangular glass enclosure with rococo flourishes on its surface hung over the bar. Lights from within caused it to glow and make the shelves of liquor bottles underneath it look like a miniature glass skyline.

Soft instrumental elevator music filled a room with mostly empty booths and tables. A businessman with papers spread out in front of him sat on one side of the bar. A waitress wearing black slacks and a red vest over a white shirt carried a tray of drinks to a pair of couples at a booth in one corner.

Dennis Abrams also wore black slacks and a red vest over an off-white shirt. He spotted me when I entered and placed a cardboard coaster with a large "S" on it in front of me as I settled onto one of the black leather stools. He extended his hand and we shook.

"Can I get you something?"

"Bourbon on the rocks. A glass of beer to chase it."

"You got it," he replied, then moved off and began filling the order. I laid a twenty on the bar and returned the waitress' smile as she walked by me.

Abrams came back with the drinks, picked up the double sawbuck and replaced it with two singles and some change. At this rate, a person could go broke before even checking in. As I took a sip of the bourbon he filled an order from the waitress and then walked back to me and leaned on the bar.

"What can I do for you, Mr. Collins?"

"Randy Tyson told me you and Jack Callahan had a bit of an argument at the party. That true?"

He made a slight adjustment to a pile of coasters in front of him before answering me. "Yes, we did, but it was nothing serious."

"Randy said someone had to step in."

"Yeah, well, at one point he got a little too close to me. I guess we might have gotten somewhat loud."

"What was the argument about?"

"Jack felt the film was skirting the truth about Big Pharma's commitment to AIDS medications. I disagreed, that's all."

"I understand the two of you left together."

"Yeah, around the same time."

"And you were still arguing?"

He paused for a long moment and stared at me. Then the phone rang and he moved off to answer it. I sipped from my beer glass and watched him. As he talked, he glanced back at me, but quickly turned away when he saw me looking at him.

He hung up the phone and walked back to where I was sitting. "Jack and I had resumed our conversation, but I wouldn't characterize it as arguing. And just where are you going with this, Collins? I mean, you're not the police. I don't even have to talk to you."

"No, you don't," I said, "but Callahan was killed early the next morning. You may have been the last person to see him alive."

"And I may not have been."

"True. So tell me what happened when you left Tyson's apartment."

"We finished what we were talking about, shook hands and I asked him if he needed a lift. He said he and Alex didn't live that far and that he could hoof it. So I headed to my car and he walked off in the other direction."

"How long had you known Jack?"

"Oh. . . five years maybe."

"So he and Alex were already married when you met him?"

"That's right."

"How long have you known Alex?"

He thought for a moment and said, "He and I go back quite a ways."

"Did the two of you ever date?"

He leaned back from the bar and again stared at me for a moment. "I don't know that that's any of your goddamn business, but yes, we did see each other for a time. Why?"

Before I could answer him the waitress called out that she had an order and he moved off to fill it. I sipped from my drink and looked around the room. A part of me didn't want to go down this road I was heading, but Abrams had had an argument with Callahan hours before his murder. Now he told me he'd had a relationship with the victim's husband. A photo in my cellphone seemed to reinforce the fact. I had a feeling that somehow, lurking amidst all these coincidences, lay the tendrils of motive.

Abrams came back to where I was sitting. He had a look on his face that told me I'd put a burr under his saddle.

"No offense, Collins, but your questions are starting to sound like you're implying I had something to do with Jack's death. If that's the case, let me tell you you're sadly mistaken."

"I'm not implying anything," I said, as I pulled my cell out of my pocket and opened the photos app. "I'm just trying to find a killer. And that means establishing a motive. Most of the time it involves sex or money. You and Callahan had an argument before he was killed, and now you tell me you had an affair with his husband."

"That was a long time ago," he said.

I pulled up the picture of him and Alex. "Then tell me how I'm supposed to interpret this," I said, as I handed him the phone.

His face froze when he saw the picture. His look almost made me think he was going to throw the phone back at me. Instead, he tossed it on the bar and got right into my face.

"A few minutes ago I was ready to give you the benefit of the doubt, Collins, that you were on the level. But I was wrong. You're just some seedy dime a dozen private dick snooping on people. Why don't you just get the fuck out of here?"

I picked up the phone and closed down the picture. "Where were you early Sunday? Say from three to five AM?"

"Home."

"Can anyone verify that?"

"I'm done talking to you, Collins."

"LAPD might want to know the answer to that question."

"Then I'll talk to them, but you and I are through." He picked up what remained of my drinks and stalked off. He threw what was left of them into a sink and walked around to the other side of the bar. Somehow I had a feeling he wouldn't want anything to do with a tip, so I picked up my change and the singles and walked out of the bar.

A CREDIT CARD GOT ME OUT of the parking structure, but not before reflecting on the fact that my ego got a kick in the ass from Abrams' kiss off. I found a meter and pulled over to the curb to digest what I'd just learned. I've been called many things in conjunction with my license, but a seedy, dime a dozen private dick wasn't one of them. Maybe I had it coming by showing Abrams that photo, but dammit, I still thought it had a bearing on the case. I entered some notes in my book and watched an elderly gent trying to capture a straw hat that had blown off his head and was leap-frogging down the sidewalk. A kid on a skateboard came to the rescue, got the man's thanks and then pushed off.

Common sense told me I had to share some of these discoveries with Charlie Rivers. He'd been generous with crime scene photos and no doubt would want to try and pry more information out of Dennis Abrams. He had the badge; I didn't. But before doing that, I wanted to check out one more thing. I pulled out my notebook, flipped through the pages until I found the address and drove off.

IMMACULATE STREETS IN THE TONIER NEIGHBORHOODS of Beverly Hills and West Hollywood like the one I'd encountered on Norwich where Randy Tyson lived don't always paint an accurate picture. Alleys, however, provide a different image. The one where Jack Callahan's body had been found was a case in point. I'd parked on a pristine street and walked around a corner to where the alley cut the block in half. About thirty feet in, two yellow strands of police tape were still present, but the winds had torn them loose and what remained were whipping around like two of those inflatable tubes one often sees in front of car dealerships and mattress stores.

One side of the alley had Dumpsters and trashcans pushed up against the backsides of buildings. Remnants of garbage protruded from several of them. Right next to the crime scene a six foot cyclone fence ran along a low hedge that needed to be trimmed. Scraps of plastic bags were impaled upon jagged metal edges. The fence was beat up and pieces of it along the bottom were missing, leaving gaps that led to holes in the hedge.

I walked up to the flapping yellow plastic and could still see stains on the pavement where Callahan's body had been found. The strands of tape were tied into links of the fence and the ends that flapped in the breeze had been anchored by a white plastic police barrier that was now lying useless up against a garage door.

It was evident these infernal winds had made a mess of LAPD's crime scene. Bits of paper and plastic littered both sides of the alley. Farther down a black SUV and a pickup were parked next to garages. As I stood there, a door opened and a blue Prius backed out. The door closed and the car drove to the other end of the alley and turned right.

I gazed at the structures on either side of the alley. Except for the backyard beyond the hedge in front of me, both sides were lined with garage doors. The yard was easily fifty feet deep before it reached a porch on the rear of a house. The murder had occurred very early in the morning, and given the damage done by whatever had caved in Callahan's head, there couldn't have been many sounds of a struggle. What in the hell had ever possessed him to be walking down this alley? Was he meeting someone? Was he with someone?

My reverie was interrupted by a flash of orange to my right. A large cat without a collar had caught sight of one of the flapping strands of police tape and was now in stalking mode. The animal crouched down, watched, head swiveling as it followed its prey. Then it pounced, grabbed the tape and batted it between its paws. The wind blew the tape up and the cat reared on its hind legs and chased it.

At the mouth of the alley a dog appeared, saw the cat and bounded in its direction, growling. When the cat heard the noise it yowled, jumped up and scurried into one of the gaps in the cyclone fence. A clump of orange fur came loose as it crawled under the fence, then the hedge and bounded across the yard.

The dog gave chase, but it was too big to make it through the gap in the fence. It lay on its belly, barking and digging with its front paws and throwing debris into the alley. Thwarted, it tried another gap but had the same result. More debris flew behind him and he finally gave up when I walked over and shooed him away.

As I turned around and started back toward the mouth of the alley, something caught my eye amidst the debris the dog had unearthed. I squatted on my haunches and saw that it was a cigarette butt.

But not just any ordinary cigarette butt.

A gold filter and about two inches of black wrapping. Sobranie Black Russian.

The brand Roy Dickerson smoked.

I reached for my cellphone, opened the camera and took a couple of close-up shots of the cigarette butt, then emailed them to Charlie Rivers. For once, I thought he might be glad to hear from me…well, not exactly.

"Collins, don't you have anything else to do but pester an officer of the law?"

"Did you get the pictures?"

"A cigarette butt? What the hell is going on?"

"Jack Callahan had a cousin by the name of Roy Dickerson. He's an actor, and he smokes Sobranie Black Russian cigarettes. He's disappeared and isn't answering his phone. I've got a gut feeling he may be person of interest in the murder."

"A gut feeling? What the hell does that mean?"

I filled him in on the fact that I'd spotted Dickerson on Santa Monica Boulevard near the gay nightclubs. That I'd seen both Alex Foster and Roy at City Walk. That he knew Alex and that he also knew that Ben Roth had given Jack the five hundred grand. I told him Dickerson's wife said he was up at Lake Arrowhead, but hadn't been seen by the people with whom he shared a cabin.

"So he hasn't answered his phone. Nothing unusual in that," Charlie said.

"He's an actor. We're tethered to our cellphones. His cousin is murdered and he doesn't show up at the guy's memorial service? Money, Charlie. Five hundred grand." There was silence on the other end of the line. "You know many people that smoke that brand of cigarettes?"

He finally said, "Nope."

"I'm at the crime scene. That's where I found the butt."

After a long silence, he said, "All right. Don't touch the damn thing. I'll be there in fifteen."

It was closer to twenty by the time Charlie's car pulled into the alley. He pried himself out of the front seat and walked toward me.

"What the hell are you doing at the crime scene, Collins?"

"Doesn't look like one to me," I said, gesturing to the police tape floating in the breeze and the plastic police barrier lying next to a garage door. He registered a look of disgust and I pointed to the cigarette butt. He pulled a plastic bag and a pair of tweezers from his pocket, squatted down and put the butt in the bag.

"God knows how long this thing could have been here," he said.

"That's true, but if Dickerson's DNA is on it, it puts him at the scene."

"I'll give you that, Eddie, but I think you're reaching." He stood up and put the sealed plastic bag back in his pocket. "I'll run this out to West Bureau. It's their case. Follow me out there. You're going to have to do your damnedest to explain why the hell you were nosing around the scene of murder. You need someone to run interference. I'll meet you there."

CHAPTER TWENTY-FOUR

———— ◆ ————

LAPD's West Bureau headquarters was on Venice Boulevard, a couple of blocks east of La Brea. I found a parking space and walked up to the front of the building where Charlie was waiting. He told me to let him do the talking; he didn't want any raised eyebrows about how I knew where Jack Callahan was murdered.

He held up the plastic evidence bag. "You sure you didn't touch this, Eddie?"

"Absolutely, but I can't speak for the dog."

He looked at me with a smirk on his face. "No, I don't suppose so, but it looks like he might have mauled it." Looking closely at the cigarette butt, I could see that it did show some signs of teeth marks.

Lieutenant Rudy Hawkins was a sturdy black man that reminded me of the wonderful character actor Ossie Davis. As he eyed the bag containing the Sobranie Black Russian cigarette butt, he looked like he was inspecting a precious jewel found in his backyard. Charlie and I sat across from him at a gun-metal table in an interrogation room. The obligatory two-way mirror was behind Hawkins. I doubted anyone was on the other side, but it was still unnerving. He gently laid the bag on his desk and glanced up at us.

"So, Charlie, you think this…" He consulted a yellow pad next to him. "… Roy Dickerson may be a person of interest."

"He seems to have disappeared. Not answering his cell," Charlie said.

"No law against not picking up a phone."

"No, sir," I said. "But his cousin was murdered. He's been left messages telling him that, but hasn't responded. I just thought it seemed kind of odd."

I'd repeated to Hawkins what I'd told Charlie when we first sat down: Roy working on a gay porno film with Callahan, and then denying that he knew his cousin was homosexual; his appearance outside the gay nightclubs on Santa Monica, and also at Universal City Walk the day I'd seen Alex Foster and Dennis Abrams together.

Hawkins listened intently before saying, "Lots of coincidences, Mr. Collins."

"Could be," I said, "but there's money involved. Five hundred grand that Ben Roth gave to his son. Unless Callahan and Foster have some sort of pre-nup, Foster stands to inherit the money."

"So you figure him for the murder?" Hawkins said.

"I don't know. He says he was home when it happened. Nobody can corroborate that. Dickerson knew about the money, and now he's taken a powder." I shrugged. "Coincidence? Maybe, maybe not."

Hawkins thought for a long moment, nodded and picked up the bag with the cigarette butt again and gave it another once-over. "I'll give you the fact that these smokes aren't that common. If there's a tie-in with Callahan, you might be right." He stood up, walked over to the door and opened it. "Hey, Faraday," he called out.

A young uniform with a blond buzz-cut walked up. "Whatcha need, el-tee?"

"Is Tollefson here?"

"He's in the head."

"Tell him to get his ass in here when he's done."

"Roger," Faraday replied, and walked off.

"Gene Tollefson's the lead on this," Hawkins said. He picked up a cardboard coffee cup from the table, finished the contents and tossed it at a trashcan in the corner. His shot missed and he cursed under his breath, then grabbed it off the floor and spiked it. The lieutenant was not happy. He sat down, leaned back in his chair, and tapped his pencil on the pad of paper, then pointed it at the evidence bag. "Mr. Collins, while I appreciate your bringing this to the attention of Lieutenant Rivers here, I'm curious as to why the hell you were at the crime scene."

"The victim's father recently disowned Callahan and hired me to find him. I did so, and he then asked me to poke around to see if I could find some answers. I told him I would, and that I'd share anything I found with LAPD. Alex Foster, Randy Tyson, and Dennis Abrams entered the picture. So here I am."

"Okay, so you 'poked' around, but that still doesn't explain how you found the crime scene," Hawkins said.

I shrugged and looked at Charlie. "Saw it on the news, Lieutenant."

There was a pause as Hawkins looked at me, then Charlie. I figured if television news had identified the scene, it would eliminate any suggestion that Rivers had been complicit in helping me.

Hawkins turned to Rivers. "That how you see it, Charlie?"

"Pretty much, Rudy." Hawkins seemed satisfied.

The door opened and a short, burly cop with a salt and pepper flat top haircut came in. He wore a rumpled blue suit that didn't quite hide a slight paunch. "What's up, Lieutenant?" he said.

"Gene, you know Charlie Rivers?" Hawkins said.

Tollefson stuck out his hand and Charlie grabbed it. "Sure do. We logged a couple years together at Rampart. How you doin', Charlie?"

"Good, Gene." He pointed to the area above Tollefson's belt. "Looks like life's treating you okay."

"Ah, what can I say?" Tollefson said, as he pulled up another chair and sat down.

Hawkins gestured to me and said, "This is Eddie Collins. He's got a private ticket."

Tollefson and I shook hands, and I immediately sensed a cop's all-too-common display of wariness with respect to private investigators, this one nurtured by the fact that one of them was on their own turf.

"Mr. Collins was hired to find our victim, Jack Callahan, which he did," Hawkins said. "And now he seems to think he has to solve his murder."

"Due respect, Rudy," Charlie said, "I wouldn't—"

Hawkins cut him off. "But maybe that's a good thing." He picked up the evidence bag containing the cigarette butt. "Because he found this at the crime scene. Don't we normally use a fine-toothed comb at the scene of a crime, Gene?"

"We did, Rudy," Tollefson said. "I don't know what else to tell you."

"For starters you can tell me you're going to put a couple of men on it and go over the damn thing again."

"Roger," Tollefson said, a sheepish look on his face, obviously not pleased with being shown up in front of another lieutenant and a civilian to boot. He took the bag and peered at its contents. "What's so significant about this?"

"Come on, Gene. A cigarette butt wouldn't have just dropped out of the sky, for crissakes. It's been smoked. It came out of somebody's mouth. Collins says it's the same brand Roy Dickerson, Callahan's cousin, smokes. Dickerson now seems to have disappeared. He might have been at your crime scene, so he might be a person of interest. You catch my drift?"

Tollefson's face flushed as he looked from one lieutenant to the other. He was a veteran cop and didn't appreciate being called on the carpet. He glared at me and opened his notebook and clicked his ballpoint.

"Gotcha. Dickerson spelled like it sounds?"

"Right," I said.

"Got a phone number, Collins? Address?"

I rattled off the numbers as Hawkins opened the door and handed the evidence bag to an officer and told him to get it over to the lab. He then reseated himself and regarded Tollefson for a moment. "So, where we at, Gene?"

Tollefson consulted his notes. "We talked to Callahan's boyfriend, Alex Foster."

"Husband," I said. "He and the victim were married."

"Yeah, right, husband," Tollefson said, the look on his face and the tone of his voice distinctly telling me the nature of the relationship was something he wasn't all that comfortable with.

Hawkins consulted notes he'd made from the information I'd given him about my interviews. "What about the movie screening and that party Callahan was at?"

"Yeah, we talked to this Randy Tyson," Tollefson said. "He gave us a list of people that were there."

"Dennis Abrams one of them?" I said.

Tollefson checked his book and said, "Right. Knocked on his door and nobody answered. No phone listed. We're looking for a cell number."

"Here," I said, and handed him my phone with Abrams' number. "I'll trade you this for his address." Tollefson gave me the address and I put it in my book. "He tends bar at the Sofitel," I continued. "He and Callahan argued at the party, and they left at the same time. Abrams offered him a ride, but Callahan said he'd walk, and they parted. I asked, but he wouldn't provide me with an alibi. I guess I pissed him off when I showed him this." I pulled up the photo in my cell and showed it to Tollefson.

"That's Foster. Who's he with?"

"Abrams," I said.

"Damn. Pretty friendly. In public, too."

I handed the phone to Hawkins. "This may indicate absolutely nothing, but it's been bugging me."

Hawkins handed the phone back to me. "Email that to me, will you? And copy it to Gene and Rivers." Tollefson handed his business card to me and I stuck it in my shirt pocket.

"So, Collins," Tollefson said, "you suggesting that Foster may have been fuckin' around on Callahan?"

"I don't know. Abrams told me the two of them had dated a while back, but when I first met Foster and Callahan, they gave me the impression their marriage was pretty solid. And Abrams got real defensive when I showed him this picture. Maybe there's something there. You've got the badge. You can sweat him more than me."

"We'll do that," Tollefson said, and looked at me as if I'd just spit in his Post Toasties. "That's as far as I've gotten," I said.

"Gene, have you canvassed the neighborhood around that alley?" Hawkins said.

"Except for the house on the corner with the backyard, the rest of the street is apartment houses with garages facing the alley," Tollefson replied. "We woke up a hell of a lot of people Monday morning, but nobody said they heard anything."

"Okay," Hawkins said. "Keep at it."

"Right. Anything else?"

"Nope."

Tollefson put his notebook and pen back in his pocket and stood up. "Nice seein' you again, Charlie," he said. "Let's get a beer sometime and catch up."

"You got it," Charlie replied.

He stuck out his hand to me and I took it. "Good to meet you, Collins," he said, his grip telling me he didn't mean a damn word of it. "I've had a run-in or two with you private guys in the past. You didn't disappoint."

"Lieutenant Rivers here keeps me on a tight leash," I said.

"Looks like you need it," he said, and left the room. Lieutenant Hawkins made a couple of notes on his yellow pad, and asked me if I could think of anything else. I said I couldn't at the moment, and we exchanged cards with the promise that I'd be in touch with Charlie if I remembered anything else. The three of us shook hands and Charlie and I walked out of the building.

"What's Tollefson's story?" I asked.

"How do you mean?"

"Not exactly Mr. Warmth there."

"You stepped all over his crime scene, Eddie. Plus the fact that Hawkins pretty much called him on the carpet in front of a civilian. I'd be pissed too."

"Point taken, but it's not like I hid anything from him. Or you, for that matter."

"Yeah, whatever," he said. We both donned our sunglasses and started for our cars.

"He also seemed to be a little uncomfortable knowing that Foster and Callahan were married."

"So?"

"How well do you know him?"

"Pretty well. Why?"

"I'm not saying this is happening, but would a prejudice like that influence his police work?"

"Ah shit, I don't know, Eddie. He's been in the department a long time. He was a year ahead of me at the Academy. Far as I know, his jacket is clean, but I can't tell you what's in the guy's head." Charlie gave me one of those glares that made it clear he didn't appreciate the comment. "Look, I'm not happy his crew missed a piece of possibly relevant evidence, but I'm not going to stand here and let you imply the department's investigation is compromised by a particular detective's personal slant on things. Those were the old days. Now the job is the job. Got it?"

"Got it," I said.

"If we find out different, we'll deal with it."

I put up my hands, palms facing him in surrender. "No problem, Charlie. My girlfriend has also been lecturing me about my attitude toward that photo, so I hear you loud and clear."

He nodded and slipped on a pair of sunglasses. "Are you done with this case now?"

"I'd still like to find Roy Dickerson. Him disappearing and not answering his phone isn't like him."

"Well, keep me in the loop, you hear?"

"Will do," I said, and we shook hands and moved off to our separate cars.

OUTSIDE ON VENICE THE WIND WAS still blowing and the heat hadn't ebbed. I let the car's air conditioning run while I emailed the photo of Foster and Abrams to Charlie, Hawkins, and Tollefson. I put his name and Abrams' address in my phone and sent Carla a text. No immediate answer, so I sat and thought about Gene Tollefson, his reaction to the photo and his apparent attitude about Foster and Callahan being married. Gay rights and marriage equality have made gigantic leaps of acceptance in this country and also in Los Angeles. But there were always going to be those who personally hadn't made those leaps. Old habits die hard, in all of us, including seasoned cops.

Then my thoughts swung around to myself, and I wondered if any of those old, submerged attitudes existed within me. As I'd told Randy Tyson, I have a lot of gay friends, Lenny Daye being chief among them. And countless actors. Why then, did I have a negative reaction to the two men in that photo I took at Universal City Walk?

A pair of young women, one of them pushing a baby carriage and the other holding a little girl's hand came walking up Venice on their way to La Brea. The little girl skipped, and tried to keep from stepping on cracks in the sidewalk. She conjured up images of a girl I'd just been introduced to, Kelly Robinson from Cincinnati. Kelly Robinson, who had a black mother and father and a black brother, and yet showed not the slightest hint of prejudice. Surely I, her birth father, shared those values, right?

As the women walked by my car I told myself to quit dwelling on it, to move on, to accept the fact that I was dead wrong about the image in that photo and that I was being politically incorrect. I could do that, but I could also not forget that a murder and five hundred thousand dollars were in the mix. My internal debate ended when my cell went off. It was Carla.

"Velvet La Rose herself," I said.

"Careful, Shamus, that's my former life."

"Damn, you're right."

She giggled and said, "Where are you?"

"Sitting outside the West Bureau Police Station."

"Have you been arrested?"

"They tried, but I pled the fifth, and they gave up." I heard another chuckle. "Actually, I'm sharing my astute investigation with the cops. What's happening with you?"

"I'm sitting in my trailer in Santa Monica missing you."

"Aww, that's nice to hear."

"I'm on standby for a couple of hours. Why don't you come out here and keep me company?"

"Will they let me on the location?"

"Piece of cake. You're my consultant."

"Sounds good," I said. "Tell me where you're at." She did, and I pulled away from the curb and started driving. Spending a little time with her was the perfect antidote to concerns about prejudice and political correctness, or lack thereof.

THE ADDRESS CARLA GAVE ME WAS a residential area north of Santa Monica Boulevard. The *Three on a Beat* production's base camp had been set up in the parking lot of a church. After finding room under a tree around the corner, I walked up to a security guard stationed at the entrance to the lot. He was big and broad and wasn't armed, but his presence indicated he probably didn't need to be.

"Can I help you, sir?"

"I'm here to see Carla Rizzoli."

"And you are?"

"A friend," I replied. My answer made no impression on him.

"This area is restricted," he said. "You might want to give her a call."

I pulled out my cell and tapped the numbers. "Hey, security's nixing my entry."

"Hang on," she said. Up ahead on the right a door to a trailer opened and Carla stepped out. She came up to the guard, a huge smile on her face. She was wearing denim shorts, a blue T-shirt and had sandals on her feet. "Hi, Bert. This is a friend of mine, Eddie Collins. He's an actor too. He's just gonna hang out with me for an hour or so. Okay?"

"If you say so," Bert said. As I walked by him, the attempt at a smile on his face seemed to be accomplished with great effort.

Carla stuck her arm through mine and led me to her trailer. Welcome cool air filled the small enclosure that, despite its size, was very comfortable. She wrapped her arms around me and gave me a deep kiss.

"There's no beer. Water?"

"Fine." I took off my hat and sank onto the small sofa. She handed me a plastic bottle and shut off the television that had been airing news footage. "How's your shoot going?"

"Good. They're doing a couple of scenes with the bad guys right now. And how has your day been? You went to the service for Callahan, right?"

"I did, and it was nice. Very simple. Got myself into a couple of donnybrooks later on, though."

"What happened?" She sat on the sofa, scooted up next to me and threw one leg over my lap.

I gave her the recap on my conversations with Alex Foster, Randy Tyson and Dennis Abrams. As I recounted the details, I couldn't help displaying the conflicting emotions that had been swirling around in my head. "I guess I didn't exactly make any friends in the gay community," I said.

"I think you're probably over-reacting."

"Really? Then why have you been giving me guff about my reaction to that picture I took at City Walk?"

"The only 'guff' I gave you is that sometimes I think you tend to jump to conclusions, that's all."

"Conclusions lead to solutions," I said. "And right now I don't seem to be able to find any of those."

"Sounds to me like the stuff you gave Rivers could lead somewhere. Don't forget, Eddie, the cops have got more leverage with both Foster and Abrams than you do."

"But in the meantime, what do I tell Ben Roth?"

She draped one arm around my neck and gave me a hug. "Hey, just remember. You told him you couldn't make any promises when you agreed to start looking, right? Whoever did this will be caught. And you will have made it possible, Shamus. *Capiche*?"

"I guess."

I ran one hand up and down the leg that was in my lap. I was reminded of the first time I'd seen her dance and had asked her how she chose the name Velvet La Rose. She'd told me to put my hand on her thigh. That had answered my question. I started to run my hand further up her leg and she playfully slapped it.

"Hey, I'm working, buster."

"You could lock the door."

"Tempting, I must admit. But I don't know how long I'm on standby."

As if on cue, someone knocked on the door. Carla got up and swung it open. A young man with a clipboard in one hand and a radio mic spanning his head stood at the bottom of the stairs.

"Oh, sorry, Carla," he said. "Didn't know you had company."

"No problem. Alan, this is my friend Eddie. He's an actor."

"Hi," Alan said, and looked up at Carla. "They said to tell you they'll probably be ready for you in a half hour or so."

"I'll be here."

"Nice to meet you," he said, and walked off.

I put my hat on, finished the bottle of water and stood. "Okay, I'm going to shove off and let you do your stuff. What time you figure you'll be done?"

"Probably late. You could hang out at my place if you want."

"Gimme a rain check. I'm beat. Think I'll catch some dinner and call it a night."

"Okay," she said, and wrapped her arms around me. "I'll touch base with you tomorrow." I kissed her and she held my face in her hands. "Don't let yourself get down, Eddie. You've done your job."

"Flattery will get you everywhere."

"I sure as heck hope so."

I patted her on the rump and stepped down out of the trailer. Bert, the guard, nodded as I walked past him. He didn't try a smile this time.

BY THE TIME I'D THREADED MY way through traffic and got back into Hollywood, dusk had started making its presence known. I popped into a favorite bar and grill and had a first-class rib eye. Cool air and dim lights led to reflection about the day's events. Despite Carla's pep talk, I found myself feeling frustrated that I hadn't made more progress for Ben Roth. I also still harbored what I guess could be called twinges of guilt over my insistence on making an issue of the photo of Foster and Abrams together at City Walk. After sitting at the bar with a glass of smooth bourbon and watching the Dodgers pummel the Mets, I finally said to hell with it; the ball was now in Rivers' and the LAPD's court. I'd call Ben tomorrow and tell him what I knew and didn't know.

The alley behind my building rivaled the one where Callahan's body had been found. I had to sidle around Dumpsters and vehicles that should have been parked elsewhere. The lack of streetlights made it a task not for the faint of heart.

When I started to turn into the spaces designated for me and my neighbors I was stopped short. Lenny Daye's car was there, next to my space, in the middle of which was a stepladder, fully extended. It stood underneath a light bulb that in the past has been dark more often than not. Tonight was no exception. It was out. Either the maintenance man had gone to get another bulb, or he'd forgotten to take his ladder with him.

I crawled out of the car, and as I moved to fold up the ladder I sensed someone behind me. Before I could turn, something heavy collided with my left shoulder. I stumbled into the ladder. It collapsed and so did I. Another blow caught me on the left side of my head. A jagged edge of the ladder scraped my right cheek and I could feel blood dripping. That's the last thing I felt before darkness descended.

CHAPTER TWENTY-FIVE

———— ♦ ————

OVER THE YEARS I'VE BEEN KNOWN to suffer from some world-class hangovers, with headaches where the blink of an eye would make a grown man cry out for mercy. Whatever the hell had hit me made those headaches bush-league. As I opened my eyes I realized I was lying on my left shoulder and it ached like hell. My right cheek stung. I couldn't figure out why, and then remembered colliding with a stepladder that stood in the middle of my parking space.

I was moving. Rather, I was *in* something that was moving. I heard a hum, a whine. My wrists were bound behind me with what felt like zip ties. My feet were also bound. I smelled rubber, dust, and a faint trace of oil. The enclosure was almost pitch black, save for pinpricks of light that bled through cracks in whatever this enclosure was.

I lifted my head and saw the glow of a white shape in the corner. Wincing with pain, I scrunched myself around to where I could get close enough to see a logo stamped on it. I focused on the lettering and saw that it was a cardboard Post Office box. Like the ones Mavis receives her collectibles in. Like the one I keep my assortment of hats and costume pieces in. Next to it was another shape. I got up close to it and saw that it was a metal box with a digital lock on the outside. Then realization washed over me. I was in the trunk of my own damn car!

Acute panic set in. Panic like I'd never experienced before. Immediately my thoughts focused on Carla. On Mavis. And on Kelly Robinson. Was I ever going to see them again? *Okay, breathe. Deep breaths.* I closed my eyes and after a moment the feeling subsided. I rolled over on my back and saw the glow of tail lights in each corner of the trunk. Flexing my wrists revealed that the ties were a bit loose, but not enough to where I could get my hands free.

I extended my legs and pushed against the side of the trunk with my feet. Eventually, I was able to partially sit up and lean my head against the other fender. That probably wasn't a good idea, since it throbbed with every slight bump of the car. I tried to think if there was anything sharp back here that I could use to cut the ties on my wrists. The only thing that came to mind was a small tool kit, but it was underneath me, where the spare and a jack lived. Absolutely no help.

After taking some deep breaths and rolling onto my right shoulder, I took stock. Where the hell was I going? More to the point, who the hell was driving? The interviews I'd conducted earlier came creeping into my consciousness. I knew I'd ticked off a couple of guys, but enough for them to want to knock me out and throw me in the trunk of my car like a spare tire? Both Randy Tyson and Dennis Abrams had jumped all over me, and when I'd shown Abrams the picture of him with Alex Foster, he'd come close to throwing me out of the bar. Foster had taken issue with me when I mentioned Callahan's gift of money he'd received from Ben Roth. Both Tyson and Abrams could find cause to retaliate against me. However, neither one of them knew where I lived. Had they followed me? They were in good shape and could deliver a blow strong enough to cause the pain I was experiencing. Then I began to wonder if the cudgel that hit me could be the same one that had done in Jack Callahan.

These thoughts swirled around in my head and only caused it to throb with every blink of an eyelid. I closed my eyes and had almost drifted off when I sensed the car slowing. It turned to the right and immediately hit a huge bump. My head collided with the roof of the trunk and I again sank into darkness.

I CAME TO WHEN THE CAR started to slow again. I squeezed my eyes shut against the discomfort caused by repeated bumps. Obviously, whoever was driving had turned off the pavement onto a gravel road. The car came to a stop. After a moment, the engine shut down and the tail lights went out. I heard a front door slam and the sound of footsteps on gravel moving to the rear. A key was inserted into the lock. It turned and the trunk opened. The beam from a flashlight seared into my eyes, stabbing me with more pain. I closed my eyes and turned my head away from the light.

"Sorry about the bumps, Eddie."

I immediately recognized the voice. It was Roy Dickerson. I could smell the smoke from one of his cigarettes.

"Where the hell am I?" I said.

"On the north side of Lake Arrowhead."

"What the hell did you hit me with?"

"A Louisville Slugger. Got me some good hits with it over the years."

"Like the one on Jack Callahan?"

"Don't know what you're talking about, buddy."

"Your cousin was beat to death."

"Yeah, I heard. The wife called me."

The light moved from my face and hit the rear of the trunk. He puffed on the cigarette, pulled it out of his mouth with his left hand and dropped the butt, then ground it out with his foot. "How'd you like the stepladder?"

"Cute. Got me out of the car."

"Exactly. You need to put some kitty litter or something on that oil spot, though. I slipped. That's why you only got a glancing blow. Threw me off my rhythm. And then some drunk came stumbling up the alley. Hell of a neighborhood you live in, Collins." He took the key out of the lock on the trunk and put the ring in his hip pocket, but kept his hand behind his back. His implication that he was almost spotted subduing me might answer why the zip locks on my wrists were loose. He didn't have time.

"Why, Roy?"

"You been sticking your nose in where it don't belong." He refocused the flashlight on my feet. "Okay, listen up. I'd just as soon drive you right into the drink, but there's no access to the lake. This is the way things are gonna go. I almost busted a gut getting you in there, so I'm going to cut your feet loose. I imagine you've got a pretty damn good headache and don't feel like running, but if you do, I've got this." His left hand came out from behind his back. It was filled with an automatic. "Are we clear?"

"We're clear."

He stuck the gun into the front of his pants, moved the flashlight to his left hand and reached back toward his right hip pocket. When the hand came around it clutched a serious looking jackknife. He juggled it with the flashlight, flipped the blade open and cut the zip ties binding my feet. The knife went back into his pocket and he swung one of my legs over the bottom rim of the trunk. I winced with pain from the movement. He moved the other leg, but neither one of them hit the ground. I sat there with feet dangling over the edge like a kid in a grownup's chair.

"Flex 'em," he said. "Get the circulation back."

I did, and gradually the numbness disappeared. Roy grabbed the front of my shirt and began to pull me out of the trunk.

"Easy, easy, goddamn it!" I muttered.

"Come on, Collins, work with me here. Scoot your ass forward when I pull."

He pulled and I scooted, grunting with the pain and bending my head down to avoid the lid of the trunk. Finally I was out and I stood. My legs quivered and my head and shoulder throbbed. Roy tossed the flashlight into the trunk, moved me away from the car and slammed the lid shut. I looked at my surroundings and saw a small cabin to my left. Beyond it, Lake Arrowhead glistened in the light of a full moon.

"This the place you share with Chuck and June Palmer?" I said.

"Nah, this is my own little man cave. The wife doesn't even know about it."

"So what are you hiding, Roy?"

"Wouldn't you like to know?" He laughed, pulled the gun from his belt, then grabbed my elbow and we started to walk down a path toward the cabin. The only sounds I could hear were night birds and the faraway bark of a dog. I could smell the pine trees and their needles crunched under our feet. The hot winds I'd been fighting all day had disappeared up here in the mountains. Just the trace of a breeze wafted through the branches.

"You told me you didn't know your cousin was gay, Roy, and yet Tabatha Preston says you worked on one of Jack's gay porn films. Apparently he wanted you to get in front of the camera, but you refused. You wouldn't go the distance. So what are you hiding? Are you gay too?"

"Shut the fuck up."

"This some romantic hideaway, Roy? Where Santa brings his little elves?"

He slapped the side of my head. "I told you to shut the fuck up!"

Pain shot through me. He shoved me forward and I almost stumbled over an exposed tree root. We came to a small porch jutting out from the front door of the cabin with the rear side of a stone fireplace to its right. Roy reached up to the lintel, found a key and stuck it in the lock. He shoved the door open, then grabbed my elbow and guided me inside.

He shut the door behind me and flicked on an overhead light. The small room was sparsely furnished. Television set in one corner. A sofa and cigarette-scarred coffee table faced the stone fireplace. A few magazines, the television remote and a plate overflowing with cigarette butts lay on top. A rack of fireplace tools sat to the right of a metal fire screen. Kitchenette straight ahead of me, breakfast booth to its right. A bathroom at ten o'clock, the back door at two. No stuffed fish or animal heads on the walls, just bare plywood. The overpowering odor of Roy's Sobranie Black Russian cigarettes filled the air. He pushed me into a folding metal chair that sat at the far end of the coffee table and adjusted my arms so that they were wrapped around the back. The movement made me gasp.

"Take it easy, Roy, for crissakes! You messed up my shoulder something fierce."

"Yeah, well, look at it this way. If I hadn't slipped it'd be worse. So deal with it." He walked over to another metal chair leaning against the fireplace. "I'm not going to bind your legs. You've still got some walking to do. Down to the water."

"What are you going to do with my car?"

"Find a boat ramp and drive it in the fuckin' lake."

"Then you're stranded. How are you going to get back to LA?"

"Questions, questions, too damn many questions. An Uber, a bus, what the fuck difference does it make?" He unfolded the chair and placed it at the other end of the coffee table, then laid his gun on it. "Don't worry. I'll work it out."

"Does that mean you've got an accomplice?"

"None of your concern, Collins."

"Who is it, Roy?"

"Just shut the fuck up. Okay?"

I started to wonder who the hell would be tied up in Callahan's murder besides Roy. He knew about the money Ben had given to Callahan, so that could lead to motive. But kill your cousin? Brutally beat him to death? There had to be somebody else involved, but who? Alex Foster? He also knew about the money. His sorrow over the loss of his husband had seemed genuine to me. And yet, there was that half a million dollars that couldn't be ignored.

Roy pulled out another Sobranie, then picked up a long wooden match off the mantle, struck it against one of the stones, lit the cigarette and threw the match into the fireplace. He sat down again and glared at me like he'd found a stray cat on his doorstep and didn't know what the hell to do with it.

"You're going to have to be more careful where you smoke those cancer sticks, Roy."

"Oh, yeah, why is that?"

"You left a pack at Jack and Alex's place."

"I know," he said.

"And you left one of the butts at the scene of the crime."

He froze. The cigarette hung from the corner of his mouth. "What the fuck are you talking about?"

"I found it when I was poking around that alley."

His eyes narrowed and he took another puff. "Doesn't prove a damn thing."

"Not unless the cops find your DNA on it."

After a long cold stare at me, he got up from his chair and went to the refrigerator and pulled out a bottle of Pabst Blue Ribbon. When his back was to me I strained against the plastic ties, and felt them give a little bit. As he walked back, he twisted the cap off the bottle and tossed it into the fireplace, then reseated himself.

"So the hot-shot private eye has been busy, huh?"

"What did you have against your cousin, Roy?"

After he sampled his beer he said, "He was a degenerate faggot."

"Is that the pot calling the kettle black?"

He shook his head and took a drag off the cigarette and flicked the ashes on the floor. After he took a healthy swallow of his beer he replied, "Not me, pal. I was only friendly to Jack because of his old man. I was glad Ben disowned the son-of-a-bitch. And it doesn't bother me one damn bit that he's gone. Those movies he made were disgusting."

"So why did you work for him?"

"I didn't know what the hell he was up to until I got there. I didn't stick around very long."

"What were you doing that night when I saw you outside the gay clubs on Santa Monica?"

"Just what I told you. Eating at Barney's."

"Do you know Dennis Abrams?"

"Never heard of him."

"I snapped a picture of him and Alex together at Universal City Walk. A few minutes later I saw you walking toward the parking structure."

"So?"

"What were you doing there? Meeting the two of them? Planning Jack's murder?"

He laughed and upended the bottle of beer. "Jesus Christ, Collins, you've got some imagination."

"So what if Jack Callahan was gay, Roy? You're an actor like me. We work with gay men. Chrissakes, we work *for* gay men. What the hell's the big deal?"

"C'mon, Eddie, the big deal is that they're all over the goddamn business. I can't tell you how many jobs I've lost because of some faggot who cast one of his butt buddies. Niggers, spics, they've all got to have a place at the table. You know, I booked a job once where I'm supposed to be on the board of directors of some big corporation. I got replaced because I was the wrong color. Some imaginary fuckin' quota. How many corporations do you know that have blacks and Hispanics sitting on the board? Or some snowflake prancing around like he's a sugarplum fairy? I'm sick of the whole goddamn mess. Get me a little money and I'm outta here."

This was a side of Roy Dickerson I'd never seen. His blatant homophobia and bigotry were surprising, and his claim was ultimately untrue. Granted, competition for acting jobs in Hollywood is pretty stiff, but certainly not made more so by people of color or gay men taking all the roles.

"So, what, Roy? You hit the lottery?"

"Something like that." He stood up, finished off the bottle of beer with one gigantic swallow and walked into the kitchenette area of the cabin.

I put more pressure on my wrists, the effort causing both my head and shoulder to throb. But the zip ties loosened a little more. He pulled another PBR from the refrigerator and walked back to the fireplace, again twisting off the cap and flipping it over the metal fireplace guard. His cell went off. He answered and listened for a minute. "Yeah, he's here." Pause. "You're only a couple of minutes away."

I made another effort against the plastic ties, but only succeeded in scraping skin off my wrists.

"All right," Roy said, and broke the phone connection. He put the cell back in his pocket, took a swallow of the beer and set the bottle on the coffee table, then walked over to me.

"Where's your phone?"

"Right hip pocket."

"Stand up."

"The chair's gonna come up with me."

He muttered under his breath, put his foot on the metal bar spanning the distance between the chair's legs, then grabbed my collar and helped me stand up. He found the phone, then repositioned me on the chair and lit up the screen.

"Who's Carla?" he said.

"My girlfriend."

"Some pretty racy texts here, Collins. You must be getting your ashes hauled pretty regular."

I wasn't going to give him the satisfaction of answering that. He uttered a guttural chortle and continued to poke keys on my cell. I twisted my wrists against the ties. Slowly, but surely, I was making progress. The question was, would it do me any good? He powered the phone down and tossed it on the sofa. "You're not going to need that anymore."

"What's the plan, Roy?"

"Thought we'd do a little night fishing."

Sitting on the shore of Lake Arrowhead left no doubt as to what this asshole had in mind. I kept trying to come up with some way to get the upper hand, but couldn't. I had to keep working on loosening those goddamn zip ties.

"You're not going to get away with this, Roy. I told the LAPD about you. When they come up with your DNA, your ass is grass."

"Only if they find me," he replied.

He pulled the pack of cigarettes from his shirt pocket, plucked one out and repeated the process with the match against the fireplace. At that point I heard the sound of a car approaching. Roy heard it as well, took a swallow of beer and walked to the door and opened it.

"Any problems finding the place?" he said.

There was no response and Roy stood back as a figure filled the opening.

Alex Foster stepped into the room and glanced in my direction.

CHAPTER TWENTY-SIX

FROM THE CONVERSATION I'D BEEN HAVING with Roy Dickerson, Alex's appearance in the cabin didn't really surprise me. But what did, however, was the realization that he'd been a party to the brutal killing of his husband. He shut the door behind him and shook hands with Roy. He wore blue jeans, sneakers and a safari jacket over a black polo shirt. Black, skin-tight driving gloves covered his hands.

"He give you any problems?" Alex asked.

"No, except for the fact that the fucker weighs too much."

Alex walked to the sofa and sat on the end nearest me. He took a box of Marlboros out of a pocket and lit one with a Bic. Then he reached into another pocket of his safari jacket, pulled out an automatic and laid it on the coffee table. He slowly exhaled a cloud of smoke and stared at me for a long moment. "You've had a busy day, Collins."

"You been following me?"

"Not me. But he has," he said, gesturing to Roy.

"So all those crocodile tears this morning were just bullshit?"

"Pretty much. Were you impressed?"

"Somewhat. Not by what you've done to Ben Roth, though."

"Yeah, well, Ben didn't care much for his own son either."

"Enough to give him five hundred grand."

Alex took another drag off his cigarette and flicked the ashes onto the small plate sitting in front of him. "And for that, Roy and I are grateful."

"So that's the money you're coming into, huh, Roy?"

"You got it," he replied, as he sat down in the chair at the other end of the coffee table. "I'm done making an ass out of myself playing Santa Claus.

Bringing flowers and candy to my agent when half the time they don't know my fuckin' name. You gotta be on Twitter. You gotta have a Facebook page. It's all bullshit. I've had enough." He grabbed his beer bottle and tilted it up.

Alex watched him and took a puff on his cigarette. "Are you through?"

"Yeah, sorry," Roy said. "It just pisses me off, the whole damn business."

"I get that," Alex said.

I twisted my wrists a tad and put a grimace on my face. "How about letting my hands loose, Roy? My shoulder is killing me."

"I don't think so," he said.

The plastic ties had lost some of their tension, but still not enough for me to get my hands loose, especially with these two goons sitting right in front of me. And now, with the appearance of Alex's weapon, my predicament had only worsened. If I could pit one of them against the other, they might shift their focus from me.

"So what's the split, Roy?" I said. "Fifty-fifty? Or are you getting the smaller piece of the pie?"

"Not that that's any of your goddamn business, Eddie, but yeah, it's down the middle."

I glanced over at Alex, his cigarette in his hand, smoke curling toward the ceiling. "You sure you want to do that, Alex?"

"As he said, Collins, I don't think that's your concern."

"Your accomplice there just had some unflattering things to say about your ex-husband."

Alex puffed on his cigarette and glanced at Roy. "That right?"

"Ah, shit, Alex, don't listen to him. He's making stuff up to get his ass out of a jam."

"Roy said Jack was a degenerate faggot," I said. "And he used the 'n' word to describe you. I'd keep an eye on him."

"Collins, why don't you shut the fuck up?" Roy said. I looked at him across the coffee table and could see that his face had gotten awfully flush. Maybe I was getting to him.

"That sounds pretty racist and homophobic to me," I continued. "I don't know for sure if he means it, though. I mean the homophobic part. He worked with Jack, and says he left when he found out he was making gay porno films. But come on, Roy, level with us. I think you just don't want to admit the fact that you're still in the closet, right? Jack offered to put you in front of the camera, but you said no. What's the big deal? Afraid you would have come up short, so to speak?"

Roy slammed a fist on the coffee table, hurled his cigarette into the fireplace and lurched to his feet. He started toward me, but stopped when Alex said, "Sit down, Roy. Don't pay any attention to him."

He fumed, kicked his chair across the room and thought about it for a moment. Then he picked up the chair, slammed it down and sat. "Collins, it's going to make me goddamn happy to take you for a boat ride."

Alex took a final puff on his cigarette, snubbed it out on the plate full of butts, and picked up his gun. He checked the action and held it in his right hand, then pointed it at me. "I take it you've known Roy for a while, right?"

"A few years," I said.

"Then you know he's got a temper. And now you're saying you also think he hasn't come out yet?"

"You'll have to ask him," I said.

Alex glanced at Roy and said, "I don't know. Maybe he just likes to shoot his mouth off."

He moved the gun so it wasn't pointing at me and slowly aimed it at Roy. The first round hit him below the left eye. The second one plowed into his chest. Roy jerked like a puppet on a string when the bullets hit him, then slumped in the chair and was still. Blood trickled down his cheek and a red splotch started to blossom on his shirt. The two shots rocked me back in my chair. The sound inside the small cabin made my ears ring.

Alex rose, grabbed Roy's gun from the coffee table and put it in a pocket of his jacket. He picked up the bottle of Pabst, held it up to the light to check the fluid level, then walked into the kitchenette, his gun still in his hand. He glanced back at me and I watched him as he poured the rest of the beer into the sink and set the empty on the counter. He looked around the cabin and peered into the bathroom. He opened the back door and surveyed the outdoors, then walked back to the sofa and sat.

He was calm, deliberate, and left me with the impression he'd just as soon shoot me as look at me. But he laid the gun down and picked up my phone that Roy had tossed on the sofa. He turned it on, and when it was powered up, punched some keys and showed me the picture I'd taken of him and Dennis Abrams.

"Dennis told me about this. Spying on two gay men?"

"No, just curious."

"Yeah, right," he said. He powered down the phone again, then laid it on the coffee table and looked at me, his eyes a steely glare.

"You were kind of rough on your pal there, Collins."

"At least I didn't kill him."

He nodded and looked at me for a long moment. "You sure you're not the one who's homophobic? Accusing Roy of hiding out in the closet?"

"I was only trying to rile him."

"Well, it didn't work, did it?"

"Guess not. Why'd you do it?"

"He was collateral damage."

"By that, you mean he did what he had to do with the bat?"

"Exactly. And five hundred grand spends better than two hundred and fifty."

"I don't get it, Alex. It looked to me like you and Jack were pretty tight."

"Looks are deceiving," he said. He lit up another cigarette and blew a cloud of smoke in the air. "Part of what Roy said was true. Jack was a degenerate."

"How so?"

"Those goddamn movies he was making. They had absolutely no redeeming value. Being black and gay, I'm confronted with enough prejudice without having to admit that I'm married to a pornographer. I wanted him to quit with that crap, but he wouldn't do it. Then when his old man laid some more money on him it was only going to get worse."

"You know the cops are not going to give up on you. You suddenly becoming the beneficiary of five hundred grand? It goes to motive, Alex."

"But they don't have any proof. They can't dispute my alibi, and they can't put me at the scene. They also don't have a murder weapon. There's supposedly a wood-chipper outside of this place. Roy told me he brought the bat with him and turned it into sawdust."

He made a good point. Without a murder weapon, LAPD was going to find it difficult to tie someone to the crime. Alex drew on the cigarette, exhaled and picked up his gun and stuck it in a jacket pocket.

"Dennis called me after you talked to him and made an asshole of yourself. He went on to tell me that Jack was argumentative with several guys at that party. It seems to me the cops have more reason to suspect them than me."

Without trying to be obvious, I kept putting pressure on the plastic ties behind my back. They were getting loose, but not enough.

"If you were so pissed off at Jack, why didn't you just divorce him?" I said. "Your marriage is legit. Your divorce would be too."

"Good point, except for one thing. Jack was in his old man's will, and the old fucker is loaded. I stay married and I'm the beneficiary. California's community property and all that. He made sure the paperwork was right. Bless his little degenerate heart."

There it was. Money rearing its ugly head again. Alex was correct. Unless there was a pre-nuptial agreement on record, he stood to inherit his spouse's assets. I didn't know if that applied in the case of murder, but if the police couldn't solve the case, it would fade into the background and a court would have to make a ruling.

Alex snuffed out his cigarette and moved into the kitchenette, looking back at me to make sure I wasn't going to make a run for it. He started rummaging through drawers under the counter, found what he was looking for and came back to the coffee table. He had a roll of duct tape in his hand and tore off a substantial strip.

"Put your legs underneath you," he said.

I tucked them beneath me and he wrapped the tape around my left leg and then the leg of the chair. Given the forty-five degree angle of the chair legs, a gap was left between my calf and the metal. He pressed the tape together in an effort to make the binding more secure. He repeated the process with my right leg and stood up.

"Not very professional, but enough to do the trick. And it's only temporary. When I've taken care of your buddy here, we'll go for that boat ride."

Fortunately, Alex didn't check the ties on my wrists. If he had, he would have noticed my persistent attempts to loosen them. Instead, he tossed the tape on the coffee table and moved to Roy. The thin trail of blood running down his cheek looked like a big macabre tear. The red blossom on his chest had stopped growing and a stain had appeared on his trousers where his bladder had voided itself. Alex bent over him, took Roy's wallet and cellphone and stuck them in his safari jacket. He then found the keys to my car and tossed them on the coffee table. He picked him up under the arms and effortlessly laid him on the floor, then walked to the front door and locked it.

"Don't think about going anywhere, Collins."

"I'll leave a note if I do," I replied.

He softly chuckled, grabbed Roy by his wrists and began to pull him toward the rear of the cabin, rumpling rugs on the way. He propped open the door with a waste basket and pulled Roy over the threshold and into the back yard, headed, I assumed, toward a boat by the shore.

If I was ever to going to get out of this mess, now was the time. I pushed against the tape with my legs, twisting them enough so the glue gave way, giving me more room to move my legs, but still leaving me basically immobile. I took stock. I was approximately two feet from the fireplace, and when I examined it, I saw one of the stones had a ragged edge. Could I do it? Before Alex came back?

Doing my best to swallow the pain in my head and shoulder, I slightly raised myself off the seat of the chair and hopped toward the fireplace. I could only move a few inches, but with repeated efforts I made it to the stone facade and twisted the chair around so the stones were at my back. I felt for the jagged edge, found it, and began sawing away at the plastic ties. I'd already succeeded in making them somewhat slack, so it didn't take too long to cut through them.

I heard a cellphone ring outside and heard Alex answer it. I grasped the loose ties in my fingers and hopped my way back to where I had started. Just after getting situated in the same position, Alex came through the back door, talking on his phone.

My only hope now was that he wouldn't pay attention to the way my wrists were bound. It was a stretch, but maybe he was in a hurry. Patience was my long suit. Would it be enough?

CHAPTER TWENTY-SEVEN

———◆———

ALEX FINISHED HIS PHONE CONVERSATION AND stuffed the cell in one of the breast pockets of his safari jacket. His gloves were covered with white dust and he had a flashlight in one hand, the kind with a handle on it that runs on a 6-volt battery. He set it on the counter and rummaged through the kitchenette's drawers, found a knife, pulled his gun from another pocket and walked over to me. I held my breath, not because I thought he was going to stab or shoot me, but rather that he would look at my hands. He didn't, put the gun in my face, bent over and cut through the duct tape binding my legs to those of the chair.

"Roy should have taken his own advice and dropped some pounds himself," he said. "Thought I was going to get a fucking hernia." He pulled the tape off, wadded it into a ball and tossed it into the fireplace. "Can you stand up?"

"Yeah, but you gotta step on the chair so it doesn't get up with me."

He put his foot on the metal bar spanning the legs and I rose, careful not to reveal the fact that my wrists were no longer bound. "You're not going to get away with this, Alex. LAPD knows I've talked to you. I disappear, they're going to come knocking."

"I don't know why, Collins. You keep forgetting that they can't tie me to Jack's murder. And they're clutching at straws if they think there's a link between you and me." He grabbed me by the elbow and we started toward the back door, his gun nestled up against my left cheek.

"What about my car? Roy said he was going to drive it into the lake. You actually think it's going to sink?"

"Oh, for crissakes, of course not. I'll park it on the main road and leave the keys in it. Some stupid asshole will drive it away. When you're reported missing and a description of the car goes out, it'll be someone else's problem."

"What about Roy's car?"

"He drove it up into Griffith Park. I picked him up and dropped him at your place. Sooner or later the cops will tie it to his disappearance, and once again it won't be my problem."

These guys had obviously put some planning into this scheme of theirs. I didn't think very deeply about whether or not it was going to be successful. Right now I was more concerned with how the hell I was going to get the drop on Alex before I went into the drink.

He picked up the flashlight and pushed me through the back door into a yard washed with moonlight. Unlike what I was used to seeing in LA, the night sky over the lake was perforated with stars. As he pulled the door shut behind him, I looked to my right and saw a cabin probably fifty yards away. No lights were on. I glanced to my left and saw another one, also dark. Next to Roy's cabin was a small pre-fabricated shed, the kind you buy at a home improvement store. Against one of its walls was a stack of firewood and several concrete blocks, along with what looked like a small wood chipper.

Alex shined the flashlight on three wooden steps leading to the ground and we started down them. Moisture had collected, making the risers slick. When my shoe hit the second step I lost my footing and fell forward. Instinct took over and I brought my hands around to break my fall. I hit the ground and Alex immediately jammed a knee into my back and pressed his gun to my neck.

"Just lay there a minute, Collins, and think about this." He rapped me on the skull with the barrel of the gun and I let out a groan from the pain that shot through my head. He shined the light on one of my hands and saw the remnant of the zip tie. "Let me guess. The stones on the fireplace? While I was dragging ol' Roy to the boat?"

"Another two minutes and I'd have been out the front door."

"Yeah, well, that's two minutes you're never going to get back." He stood up and kicked me in the ribs. "Get up." I struggled to my feet and he stuck the gun into my left ear. "Nice and easy. Down to the boat."

"Why don't you just pull the trigger now, Alex? Save you a lot of trouble."

"I busted a gut getting Roy down there. You can push the fat fuck over the side."

We made our way on a dirt path toward the water. Roy's heels had created two ruts running through the center of the path. I looked ahead of me and saw a boat with an outboard motor tied up to a dock, its bow pointing offshore. It had five bench-like seats. Roy's body was draped over the middle one. His claim that there wasn't beach access proved to be true. The shoreline stretching in both directions from the dock consisted of sharp drop-offs choked with brush. The wooden dock was old, weather-beaten, and creaked as we stepped onto it. Planks ran the length, moonlight picking up the shine of moisture covering them.

As we approached the boat, the moon glow provided enough light for me to see two concrete blocks on the boat's deck. One of them had a piece of rope tied to it. The other end was knotted around Roy's waist. When we got to the middle of the boat, Alex stopped.

"Get in and sit on the seat next to your pal," he said, as he prodded my beat-up shoulder with the barrel of his gun.

I winced and put my left foot over the gunwale. As I started to reach for an upright pole anchoring the dock to hang onto, I instead grabbed one of Alex's ankles and pulled, hoping I could throw him off-balance. He slipped on the wet surface and kicked me in the head with his other foot. I hung on, but let go when a bullet pierced the wooden plank in front of my face. The explosion of the gun made my ears ring and I recoiled and fell back into the boat, landing on my sore shoulder and looking into Roy's mangled face.

The smell of rotten fish filled my nostrils, along with the dead man's bladder and bowels having been voided. When my weight hit the boat it bobbed slightly and water lapped at the sides. I pulled myself upright and sat down facing Roy's body and the stern. Alex squatted on his haunches, the gun leveled at me. He shined his flashlight into my eyes and I put one hand in front of my face.

"You're beginning to piss me off, Collins. Maybe I should just shoot you right here and now. But since you're such a stubborn asshole, it's going to give me great pleasure to see you throw yourself into the drink." He turned the flashlight off, tossed it into the boat and stood up. "Now, very slowly go to the bow and untie the line." I got up and stepped over the seat and did as he asked, watching him as he followed me along the deck. When the line was free, he gestured with the gun for me to sit. I returned to my seat, sank down and stared at the other concrete block at my feet, the one with my name on it. Still with the gun on me, he walked to the stern and climbed aboard.

"Two blocks, Alex? Looks like Roy was planning on sending you into the drink along with me."

"Wrong, Collins. I pulled one off that pile next to the shed."

That explained the white dust on his gloves and the longer amount of time he'd given me to get the zip ties cut. With his gun still leveled at me, he stepped aboard.

"Don't give ol' Roy that much credit. He at times may have been a float short of a parade, but he knew he wasn't going to be able to get his share of the money with me out of the picture."

Underneath Roy's mangled head lying on the seat in front of me sat a metal tackle box. Curled next to it were several more feet of rope. A closer look revealed it wasn't rope, but rather stringer cord, the kind an angler would run through the gills of a fish and drop over the gunwale into the water. Two wooden oars lay across the seats on either side of the boat. On the deck next to the motor was an anchor in the shape of a metal disk and attached to a length of heavy rope that was tied to a cleat in the boat's deck.

Alex untied the stern line, leaned over and pushed the boat away from the dock. His effort put us six feet into the lake. He sat down next to the outboard motor and pushed a button. The engine sputtered to life. He throttled it down so it sounded like a purring sewing machine.

"For someone who told me he wouldn't be caught dead fishing, you look like you know your way around a boat," I said.

"Yeah, well, when your old man practically straps a rod and reel into your hand, you've got no choice. Old habits die hard."

We slowly pulled away from the dock, the motor making only a tiny wake. I didn't see any other boats on the lake, but that didn't mean there weren't any. It had been a while since I'd been up here. Some years ago I managed to land a couple of days on a low-budget potboiler that went straight to video. I remember a guy on the crew telling me how Lake Arrowhead got its name. A long inlet pointing north by northwest on a map looks like an arrowhead. Roy's cabin was along the north side, and as we made our way to the center of the lake, I could see that access to the water was hampered by dense foliage and steep embankments on the shore.

Apprehension welled up in me. I thought about jumping overboard, but knew Alex would shoot me as soon as I made a move. Since he'd already fired a round into the dock, he obviously wasn't concerned about the sound of a gunshot. Besides, with fishing and hunting being major sports up here, I had a feeling the sound of gunfire would go unnoticed. I leaned over the gunwale and looked into the black water.

"Don't even think about going for a swim, Collins. You wouldn't get far."

He took his hand off the tiller, steadied it with his knee, then fished out another cigarette and lit it with a lighter. The flare bounced off his black face, the expression on it benign, stoic. The flame went out and he stuck the lighter back in a pocket and grabbed the tiller again. We glided through the placid water, both his gun and his stare fixed on me.

"When did it start, Alex?"

"When did what start?"

"The hatred."

He took a deep drag on the cigarette and stared at me for a long moment. "I don't remember exactly. Growing up as a black kid in Bakersfield was the pits. I was always the last one chosen for the pickup baseball team. I used to find pictures of monkeys and apes stuffed in my locker with my yearbook picture glued over the faces. I was ostracized, laughed at, ridiculed. Then when I realized I was gay, it got even worse." He paused and exhaled a cloud of smoke that quickly dissipated with the movement of the boat. "You've never experienced much rejection, have you, Collins?"

"Are you kidding? All the time. I'm an actor, remember?"

"Nah, bullshit. Not the same thing. You guys do your little auditions, jump through your hoops, and leave it behind you at the door. With me, feeling like a second-class citizen became a way of life."

"In Los Angeles? That doesn't strike me as being the way things are."

"Yeah, well, you're on the outside looking in. Different ball of wax in my shoes."

Off to our right the running lights of another boat slowly glided to the far shore. Alex slowed a bit, and when he saw the boat disappearing, resumed his speed.

"I don't get it," I said. "Jack surely gave you support. You must have loved him."

"At first. But it didn't take long for me to see that he started to think of me as a token. Having a black gay lover made him appear chic, edgy, politically correct. I began to feel like I was his house nigger. Then he started making those goddamn movies. Soon there were affairs. One-night stands. He didn't think I knew, but I did."

"Why did you stick around?"

"Simple. Money. Makes the world go around, as the song says."

"But murder? Seems to me you're pushing the envelope."

"I didn't murder anyone," he said, and gestured to Roy. "Roy was more than happy to do the deed."

"I poked around the crime scene and found a butt from one of those Sobranies he smoked," I said. "If LAPD finds his DNA on it, it's only a matter of time before they make a connection."

He finished his cigarette and flicked the butt over the side of the boat. "I don't know how many times I've got to go over this with you, Collins. They can't disprove my alibi, they can't put me at the scene, and they don't have a murder weapon. Use your head. You're supposed to be the fucking detective."

He throttled the motor down and shut it off. The boat drifted for a few feet and then came to a stop. There was no breeze and the night was deathly quiet, except for the faint sound of music coming from Lake Arrowhead Village on the south shore of the lake. Still pointing the gun at me, Alex got up from his seat and stood over Roy's body.

"Time for Roy's swim," he said. "First the body, then the block."

After a moment, I stood up and began sliding Roy's body along the seat toward the port side of the boat. I draped his legs over the gunwale, then grabbed his shoulders and pushed him up and over and he went looking for Davy Jones's locker. The tether rope slithered over the gunwale, but jerked to a stop when the cement block rammed into the side of the boat. The impact caused Alex to teeter a bit.

"Now the block," he said. "Nice and easy."

I grabbed the piece of concrete with both hands, lifted it to my waist, and looked back at him. He gestured with the gun and I tossed it into the water. I let the momentum of the throw propel me into the side of the boat. I took a firm grip on the gunwale and pulled back, causing the boat to rock. Alex reeled with the movement, lost his balance and fell to the deck on his back. The gun dropped from his hand and skidded into the corner next to the anchor.

I reached down, grabbed one of the oars, and as Alex stretched out to retrieve his gun, I took the oar in both hands, wound up, and slammed the flat end into his back. Pain shot through my left shoulder. I stepped over the seat in front of me, swung again and hit him on the back of his neck. He grabbed the end of the oar before I could retrieve it. We jostled with it for a few moments, both of us trying to wrest it away from the other. He pushed me back and I stumbled over one of the seats and lost my balance.

When he saw me trip, Alex again lunged for his gun, but then he tripped over one of the seats and broke his fall with his hands. I righted myself before he did and leaped over the seat, raised the oar like an axe and brought it down on the top of his head. He crumpled to the deck, groaning, holding his head.

I dropped the oar, reached down and picked up the concrete block meant for me. My bum shoulder made it hard for me lift it very far, but I managed to get it over my head and heaved it at Alex. He'd picked up his gun again and was turning to face me when the block smashed into the left side of his face with a sickening thud. He sank to the deck and lay there, silent and still.

I reached down, grabbed his gun, tossed it toward the bow and then collapsed. The pain that shot through my shoulder and head almost made me lose consciousness. I took several deep breaths and looked at Alex. He hadn't moved.

I groped for the fishing cord underneath me. There were four strands, each about three feet in length. I grabbed two of them, stepped over the seat in front of me and tied Alex's feet together. He stirred momentarily, but didn't come to. His forehead had a noticeable dent in it and considerable skin was scraped off. Blood dripped from his nostrils and left ear. I checked for a pulse, found one, then rolled him over, wrenched both arms behind him and tied his wrists together with another one of the fishing cords.

When his arms and legs were bound, I dropped the anchor over the side.

I remembered the crew member telling me that Arrowhead was a deep lake. That anchor wasn't going to hit the bottom, but it was heavy enough to keep the boat from drifting too far. I rolled Alex over again and rifled through the pockets of his safari jacket. I found his cellphone and turned it on. I couldn't tell for sure how many bars there were, but I dialed the three numbers anyway.

"This is 911," a female voice said. "What's your emergency?"

"I'm in a motorboat in the middle of Lake Arrowhead. A man has been thrown overboard and I'm looking at the guy who did it."

After a pause, the dispatcher said, "Do you know your location, sir?"

"I don't. You'll have to ping this cellphone."

"Oh. Ah. . .okay." I could tell by the sound of her voice that she was responding to something unfamiliar to her.

"I'll leave the phone on, and I've got a flashlight. Tell them to look for it. They'll figure it out."

CHAPTER TWENTY-EIGHT

———— ◆ ————

THE ER DOCTOR AT MOUNTAINS COMMUNITY Hospital was named Julie Atkins. When I'd told her what had happened, she looked at me in disbelief. I assured her it was true. She did some tests and finally concluded that I had suffered a mild concussion. No surprise there. Roy Dickerson had been a heavy hitter. After putting my left shoulder through several painful maneuvers, the good doctor said it didn't appear as if anything was broken, despite the fact that the joint looked like someone had used it to display paint samples. She gave me a sling and told me to try and keep it immobile. I was relieved when she told me I didn't need to spend a night in the hospital, but she suggested—no, warned—that I should rest for several days. She gave me the name of a colleague in Burbank for a follow-up visit. Fortified with my sling, some sample pain pills and a prescription for more, she'd sent me on my way.

San Bernardino County Sheriff's deputies and local police were waiting for me at the hospital's front door. It had taken the better part of an hour for them to find me in the boat, the flashlight's battery almost dead. Alex Foster had briefly come to, spat obscenities at me, struggled against his bindings and promptly passed out again. I myself had almost lost consciousness a couple of times and was shivering from the cold when the boat with the cops arrived.

The first question the police had asked me when they'd coasted up was why the hell hadn't I started the motor and headed for the shore. The looks of incredulity on their faces disappeared when I told them I was sitting on top of a crime scene. Would they rather send their divers on a wild goose chase looking for a body, or did they think it made more sense for them to anchor the boat and come back in the morning? They agreed with me, threw one of their anchors overboard and secured it to Roy's boat, after assuring me the tether was long enough to hit bottom.

By the time the police ushered me into an interrogation room and set a cup of tepid coffee in front of me it was two-twenty in the morning. I told them where my car was, along with the keys and my cellphone. They brought in a phone, plugged it into a jack on one of the walls, then left me alone so I could make a call. After three rings, she answered, her voice thick with sleep.

"Hello?"

"Carla, it's me."

"Eddie?"

"The same."

"It's the middle of the night. Are you okay?"

"I am now," I said, and went on to tell her what had happened.

"Oh, my God! Are you still up there?"

"Yeah, I've got to sort everything out with the police. They said they'll get my car, but I don't think I should drive. They're going to put me in a motel for the night and interrogate me in the morning."

"I've got an early call, but maybe I can get it changed."

"No, no, you have to work."

"I'll tell them it's an emergency."

"Honey, no. Listen to me. You and I both know how important this job is to you. It's a no-brainer. You have to be there. Here's what you do. Call Mavis, tell her to get Reggie and drive up here. When I find out where they'll put me up, tell her I'll call her sometime in the morning, okay?"

"All right, but I wish I could be there with you."

"So do I, but I'll see you soon. Go back to sleep, if you can."

"Fat chance, but I'll try. Love you."

"Right back atcha," I said, and hung up.

I popped a couple of the pain pills, washed them down with the coffee and laid my head on the table. The aches had subsided somewhat, but I still felt like I'd been scrimmaging with the Rams. After a couple of minutes, the door opened and Sheriff's Deputies Matheson and Burke stepped in. Matheson was burly, all business, and Burke was a tall black man with a shaved head. They were two of the crew that had seen my flashlight and brought Alex and me to shore. Burke gave me another cup of coffee and a bottle of water, then they sat down across from me.

"You've had a hell of a night, Mr. Collins," Matheson said.

"At least I'm not at the bottom of the lake."

They nodded and for the next fifteen minutes or so they had me outline in broad strokes what had transpired from the time Roy had bought me to the cabin. When I finished my coffee, they took me to a nearby motel, checked me in and told me they'd be back around nine o'clock.

Before he shut the door, Matheson said, "You're going to be here in the morning, right?"

"No wheels, deputy. I'm not going anywhere."

"We'll have your car by then," he said. "Get some sleep."

He shut the door. I slid the dead bolt home, took off my shoes and collapsed on the bed. Sleep followed immediately.

THE PHONE JARRED ME AWAKE. I looked at my watch. Seven-thirty. A woman from the front desk was on the other end of the line. She said the deputies had told them to give me a wake-up call. I offered my thanks, rolled out of bed and let the cobwebs clear. My head and shoulder felt better, but I took a couple more pills, then stripped and stood under the shower until the water started to cool.

The motel offered a buffet breakfast. I set a cup of coffee and an orange juice on a table, then dished some scrambled eggs and link sausage onto a plate, sat down and watched a young mom and dad try to settle an argument with their two tots as to what the plans for the day were going to be. Back in my room I tried my office number first, but Mavis wasn't there yet. She answered her cell after a couple of rings.

"Eddie? Carla just called me. What the heck happened?"

I recapped the events of yesterday. She listened and was silent before telling me she'd track Reggie down and be here as soon as she could. Reggie was Reggie Benson, a guy I'd been in the Army with and who'd saved my life on one particular night in a Korean village. A few months back I'd found him on the streets in Santa Monica, given him a leg up and now I considered him to be my quasi operative in my investigations. I told Mavis I'd call her back when the police retrieved my cellphone.

The knock came at five after nine. I switched off the *Today* show and swung the door open to see Matheson standing there with another deputy, a Hispanic whose badge identified him as Valdez. Matheson handed me my car keys and my cellphone.

"Thanks," I said. "Any sign of Dickerson's body?"

"Divers are out there as we speak," Matheson replied. "Shall we go?"

I finished off the coffee and put the paper cup in the wastebasket. I held up the key card. "Should I leave this here?"

"Keep it for now," he said.

I closed the door behind me, followed the two deputies to a patrol car and we drove to the sheriff's station. For the next two hours Matheson and Valdez grilled me about everything that had happened yesterday. I gave them the names of the two LAPD lieutenants. I told them about Jack Callahan's murder. The cigarette butt I found at the crime scene. Roy's relationship to Callahan and Ben Roth. Dickerson clubbing me with the bat. I described where Roy had been sitting when Alex shot him. They said they'd found one gun in a pocket of Foster's safari jacket. I told them it belonged to Dickerson, and that I'd tossed Alex's toward the bow of the boat. I said that I thought the bullet into Roy's head had exited. The one in the chest I wasn't sure about.

When I gave them this information, Valdez left the room to make phone calls. After several minutes he returned and said the crime scene team had retrieved the slug that had gone through Roy's head. Dickerson's body had been found and was in the morgue. He also relayed the information that Foster's condition was critical. The doctors had induced a coma because of swelling on his brain. I suppose I should have felt some twinge of guilt for smashing in his head with the concrete block, but the news left me indifferent.

Matheson and Valdez left no stone unturned. At one point, after going through the events for what seemed like the tenth time, I told them that my headache had returned with a vengeance and wondered how long they were going to keep me in the hot seat. They responded by saying that they had what they needed from me for the time being, but that they might want further details. We exchanged business cards and they dropped me back at the motel.

I called Mavis and told her where I was. She said she'd talked to Reggie and that they'd be there as soon as they could. Housekeeping had done up the room, so I laid down on the bed and thought back on what I'd gone through the day before. The service for Jack Callahan and his father's regret that his son's martini shot had come before his own. I recalled Alex Foster and his apparent grief over the loss of his partner. The tears had seemed genuine, and it amazed me that they were only masking hatred. The casual manner in which he'd pulled the trigger twice and disposed of Roy Dickerson's body had scared the hell out of me. I was certain the realization that I'd come damn close to having my own martini shot was going to stay with me a long time. Probably forever.

MY CELLPHONE WOKE ME UP. A glance at my watch revealed I'd been asleep for an hour and a half. The screen said it was Mavis.

"We're almost there. Traffic was a bitch."

I gave her the room number and twenty minutes later she knocked on the door. Reggie stood behind her and followed her in. The hug she gave me seemed to be more enthusiastic than I'd remembered of late, but was also more welcome than any I'd ever received from her.

She stepped back and looked at me. "My God, aren't you tired of getting beat up like this?"

"You think I should retire?"

"Might not be a bad idea," she said.

Reggie always seemed to be rather shy by nature, but the embrace he gave me belied that trait. "How ya doin', Eddie? Man, you been through some shit, huh?"

"I needed you at my back, Reggie."

"Yup, yup. Next time, okay?"

"Are you ready to go?" Mavis said.

"Yeah, just let me check in with the sheriff first." I called Matheson and told him I was ready to head back to Los Angeles and asked him if that was all right. He gave me the okay, but said I would no doubt be called for further details as their investigation progressed. I assured him I'd do everything I could to help them, and we broke the connection.

Mavis suggested that Reggie follow her as much as possible. Since I'd rescued Reggie from the streets, I'd helped him get a driver's license and let him use my car to get himself back to where he could handle Southern California freeways.

"You ready, Reggie?"

"Let's hit it," he said, a big grin breaking out on his face.

We started down the mountain, and by the time we got to the 210 Freeway heading west he'd more than proved his mettle behind the wheel. We drove in silence for a long stretch, my head tilted back, filled with images of Roy Dickerson sinking into the depths of Lake Arrowhead. At one point I took a deep breath and straightened up in my seat.

"You okay, Eddie?" Reggie said.

"Yeah. Just trying like hell to get last night out of my head."

"Yup, yup." He paused and negotiated the car around a big rig. "Sounds like that Alex guy had your number there for a minute, huh?"

"Scared the crap out of me, Reggie. Almost like that night in Korea when that damn sergeant came at me with that knife."

"Yup. Good thing the guy didn't have a gun."

"And even better that you were there." Reggie nodded and I reached over and popped him on the shoulder. "Do me a favor, okay?"

"What?"

"Remind me never to go up to Lake Arrowhead again."

"You got it," he said, and we both laughed as we sailed on by the first Pasadena exit.

Mavis was already behind her desk at Collins Investigations when Reggie and I walked through the door. Without further ado, she ordered me to seek out Mr. Murphy's bed. I complied and she said she'd take Reggie back to his apartment before filling the prescription for the pain medication. They left and I sent Carla a text telling her I was home safe and sound. After a minute or two, she replied and said she'd be over as soon as she was finished shooting. As I kicked off my shoes and climbed onto the bed, I decided her arrival would be the best thing to happen to me in quite a few hours.

CHAPTER TWENTY-NINE

———— ◆ ————

BEN ROTH SAT IN HIS EASY chair, iced tea at his elbow. He stared out the sliding glass door in his apartment watching two squirrels in combat over some morsel. He was quiet, subdued. Three days had elapsed since the events up at Lake Arrowhead. On the first of those I'd followed Mavis's orders and confined myself to quarters, immersing myself in daytime television, a pursuit bound to challenge anyone's sanity. I tried napping, but many times was jolted awake by images of the boat, concrete blocks, and Roy Dickerson sleeping with the fishes. Carla had made a couple of runs to a deli and provided me with some tasty chicken soup and sandwiches. She'd also contributed greatly to my peace of mind and helped me sort through the display of hatred and violence I'd witnessed.

Ben took a sip of his tea and set the glass down, then erupted into a cough. He put his handkerchief to his mouth and went through a series of wheezes and snorts.

"Went down the wrong pipe, Ben?"

"Ah, crap, everything goes down the wrong pipe these days." He blew his nose and stuffed the handkerchief back in his shirt pocket. "They might as well hook me up to a goddamn needle. Probably will happen soon enough." He struggled to his feet and shuffled over to the glass door and slid it open a couple of feet. "Better get some fresh air in here, in case I start breaking wind."

He walked back to his chair and I had to restrain myself from chuckling. His frequent comments about his plumbing and bodily functions were amusing. I'd filed them away for the day when I'd be trying to keep a career afloat by playing coots and old codgers. Ben had been filled in on what happened up at the lake, and he'd been stunned. First of all by what Alex Foster had done, but even more so about Roy Dickerson being the one who had killed his son.

He sank down in the chair and let out a huge sigh, then sipped more tea. "You hear anything more about Alex?"

"Matter of fact, the sheriff up there called me this morning. They brought him out of the coma. Apparently he hasn't said anything."

"And probably won't, the fuckin' guy. My lawyer was here this morning. I changed my will so he don't get a goddamn cent."

"Good idea, Ben."

"What do you think they'll charge him with?"

"Conspiracy to commit murder, most likely. I don't know that they've sorted it all out yet. And apparently the doctors don't know the prognosis on his condition."

"Yeah, I suppose." He sipped from his glass. "What about you?"

"I'm all right. Headaches are starting to disappear."

"I fell off a horse one time back in the day. They said I had a concussion. The goddamn studio wouldn't lift a finger to help pay for the bills."

"Things have changed, Ben. For the better, I might add."

"If you say so." He lifted the glass to his lips and carefully took another swallow. "You know what bothers the hell out of me, though?"

"What?"

"Roy. For the life of me I never would have figured he'd do something like that. He used to take me fishing up at that damn lake. I'll bet you a sawbuck I sat in that cabin where you almost bought it. Unbelievable. I mean, he was like a son to me, for crissakes."

"Greed does strange things to people."

He looked at me and a grin formed on his face. "You're full of platitudes today, aren't you, Collins?" I shrugged my shoulders. He laughed and picked up his writing board from beside his chair, then grabbed his checkbook and ripped up the check he'd attempted to give me earlier. "How much do I owe you?"

"I didn't come out here to collect, Ben. I wanted to see how you're doing is all."

"Aw hell, I'm okay. 'This too shall pass,' as my urologist keeps telling me." We shared a laugh and he wrote another check and handed it to me.

"Whoa, whoa, this is too much."

"Consider it your inheritance," he said, and let out a guffaw, which provoked more coughing. "Aside from your medical condition, how are you otherwise, Collins?"

"What do you mean?"

"Any guilt for what you did. To Alex?"

"At first. Then I thought it through and realized it was him or me."

"That's usually what it comes down to," he said, and sipped more tea. "Well, I really appreciate what you've done. And I'm sorry as hell about what it put you through."

"Comes with the territory," I said, as I stood up.

"Enough with the goddamn platitudes," he said, then struggled to his feet. We shook. His grip was that of a much younger man and he took my hand in both of his. "You take care of yourself, hear?"

"I will. You do the same." I opened the door and walked down the hall. As I turned the corner I looked back and saw him standing in the doorway.

"Drop in from time to time, if you want," he said. "Mystery meat is always on the menu."

We shared another laugh, I flipped him a salute and headed for my car. My getting to know Ben Roth had made a big impression on me. He was a survivor. Not only of the Hollywood hustle, but of life itself. Nothing demonstrated that fact more than the way he dealt with the violent murder of his son. One could learn a lot from a guy like him. I'd like to think that I had.

CARLA'S TV SHOW DIDN'T SHOOT ON the weekends, so we had a couple of good days together. From time to time, I was haunted by the memories of what I'd been through up at that lake, but her arms wrapped around me and her cheek next to mine did wonders to dispel them.

The effects of the concussion and my bruised and battered shoulder receded with every passing day. I made an appointment with the Burbank doctor Julie Atkins had referred me to. His prognosis was encouraging. After learning what had caused my mild concussion, he broached the possibility of PTSD and gave me some literature on it. I looked it over, and while I didn't think symptoms existed in my case, I promised him I'd get back to him if I began to think differently.

Mid-week after visiting Ben Roth I got another call from the sheriff's office in Lake Arrowhead. A San Bernardino County Assistant DA was going to be there and wanted to interview me about what had happened. Alex Foster had been moved to a hospital ward in the county jail. His condition had improved somewhat, but his motor responses were still shaky. I tamped down any feelings of guilt about crippling another human being. *You made your bed, Alex, you lie in it,* I thought, and then smiled when I remembered Ben's warning about platitudes.

So I picked up Reggie and we had a nice trip up to the mountains. He drove part of the way and looked at me with a trace of anxiety in his face when I suggested I could maybe lend him some money and we could start looking for a car of his own. Given the jungle of LA freeways, where weapons on wheels reign supreme, I could appreciate his trepidation.

Mark Dwyer was the DA's name. His John Lennon glasses kept slipping down his nose as he talked to me. Based on his performance with me, I had no doubt he would be a worthy advocate in front of a jury. In fact, I thought he was going to ask me what I'd had for breakfast that morning and what the writing on the cereal box was. Finally he seemed satisfied, and told me that I'd probably be subpoenaed when Alex went to trial. I told him I'd welcome the opportunity to testify against him.

On the way down the mountain with Reggie behind the wheel, I started to doze when my cellphone went off. The screen said it was Morrie Howard, my long-suffering agent.

"Bubbeleh, how's the head?"

"Still on my shoulders. What's up, Morrie?"

"Good things come to those who wait. *Shades of Blue* called. They want to book you for next week. Please tell me you're available."

My heart skipped a beat, and I said, "I'm the walking definition of the word."

"Terrific. I'll send you the wheres and the whens."

He hung up and I turned to Reggie. "Good news, buddy. Maybe that car of yours is closer than you think."

He held up his hands and shook them as if he was demonstrating nervous trembling. Laughter carried us to the freeway.

I showed up at the Universal lot the following Monday morning and couldn't remember the last time I'd felt that good to be back in front of the camera again. The set was friendly, the stars didn't regard me as an amateur, and a couple of producers told me this Internal Affairs officer I played could conceivably show up again. Of course I'd heard that mantra many times before, but considering the fact that I'd recently been confronted with the possibility of my own martini shot, his words were especially welcome.

August evolved into September and the NFL in full bloom. Charlie Rivers and I acted like rabid fans when I made good on my Rams tickets. A grand jury indicted Alex Foster and I testified before them. The defendant appeared in court sitting in a wheelchair. He glared at me and at times appeared like his mind was somewhere else, which it very well could have been.

On a crisp Sunday morning Carla and I were digesting the morning paper at her place when she said, "Oh, no. Eddie, look at this." She handed me the section of the paper she was looking at. A story below the fold reported the death of Ben Roth, longtime actor and resident of the Motion Picture Country Home. I'd dropped in on him a couple of times since July and he was still full of piss and vinegar, albeit not as much. Now he'd finally had his martini shot.

I did three more episodes of *Shades of Blue*. The Internal Affairs investigator I portrayed could conceivably be a recurring character, depending upon how honest the show's cops were. Carla's series had gotten an order for six more episodes and she was walking on air. We had long conversations about leaving Mr. Murphy's bed behind and getting a place together. Even though we were serious, we both dropped hints that maybe a step like that should be taken with measured thought.

ON A TUESDAY AFTERNOON I STEPPED off the elevator and saw an elderly man standing outside Dr. Travnikov's office looking down at the psychedelic carpet that covered the hallway. He glanced up at me as I approached.

"Interesting choice of carpet," he said.

"Why is that?"

"Well, if one wasn't particularly ill coming up here, a few minutes staring at this would definitely justify your doctor's appointment. Psychology at work, perhaps?"

"Works for me," I said, as I pushed open my office door. Over the past several months our landlord's choice of floor covering had been called many things, but this was a first. Mavis was at her desk and looked up as I came in. She handed me a clump of mail.

"Howdy, Boss Man. Somebody taking you to court?"

"Not to my knowledge. Why?"

"It's on the top," she said, and pointed to the first envelope in front of me.

I looked at the return address. It was from the law offices of Ross, Mathius, and Wilson, names completely unknown to me. I sat in one of the chairs in front of her desk and she handed me a letter opener. I sliced it open and unfolded a glossy piece of stationery. As I read, my jaw dropped and I glanced over at Mavis, surprise washing over me.

"Well?" she said.

I held the letter up and read the following: "*We request your presence in our law offices at ten o'clock, Wednesday of next week. You have been named as a beneficiary in the last will and testament of Benjamin Roth.*"

"Oh, my God," Mavis said. She took the words right out of my mouth.

DRESSED IN MY ONLY PRESENTABLE SUIT, I appeared at the law offices out in Woodland Hills and was ushered into a conference room dominated by a highly-polished oval table the size of my office. Ben's three friends, Jerry Daniels, Paul Baker, and George Higgins, were there. I'd seen them at Ben's funeral a few weeks back, and they looked like they'd taken the news of his death quite hard. Now they seemed to be in better spirits and we shook hands and exchanged warm greetings. Two women and three other men were in the room, none of them familiar to me.

We all sat on one side of the table across from two lawyers. In sonorous tones they proceeded to reveal the contents of Ben's will. A large sum was left to the Motion Picture Country Home, along with a sizable contribution to the SAG-AFTRA Foundation. Ben's three amigos were all overcome when the lawyer named them each as a beneficiary of Ben's generosity. However, their surprise paled in comparison to mine when I heard that Ben had left me two hundred and fifty thousand dollars.

A few days later Reggie almost broke into tears when I handed him the keys to a smart little red Subaru. Both Carla and Mavis accompanied us to the dealership and we then proceeded to celebrate his new ownership by a trip to a Mexican restaurant and a few rounds of margaritas. When I got back to my office, I enlisted Mavis's help in writing a letter to James Robinson.

Three days later I was behind my desk when the office phone rang. Mavis said it was for me and I picked up the receiver.

"Eddie Collins."

"Eddie, it's Jim Robinson."

"Hey, Jim. How you guys doing?"

"Well, frankly, we're a bit stunned after getting the mail this morning."

I'd had a discussion with Carla and Mavis, and they agreed with my decision to send half of my inheritance to the Robinsons for a college fund for Kelly. Jim raised some objections over the phone, but I wouldn't be dissuaded.

"I don't know how far the money will go, Jim, but maybe you can stick it into something where it'll grow a little."

"Eddie, your generosity knocks both Betty and me for a loop."

He continued to offer objections, but in the end I was able to persuade him to keep the money. He thanked me profusely and we ended our call. I looked up and saw Mavis standing in the doorway to her office, a smile on her face.

"I'm proud of you, Eddie."

I replaced the phone on its pedestal, leaned back and put my feet up on the desk. "I hope it helps them. That kid deserves the best. Seeing her in contrast to all the crap spewed out by Alex Foster and Roy Dickerson makes me think it's the right thing to do."

A FEW EVENINGS LATER OVER PIZZA at Carla's and the Rams on television, I happened to suggest that maybe with the remaining money I could put a down payment on a condo or something.

"Are you serious?" she said.

"Yeah, sort of. What do you think?"

She wiped her mouth with a napkin. "You think we can put up with each other on a daily basis?"

"We could work at it."

"What about your office?"

I sipped from a bottle of beer in front of me. "I don't know. I could keep it. I'd hate like hell to get new business cards made up. New Yellow Pages listing. All the important stuff, you know?"

She laughed and glanced over her shoulder at me with a grin on her face. "Not to mention still having your own man cave, huh, Shamus?"

"Well, there is that."

She leaned in to me and planted a sloppy kiss on me. "I think we should take it under consideration. Now that I'm a working actress I can give you some help."

"Might be a good idea, since I'll probably never work again."

"Oh, stop!" she said, and playfully punched me in the stomach.

We horsed around for a couple of minutes until we were interrupted by my cellphone. There was an email from Kelly. My face broke into a huge grin. We'd exchanged a few over the months, including mine about the television gig. But this one was different. It had an attachment that was a video. I showed it to Carla. She told me to email it to her so we could look at it on her laptop. Since that was above my pay grade, I handed the phone to her and told her to be my guest. She completed the task and went into the bedroom for her laptop.

Snuggled together on the sofa, we opened the attachment. The faces of Kelly and her brother Troy filled the screen. In the background was an athletic field. Both of them grinned and mugged for the camera.

"Hi Eddie," Kelly said. "And hi, Carla. We just know you're watching this together." They both giggled and she went on to say that her soccer team was getting ready to play, and that she'd be back with the recap. She ran off and the film faded out, then came back in showing her running down the field, the ball in front of her. She passed it off, got it back, and sent the ball flying into the net. Hands went into the air and she jumped into the arms of one of her teammates.

The video faded out again and then came up showing Kelly holding a trophy, flanked by her brother. Standing behind them were James and Betty Robinson, huge grins on their faces and porkpie hats on their heads. Kelly moved closer to the camera and said, "Eddie, we're going to the regionals. You have to come and see us. Love you." She went back and stood beside her brother, who wrapped his arms around her. Her parents waved at the camera, shouted greetings and the image faded out. I sat staring at the computer as Carla closed the video.

"Amazing," I said.

"What's amazing?"

"She's surrounded by her family, all of them black, and it's not even an issue with her. Then I think back at all the goddamn hatred and bigotry Alex Foster and Roy Dickerson churned up. I don't know, Carla. Maybe those two kids have the answer."

She draped one arm around my shoulder, leaned over and kissed me on the cheek. "Let's hope so, Shamus."

THE EDDIE COLLINS MYSTERY SERIES

BOOK ONE

PI and part-time actor Eddie Collins is hired to investigate the death of his ex-wife, Elaine Weddington, on the set of her latest B-movie. As Eddie follows the trail of clues, he realizes how little he knew about his ex, who was surrounded by jealousy and intrigue. And now the killer wants him dead too.

BOOK TWO

Hollywood PI, sometime actor Eddie Collins receives an SOS from Mike Ford. His Oscar has been stolen during a home invasion and his girlfriend drowned in the swimming pool. Did she surprise the burglar? All the dots connect around a movie Ford directed and acted in: *Red Desert*. Is a person associated with the shoot harboring a deadly grudge?

BOOK THREE

Carla Rizzoli and PI Eddie Collins were once cast on the same TV show. He has never forgotten her. Now Carla needs Eddie to find her missing brother, who warned her in a note to "watch her back." Carla, now an exotic dancer, has a role in a B-movie, and Eddie is driven by more than a paycheck to protect her, no matter what the risks.

CLIVE ROSENGREN IS A RECOVERING ACTOR. His career spanned more than forty years, eighteen of them pounding many of the same streets as his fictional sleuth Eddie Collins. He appeared on stages at the Great Lakes Shakespeare Festival, the Guthrie Theater, and the Oregon Shakespeare Festival, among others. Movie credits include *Ed Wood, Soapdish, Cobb,* and *Bugsy.* Among numerous television credits are *Seinfeld, Home Improvement,* and *Cheers,* where he played the only person to throw Sam Malone out of his own bar. He lives in southern Oregon's Rogue Valley, safe and secure from the hurly-burly of Hollywood.

Rosengren has written three books in the Eddie Collins Mystery series: *Murder Unscripted, Red Desert,* and *Velvet on a Tuesday Afternoon.* Books one and two were both finalists for the Shamus Awards, sponsored by the Private Eye Writers of America.

Visit him at his website, www.cliverosengren.com.